"In language both poetic and spare, *Finding Caruso* tells a compelling story of passion, despair, and redemption. Kim Barnes has written a great novel of the American West, one that will thrill you with its deep beauty and dark grace."
                                                                —Brady Udall,
                                            author of *The Miracle Life of Edgar Mint*

"The underlying tensions and deftly wrought metaphors gather quickly in ways complex, beautiful, and heartbreaking, all told in Barnes's steady, diamond-cut prose and stripped dialogue . . . wonderful supporting characters . . . What raises the quality and the stakes in *Finding Caruso* is Barnes's absolute mastery of Buddy's churning, on-the-cusp-of-manhood emotions."
                                                —*The Atlanta Journal-Constitution*

"An accomplished novel."   —*Seattle Post-Intelligencer*

"Here is a story of brothers learning to be men—a story of young men learning to be wise. *Finding Caruso* is a song elevated to psalm."   —Mark Spragg, author of *The Fruit of Stone*
                                                and *Where Rivers Change Direction*

"Barnes first evoked the spectacular Idaho timberlands in her unforgettable memoir, *In the Wilderness*, and now ably switches to fiction . . . [she] is as fluent in provocative metaphors as she is in scenes of profound conflict and revelation."   —*Booklist* (starred review)

"Solid, evocative . . . poignant writing about first love . . . Barnes's rich, multilayered prose makes this an engaging read."
                                                                —*Publishers Weekly*

"Barnes, a published poet, skillfully uses language to paint an affecting picture of the rural West and its lonely inhabitants."
                                                                —*Library Journal*

continued. . . .

For Bob, who continues to teach and inspire in every way

For the Barnes boys and their sister:
Although this is not your true story, it is your true voices that I hear—

ACKNOWLEDGMENTS

Thanks to Claire Davis, who kept me going with early-morning calls and late-afternoon glasses of wine. Robert Johnson fed me encouragement while I fed him another helping of garlic chicken. Keith and Shirley Browning, Mary Clearman Blew, Judy Blunt, and Christy Thompson offered advice and inspiration; Steve and Connie Evans, Karla Steele, and Jeanette Weaskus provided much-needed information and insight. Thanks to Gary Miranda, who years ago shared with my husband and me the story of his grandfather Salvadore Miranda, the rightful Celery King. And to Ronnie Gilbert, a special note of gratitude from one writer to another: Thank you for sharing your words and voice.

My summer troupe—Collin Hughes, Buddy Levy, Lisa Norris, and Jane Varley—offered encouragement and criticism in just the right measure. Thanks to Sally Wofford-Girand for her good sense and strong patience, and to Marian Wood, who recognizes the song I mean to sing.

To Bob, Philip, Jordan, and Jace, and to my parents—again, I am thankful for all the hours you've given so that I might do what I love, surrounded by people whom I love, in this place that I love. I am blessed.

I am grateful to the Idaho Commission on the Arts for the fellowship that allowed me room to write and breathe.

Ch'ella mi creda libero e lontano.

Let her believe that I am free and far away.

—from GIACOMO PUCCINI'S *La Fanciulla del West*

We have no choice but to forgive ourselves.

—WILLIAM KITTREDGE

FINDING CARUSO

Kim Barnes

CHAPTER ONE

August, sky paling. The humid Oklahoma air crowds in. The chickens have breasted their bowls of dirt; the hounds lie heat-sick beneath the porch. The smoke of Lee's cigarette does not rise but haloes around us. Only our father moves in the stillness, and the mare with him, a dance of retreat and retrieval.

"It's bad this time," Lee says.

I have come to join him at the fence, where we stand and watch our father trying to saddle the pinto mare.

We are brothers, Lee and I. Will always be. I am ten. He is seventeen. It is 1950, and our father is three days dry and angry. With the mare, who will not stand for the cinching. With our mother, who has turned him from her bed until he promises sobriety; with the two boys who have witnessed each new failure of strength and will.

His hands fist and tremble. The mare remembers punishment, cannot stop her nervous shying away, the flinching each time he elbows her gut.

I should go now, I think. Now is the time before it's too late. But like Lee, I cannot turn away. As though it is not the mare but we who are tethered to the man by bit and bridle. As though we know that it is different this time, that there will be a final telling of this story.

Behind us, the *churg-churg* of the wringer washer, the distant smell of bleach and bluing. The corn stands hollow, stick-brown. Our father bites the butt of his cigarette, lashes the mare with the reins—across her shoulders, her soft pied face.

Lee feels what I mean to do. He grabs my arm, says, "Don't."

Our father pulls her nose-to-neck, grabs the horn, has one foot in the stirrup when she bolts. He hops once, twice, then goes down, caught and dragging. His arms flail out, his body bounces across the rough pasture. They will not go far—it is a small farm, sufficiently fenced—but on the second round his foot comes loose of its boot. The mare finds the farthest corner, stands white-eyed and blowing.

Bastard Creek slews red and thick along the field's north margin. It has rained, but no one knows just where. I think I can smell it, silty and fresh, mixed with peachleaf, soapberry, nightsoil. I smell Lee's sweat and my own, the mare's sharp odor of fear.

Our father rises, limps his way to the barn. We hear the cough of the Ford pickup, see him coax it out in an oily fog. He's given up, I think, he'll drink now, and some part of me is glad. He revs the engine smooth, slips the clutch, but instead of turning for the road, he steers for the pasture. The truck jerks forward across hummocks and rock pockets, our father jouncing behind the wheel, head knocking the roof.

I am curious, wondering what he brings, what he means to take away, realize as the Ford picks up speed that he's gunning straight for the mare. He hits her hard, knocks her through the fence, rails splintering, raking the fenders.

"Hold," Lee says, and I do because I cannot imagine what else.

The mare is on her side, legs churning. Our father pulls rope from behind the seat, lashes her hind hooves, throws the other end over a fat limb of hickory, ties it to the bumper, backs the truck until she hangs suspended.

We watch him step out with the tire iron, hear the crack of ribs, the horse's screams. Her joints tear, lungs collapse beneath the visceral weight.

Our father exhausts himself, drops the iron, uses his fists, and I think I can hear this, too, although by now I am humming along with Lee, our voices growing together, louder and louder. No words, just the vibration at the back of my throat, deep in my chest. We are singing with our mouths closed, *wildwood flower, wildwood flower,* over and over as our father weakens, until he cannot lift his arms, unties the rope, backs away from the black-and-white body still heaving in its bright pool of blood. We hum a little quieter as we watch the Ford disappear toward town, quieter still as we kneel by her head, all the long while it takes her to die.

There will be no burial, except, perhaps, in memory. What can be done with so much flesh and bone? Consider the tractor repossessed, the single good shovel, the ground dry and packed to stone.

The gut rumbles, begins its bloating. We stand, look toward the small shack where our mother knows or does not know. We remove the saddle and blanket, the bridle and bit, smooth the mane. We leave the horse to crows and foxes, knowing what we do of the world's justice.

By the next day, the moist breeze comes sweet with rot, settles in with us at breakfast, stays through lunch and dinner. We clear our plates, lick our bowls clean. We sleep with our windows open, the death of the mare a dream we cannot wake from.

When our father returns three days later, sick on corn whiskey, we watch him once again rope the mare's hind legs, see him turn away long enough to vomit yellow bile. He puts the Ford in first gear, meaning to drag her to the bone pile, but the hocks pop and separate. He takes her in pieces—hind legs, forelegs, head—until all that is left is the body, swollen and grim. But now there is nothing to tie on to. He circles once, twice, kicks the belly hard.

"Move away from the window," our mother says. Some things are better not seen. But we stay. We are rooting for the mare. Obstinate. Impossible.

"Deadlock," Lee says. "Dogfall."

Our father disappears into the barn, comes out lugging kerosene. He douses what remains, soaks it good, stands back as the flames jump high and clean then recede to a deeper burn. He looks toward the window, lights another cigarette, moves to the trough, splashes his face, the back of his neck.

"Best not be standing there when he comes in," our mother says. "Dinner's about on."

Lee looks at me, tips his head toward the door. "Let's go," he says. He means a walk, a long loop around the fields, maybe a turn into town for a soda. Away from our father, the greasy smoke.

But how can I leave our mother alone with what comes next? I tell Lee to go ahead, and he does, because he can. We sit at the table, my mother and I, hands in our laps, waiting. She keeps her eyes closed, as though in prayer. Through the window behind her, I watch the sky darken, the fire's slow licking.

That night, I will rise to a new moon, leave Lee sleeping on the floor, make my way to the smoldering mound, feel the ground warm beneath my bare feet. I will imagine for the first time a wild ride away, the mare young and alive beneath me. But when I awake, stiff and shivering, to the rough nudge of my father's boot, the dream is forgotten, the fire dead.

I will turn from the charred cage of ribs to my chores, see in the distance the black scavengers at the bone pile, know they have already taken the eyes, preened the teeth for tongue. And this is what I will not forget: their raucous delight at such plenty, how they feed and feed, skull and femur fallen into strange symmetry— a stick horse running, honed and glistening, somehow new. Like the bones of an old song remembered. Like this story, whittled back to its beginnings, and at its heart the emptiness, the loss, that might tell you the whole of who I am.

Who I am: Buddy Hope, once that child, now this man. The drunkard's son. Young brother of Lee. Nothing more or less until that summer of 1958, when Irene walked into my life, planted desire deep in my marrow, vines even now twining so that I rise each morning rooted in memory, unfolding to sun or snow but always to the absence of her.

I abide in the whisper of wind through an old mare's bones. I exist in this place Irene made for me, surrounded by those she meant to love and shelter. I try each day to be more of the man she dreamed I might be. I dream, and still she is here with me, making me new again, giving me this story to tell, and the voice to tell it. Every word is her name.

CHAPTER TWO

Before Irene, there remains the story of the boy I was, and so let me begin again in Oklahoma because that is where I left the bodies of my mother and my father and some part of myself dead, where even before their lives ended I had lost any sense of possibility, my world circumscribed by the simplest of needs: food, shelter, my mother's love. Having these things, I lived out my childhood days with my eyes fixed on the present: no hour seemed more or less desirable than the next; any dreams I might have had of a life made better by different circumstance slipped from my conscious mind the moment I rose with the sun to attend to my chores.

We sharecropped a small farm west of Tulsa, broomcorn and cotton, enough to make the landowner some money and buy what we could not raise or grow. Of those times, this is what pleasures me most to remember: summer, the chickens and hogs gone quiet, the tractor in the barn; my father taking his fiddle to the porch, leaning his chair against the clapboard, starting slow— a few slips across the strings, then a pause to look out over the fields and creek gully, as though for a sign. My mother, flour-sack apron tucked in her dress belt, would stand in the doorway, start the little hum in her throat. Lee brought his guitar, took his place beside me on the wooden steps. When the right time had come, my father let the bow stay its glide, my mother began in her high, lovely soprano, and Lee and I joined in, the song pulling our voices together. We sang loud and clear through the jigs, my father banging his boot against the porch boards. The ballads were my mother's favorite, and we let her lead, our boys' voices blending in a harmony that had been in us since the moment our parents came together and planted the music in our bones.

Through spring tornadoes and winters blighted with frost, it was music that sustained us, kept us believing that the next year's crop would bring with it promise of better times, the means to leave the little house with its tilted porch and head for Oklahoma City, where men made more wages in a week than my father made in a season. Never so poor that we couldn't make music, my mother said, believing in her good Baptist way that the truest riches lay somewhere just beyond the horizon.

But nothing got better. The clay-ridden soil my father tilled caked beneath the gentle rain, then cracked in the next hour's sun. We watched him rise each morning, drink his coffee at the window, saw the way his face, deeply creased, had come to mirror the land. The corn sprouted, wilted, and died. And then, when its needed time had passed, the rain arrived, pooling atop the hard-pack, swamping the potatoes. Or the hail came down, beating the bolls from their stems.

By the time I was in school, my father had quit singing. Instead of relaxing on the porch, he spent his nights at Mackey's Crossing, hunched over whiskey with other men, the only thing that mattered the drink in front of him, and the next.

My mother pleaded, prayed. She banished my father from her bed, and when he shrugged and slept like a dog curled tight on the porch, she begged him back in. She sent Lee to the bar, scolded when he returned alone, but what could he do? Our father was a tall man, more length than Lee could willfully shoulder, and it was not in Lee to command him to the pickup like a child. "He'll come home when he's ready," Lee would tell our mother, then pull her into a two-step, joshing her out of her sadness with a lighthearted rendition of "Jig Along Home."

I'd stay at the table, or lean against the wall, delighted and alarmed by the vision of my mother and brother twirling and dipping around the room, my mother's dark hair released from its pins, falling into ringlets as she protested, then laughed, and finally, fell into a chair and cried. And then Lee's tone would change, he'd rub her shoulder, say, "Here now," sing a lullaby until she wiped her eyes, gave a brave smile, and found her way back to the kitchen, where the just-baked bread remained uncut, the butter cooled in its crock. Other times, Lee could offer no more solace and headed out the door himself, bound for a tavern farther down the road, or the house of a girl who might hum him a song of her own.

Those nights with both Lee and my father gone, my mother became someone else to me, perhaps believing that she was all that was left standing between her younger child and the bitter world outside. She'd straighten, smooth her apron, say there was nothing that a little sweetness wouldn't help. She'd butter a slice of warm bread, sprinkle it with sugar, hold it toward me with a ceremonial nod, as though proffering a potent remedy.

When he turned eighteen, Lee joined the Air Force, trained as a flight mechanic, came home wearing blue, his cap at an angle, taller now than most men. So handsome, my mother said, in that uniform, the way it set off his eyes, and all that dark hair. I'd peer into the bathroom mirror, see my own hair so white Lee called it cotton—and my eyes, brown instead of blue. It had been generations since a Hope child's eyes had not lightened, and I began early on to make my way through the world with my gaze cast downward.

Though he never saw combat, I heard him tell of wondrous things—the ocean below the belly of his plane, the bashful girls of Seoul, the lights that lit up the sky above L.A. But none of it made any difference in Lee. He'd shrug, say that it seemed to him people were just about the same all over, and that nothing was as pretty as a cotton field in spring, no girl more fun than the one just down the road, who milked her father's cows in her nightgown.

Lee brought me coins with strange markings, silver wings that he pinned to the gallus of my overalls. He brought my mother tiny vials of perfume that she arranged unopened on the sill of the kitchen window. He handed my father miniature bottles of Jack Daniel's and Smirnoff, perfect in their detail. Later, I'd find the empties scattered about the barn, or left in a tidy pile in a corner of the outhouse. I gathered them carefully, ranked them like soldiers along the fence's top rail, shot them one by one with my .22.

When Lee returned for good, we'd lost our lease, though the owner didn't have the heart to evict a woman and her young son when the man on whom they depended—the man who had once felled a stubborn steer with a single fisted blow—could no longer raise his hand against the flies that settled on his eyes and lips those mornings we found him laid out on the porch, bottle snugged against his chest.

The more my father drank, the more my mother cried, the more animated Lee became, as though he believed his loud singing and quick dance might drown out the shrill grief and fear that filled our days. My father stumbled through his morning's work, the bucket rattling in his hand, the match he struck to light the lantern trembling above the wick. He had once been a patient man, but now my smallest error warranted his wrath. A tool left outside its box brought him striding from the barn, his belt already stripped. Any word I uttered was sass, my silence an insult.

When Lee was home, my father seemed less inclined to rage. Lee kept him soothed with offerings of whiskey or rum, meted out like rations to the poor. In Lee's absence, it was my mother who attempted to intervene, but her protests were useless. Best that I not be seen at all. "It's not your fault," my mother said. "I hope you can remember he was a good man."

I rose early, met the school bus a mile down the road. I studied in a nest of abandoned machinery behind the barn. At night, I shadowed the doorway, watched my mother's face for signs: a nod meant the way was clear; a tight mouth and widened eyes meant go. Sometimes I climbed the oak outside the bedroom I shared with Lee, slid through the window, slept with my stomach empty rather than risk putting myself within reach of my father's fists. I learned to stifle my babyish sobbing, learned, too, that any moment of pleasure would be followed by pain. In my child's way, I came to believe that one brought on the other, began to greet any small joy with distrust.

Those nights my father disappeared down the road, I felt the house itself let loose its breath. I ate the sugar my mother now spooned onto everything—pancakes, the gift of watermelon from a neighbor's patch, the ham donated by the Tri-Creek Ladies Guild. Our coffee was syrup, our tea like honey.

Lee didn't say a word as he stepped over our father's sleeping body on his way in or out the door. He was looking for work, but jobs in town were few. Though our mother argued against it, Lee knew he'd have to go to the City, leave me to tend to our parents and what was left of the farm. He hated the idea of it, he said, hated leaving us again as much as he hated the prospect of hauling another man's garbage, shining a rich man's car. His days in the Air Force had taught him this: he did not serve well. He'd take me for long back-road drives in the red-and-white Chevy Bel Air he'd bought with his GI paycheck, tell me that there were few things worse than answering to a man not your equal. "Got to be your own boss," he'd say. "Only way to have any peace at all." I'd breathe in the musty air, hear the whir of cicadas rise and fall as we passed the dense groves of pecan and blackjack. With Lee behind the wheel, the two of us meandering the dark country boundaries without destination, I felt suspended, safe for a while.

After my father bartered our hens, eggs, and last jar of cream for whiskey, leaving us with nothing but a slab of bacon and a few cups of flour, my mother fried the meat, mixed the flour and grease, enough to stave off our hunger until Lee wore his work boots into town and came back barefoot, a fat white hen under one arm, a young banty rooster under the other. He sang the next county fair in borrowed shoes, drove to town with his earnings, returned wearing a pair of fancy Acmes, tooled black leather inlaid with wings of red and white. "These boots are going to take me places," he said. "They're going to take me far."

When he announced that we had a job come Sunday, my mother dressed me in my father's old suit, took up the sleeves, hemmed the trousers. Lee stepped from the back room in full uniform, regulation except for the new boots. We drove into town, sang twenty-five choruses of "Amazing Grace" while mourners filed by the waxen body of the dead man. After the funeral, the undertaker handed us each a five-dollar bill, told us to come back the next weekend. Busy times, he said, shook his head and smiled.

"This is what we do, Buddy." Lee leaned forward over the steering wheel as though coaxing a reluctant horse. "Better than shoveling coal, I'll damn sure tell you. All we got to do is get up there and sing."

We sang Methodist weddings, high school dances, Catholic fish fries. At the American Legion Hall, men cried when Lee straightened his cap and belted out "Glory, Glory, Hallelujah" while I hummed plaintively in the background. At the sock hop, I was too shy, too aware of my classmates' assessing gaze to offer more than a thin quaver of melody. Lee finally told me to go on down, then dragged out a doleful "You Send Me," stroking the microphone, lolling his head, until the girls at the foot of the stage squealed and their boyfriends glared from the back of the gym. I knew them all but kept myself separate, like them in age only. But I was Lee Hope's little brother, and some shine rubbed off on me.

Still, when he handed my mother the money with the same

earnest gesture with which she fed me the sugared bread, I watched the way her eyes stayed on him, the love no more than she offered me, but different somehow. It wasn't jealousy that gripped me then, but a sense of my own limitations. What could I give that would bring such light to my mother's face?

Everywhere we sang, people told us how good we were, how we were headed for the big time. But it was my brother whose attention they tried to catch. Even as my legs lengthened, I felt myself becoming small beside Lee. I'd stay just a little behind him, give what harmony he needed.

I understand now how the responsibility Lee shouldered must have eaten at him, how the smile he shined on us must have faded the moment he left the house, those times he disappeared in his Chevy, came home happier and smelling of perfume. Or he'd return smelling of possum, the dead animal he'd swerved to hit dangling from his shoulder. Sometimes he didn't return at all, and I'd be sent to fetch him, just as he'd been sent to fetch our father. "You *are* your brother's keeper," my mother scolded whenever I complained. Like everyone else, my mother was charmed by Lee and could never shame him without shaming herself. His drinking and carousing were not vices but preoccupations: he was headed for better things and needed more room than the rest of us. He needed special consideration, special care, as though his being wounded would wound us all.

There was another side of Lee she did not see—those times when he seemed bent on charity, allowed me to tag along on his date with one girl or another, then goaded me to madness with out-of-school tales: the time I cried because our mother had washed the me-smell from my favorite blanket; the frost-licked morning I'd stumbled half awake toward the outhouse only to lose my way, so that when he came to find me, I was standing at the row of laying boxes, oblivious to the clack of hens whose nests I filled with piss. I understood that what Lee meant by his tellings was not to entertain but to extract some price for my being there. A fight was what Lee wanted, but when I did lash out in a foolish attempt to defend myself, this is what I learned: taking me down, beating me, released something awful in Lee that made us both ashamed.

There came a time when I could hardly remember the brother Lee had once been, the boy who had locked himself in the outhouse whenever our father caught one of the barn cats raiding the hens and chicks. I'd watch in my own state of dread as the cat was snatched up by its tail, then swung against the big oak, blood and brains spraying the grass. "Sissy girl," our father would call, and laugh, while from behind the closed door came the sound of Lee singing "Wildwood Flower" at the top of his lungs. Later, in the bed we shared, I'd feel the shudder, hear the muffled sobs. I'd pat his head or press a hand to his shoulder, just to remind him I was there. Soon it embarrassed me to show such pity, and I came to believe it embarrassed him as well, and so we'd lie there, Lee with his face to the wall, I on my back, silently willing him to sleep so that one night's sorrow might end.

When Lee started winning talent contests, playing grand openings, I took on his share of the chores, mucking the barn, taking my father's hounds to hunt the woods for squirrels. Lee came home bright-eyed, shiny with sweat, bearing boxes of oranges, tins of ribbon candy. He'd encourage our father toward the galvanized tub, get him shaved and at the dinner table, ply him with jokes and anecdotes until the tremors set in and the iced tea rattled in its pitcher. And then Lee would slip him outside, hand him the flask, give him a ride into town. What use, he said, in fighting what couldn't be beaten?

Lee was playing at the Grange Hall the August evening my mother discovered she was out of sugar. The next day was my seventeenth birthday, and she needed to make the cake. I said I'd walk down the road, see if Mrs. Fraeney had a cup to lend. But no, she needed more than a cup—she needed a pound at least, not just for the cake, but for the week ahead. How could she keep a house without sugar?

It was then that my father rose from the couch, said we were acting like he wasn't sitting right there. It was *his* goddamn pickup. He'd drive his wife into town.

My mother gauged the steadiness of his knees, the list of his shoulders. He adjusted his trousers, rubbed his mouth. "Maybe we can get us an ice cream, Sally," he said. "How long's it been since I bought you an ice cream?"

"Let me freshen up a bit," my mother said. She came back from the bedroom patting her hair, cheeks rouged, lips colored. It struck me that I hadn't seen her leave the house for a long time.

I watched them get into the pickup, saw that my father kept a straight line down the road. I turned to the sudden silence, decided I liked it fine. I spooned a dollop of jam onto a biscuit, poured a jar full of milk. I had hay to pitch, but what drew me was the couch my father had vacated. I stretched its length, smelled the faint sourness of his body. Though I knew there would be no presents, there would be my mother's attention, white gravy on our bread. My father had seemed suddenly new to me, woken not from a nap but from a long sleep. Maybe he would bring out his violin, take it to the porch. Maybe this was when things would change.

I woke to the sound of Lee's Chevy, his too quick stomp up the steps. He didn't have to tell me anything.

My father hadn't slowed when he came to the sharp turn onto the bridge. The pickup sailed from the road in spite of its heaviness, arced into the dry creek bed. Our mother, who had never tasted a drop of alcohol in her life, died pinioned against the dashboard. Because he was drunk, the doctors said, because the liquor in his body kept the heart pumping and the muscles relaxed, my father lived a few hours more, long enough for Lee and me to see the arm angled against itself, the rib cage busted, the crush of bone that was his face. Lee held me hard at the shoulders, as though he knew I felt some part of myself slipping away, as though he might lose me in the dark.

When we left the hospital that night, Lee never said a word but drove Route 66 straight to the City, bought me a burger and fries, then popcorn at the drive-in movie, where we watched *Around the World in 80 Days*. He ordered double-scoop chocolate for the trip home, let me sleep in the car while he went into the house, where he found the dough our mother had left to rise. He fired the cookstove, wiped the counter, swept the floors while the loaves baked. When I woke, he led me to the table, sat me down before a plate of hot bread, a mug of sweetened coffee. It was then that I dropped my head and cried, and he let me, going on about his cleaning, singing a soft song as he stepped to the door, scattered corn for the chickens. I'd loved him then, and nothing in that ever changed.

We sold all that was left of the farm: the chickens, the eggs beneath them, what meat remained in the smokehouse. Sold our mother's oak table and our father's fiddle, his two bluetick hounds, chains and all. The only things we kept were the two guitars—Lee's Gibson, and the older one he'd first learned on and given me, blond wood scratched from the hours he'd played in the hayloft and down by the creek, the neck worn smooth by his hand.

It was 1957, and there were places in the country still booming. An Air Force buddy of Lee's said there were jobs to be found in the Texas oilfields and in the Northwest—cutting timber, driving trucks, working in the mills. Lee flipped a coin. "Heads, we go west. Tails, we make friends with the ol' boys down south." We watched the quarter spin up, land in the red dust at our feet. "Heads it is!" Lee hooted. When I bent to pick it up, he scuffed my hand aside. "Leave it there," he said. "Maybe it'll grow something."

We loaded the guitars, our clothes, a few sandwiches wrapped in wax paper into the Chevy and headed north, warbling our way across the Panhandle of Oklahoma and into Kansas, where we spent one night in a homely campground, both of us laid out on the car seats, doors open to catch whatever breeze might come our way. A gentle tune had floated in—the group of Mennonites we'd seen earlier loading a picnic table with baskets of cold chicken. They'd circled around a campfire and were singing their hymns, and Lee and I joined in, low enough to keep their voices in our ears, the air just cool enough to soothe, my brother close and familiar.

We kept up our singing—"Bill Grogan's Goat" through Colorado, "I'll Fly Away" across the Utah line, the long miles of southeast Idaho. We ran out of money in Boise, and it was there I left my guitar, pawned for six dollars. The Gibson would have brought more, but neither of us thought to sell it any more than we'd have thought to sell Lee's soul.

From Boise, we headed north, following the Payette River and then the Salmon through the settlement of Riggins, the row of small houses, rough mill, and tepee-shaped sawdust burner set deep in the V of the canyon. Just past Lapwai, we turned west, picked up the Clearwater River, which paralleled the highway. Just before Snake Junction, Lee spied a large building, a sign that read "The Stables," and then, in smaller letters, "Dancing Liquor Music Live."

A bar, Lee said, was the best place to get the lowdown. I waited in the car, marked the erratic lay of the land, the isolated acreage surrounding the nightclub, the Y west of town where the Snake River joined the Clearwater. When Lee finally emerged from the bar in the company of a short, compact man, both of them three gins under and grinning like fools, I knew that we'd get no further and that whatever money Lee earned would come not from the lumber line but from the stage.

A new place—a good place, Lee said. We were lucky. But what I saw before me did not look like anyone's good fortune. I could hardly take in the broken landscape, its deep clefts, the fractured rise of mountains to high prairie. There was too much dimension to be absorbed, and I found myself disoriented by the depths and distances my eyes had to follow. I set my jaw, pretended to study the mill that sat on the far floodplain, huffing its sulfuric smoke, draping the valley in a brown haze. Already, I hated the smell of it.

I was a boy, believing only what I could taste, touch, see, and I could not have known that my future lay not in the land or the hands of any man but in the heart of a woman whose journey would intersect with my own. Even as I leaned back, closed my eyes against the banking sun, she was making her way home, across the Ohio, the Wabash, the Missouri, the Bighorn; through Billings and Butte and over the Bitterroots into Idaho. Through cornfields and wheat fields and the split-open hearts of mountains; past battlefields and the creaking machinations of derricks and refineries; along the edges of boreal forests and the black snags of cedar left by the great fire of 1910—she was driving hard, counting the miles, the hours, the days until she reached that place she loved more than any other, bringing that love with her, bringing it to me.

CHAPTER THREE

Spud, who owned The Stables, gave us a room at the back of the building that had once been an icehouse but now held stacks of cocktail napkins and old beer signs. He and his longtime bartender, Harvey, a burly man with a cauliflower ear, brought in two single beds and an armful of Pendleton blankets, pillows and sheets and an electric lamp, its shade stenciled with cattle brands: Circle 2 Bar, Running O, Sunny Jim, and my favorite, Snake in Moon—a hollow crescent shot through with a serpent.

Lee took charge of the Golden Spurs, the band whose former lead guitarist had run off with Lila Rafferty, a half-famous platinum-haired singer whose tour had brought her to Idaho. She'd dragged her act through Snake Junction like she was trolling for catfish, heavily baited and hitting bottom. No one was sorry to see her and her catch hit the road, headed toward Missoula.

The Spurs seemed happy to have Lee at the helm. The steel player, Floyd, was a quiet man nearing forty, with silver-capped teeth and cool gray eyes, who had about him the sweetish odor of someone who was often ill. He sometimes wailed along with the mournful, drawn-out notes he wrenched from the strings beneath his fingers. Lee said he could wring the tears out of pig iron.

Dean, who wore his muddy hair slick and his sideburns long, played drums and seemed a good enough man when sober, but I'd heard stories of him drunk—a "mean drunk," Harvey said, and I knew what he meant by mean: a man whose violence was mixed with cowardice, who would turn his fists on a woman.

And that woman was Laurette. Black hair piled high on top, a long swing of it down her back. She played bass, wore sequined outfits, white or pink or soft blue, hats and boots to match. She'd been a rodeo queen ten years before, and folks in Snake Junction still remembered her on her Appaloosa, doing the slow wave for the crowd. She never seemed comfortable, even offstage, and for that there were two reasons: she'd lost her crown when word got out she was pregnant by a second-rate bronc rider, and because she was married to Dean.

Even though Dean had taken a vow of sobriety, Laurette feared him. I saw the way she kept him at the corner of her eye, quick to listen whenever he called her name. In her tense stillness, I recognized something of that boy I'd been beneath my father's hand. I carried her baggage, opened her door, as if I believed I was aiding her small escapes. But for Laurette, there was no barn loft, no thicket of oak, in which to hide.

It seems to me that I should remember more of her than I do, but she took so little space, drew so little attention to herself, it was almost as though the moment I met her, she was already gone. Within a year of our arrival in Snake Junction, she was dead, and like the birth of her fatherless child, her death came shrouded in secrecy and shame.

Until Laurette's death, I must have believed that death arrived unbidden. Sudden, like the spring of a cat, the snatch of a man's hand, the curve of road disappearing. Or slow, like the cancer that ate away the jowls of my grandfather so that his teeth glinted through the open wound. But never welcomed. Never courted like a lover in whose arms you might find comfort. Because that is how she died—killed not by rage or even by desire, but by her own sweet will. That is what I believe now. That is what I know.

But there were months yet to come when I felt empty of death, the newness of the land weighing against loss, and in Laurette's absence, Irene.

Word spread that the Spurs had a new voice, and soon a good Saturday night meant no empty tables, no room at the bar. Those were the nights the doors were left open so that the couples waiting to get in could hear what they were missing. Often they stayed right there, dancing in the gravel, having their own good time. Lee would sing a little louder, say, "This song's for all our good friends out there under the stars," and they'd love him for it.

I'd lie on my bed, hear Spud's voice booming through the cavernous building, "Welcome, ladies and gentlemen, to The Stables! The biggest dance floor this side of the Mississippi!" and I'd feel my own heart jump with excitement. Yet every time Lee urged me to join him onstage, I'd shake my head. I could tell that underneath his encouragement was a secret wish that I'd let him go this alone. Some part of me knew, too, that though I could hold my own on a sun-warped porch or in a wind-whipped car, I no longer had the desire or the courage to share the spotlight with Lee. He had the looks, the voice, the charm. He could pull in an audience and hold them, especially the younger women who sat close to the stage, smiling up, leaning forward, crossing and uncrossing their legs, rocking the table. Even from the dance floor, in the arms of their partners, waltzing, two-stepping, doing the jitterbug or bop, they followed Lee with their eyes, moon-faced in the spotlight's shadows. Every woman wanted to take him home, feed him, be fed by him. He was the man every other man wanted to be.

I'd look at Lee up on that stage and for a moment not recognize him, like a photograph of someone I almost remembered. Sometimes, after the bar had closed, after he'd been out with a woman and come back, I'd wake to find him sitting on the edge of his bed, looking weary, bewildered. "It's nothing," he'd say. "I just need some sleep."

After a while, he quit asking me to sing, and I quit remembering that I'd once been there beside him, joining in a harmony our mother said was the prettiest in the world.

While Lee practiced days and played nights, I wandered the town of Snake Junction a mile west, big enough to have several churches and schools and a sign that read "Welcome to Snake Junction, pop. 12,985, home of Will Rapich, World Champion Log Burler."

I discovered that Snake Junction was a town in three parts.

Downtown spread out along the river. On the benchland just above the floodplain, doctors and lawyers built their small mansions and set granite lions to guard their verandas. A few blocks south, before the basalt hills gave way to a plain of rich soil, millworkers and clerks raised their families in modest bungalows. And then the area known as the Vineyards, a scrabble of old homesteads and rural occupations: ranches of fifty head spilled over into one-family farms; acres of apple, apricot, and cherry trees turned the spring air to honey. What grapevines remained clung to the sandy ground in a terrace so old, few could remember the first planting, though they never forgot the grapes themselves, the children coming home from play, fingers and mouths stained black.

Goats picketed in front yards to keep down the grass; chickens dusting themselves beneath boughs of juniper; children running barefoot from home to store, clutching pennies that would buy them a day's worth of hard candy from Falco's Tack and Feed—the Vineyards seemed most like home to me. One paved road cut through the center, the most direct path to and from downtown, but it was the gravel streets, the alleys lined with burn barrels and stacks of old tires, where neighbors met and traded important news and essential gossip. Vineyards girls spent their summers on horseback; boys excavated their way into backpasture garbage heaps, discovering old pots and empty bottles, which they lined up and shot with their Daisy Red Ryders.

The fastidious downtown businessmen who opened their stores at ten a.m. with keys that jangled against the coins in their pockets kept themselves separate from such Vineyards men as Bernie Scaggs, owner of Scaggs's Slaughter and Storage, who threw open his door each morning at five to let the bloody air out and the fresh air in, who feared nothing at all because he had enough meat to survive any Depression but who died anyway, his femoral artery severed by the slip of his perfectly honed knife. Cutie Pie's Café, where cattlemen and anyone else in need met at dawn to cure their hangovers with platters of brains-and-eggs; Rosie's Drive-In, where Rosie herself, white hair braided and wound like a kuchen, made hamburgers to order and always with a side of fried onions; Merle's Drug, where the first step in was over the ancient milk-eyed border collie that had appeared one day and decided to stay, lifting its head only to words in Spanish, which caused the children to cry *"Toro! Toro!"* each time they biked by.

The single high school anchored and blended the town—the building where every local child came to be called a Snake Junction Warrior. I, too, was expected to join the educated ranks, become part of the tribe that whooped through town during the homecoming parade and kindled the traditional bonfire at the confluence of the Clearwater and the Snake. But I had no desire to join the line of teenagers that serpentined down Main Street dressed in letter jackets and war bonnets. Their giddy play seemed foolish to me, bound to bring on hell.

When school opened that fall with no mention of my truancy, I began to relax. Having surveyed the town to the west, I contemplated what lay east. Spud had told me that The Stables was built on reservation land. Later I would have time and reason to think of the Nez Perce who once camped on the very spot where my brother and I slept, their blackened fire rings, flint chips, and arrowheads buried somewhere beneath the building's foundation, but I saw little sign of Indian life. The Nez Perce kept to themselves in the tribal town of Lapwai, ten miles southeast of The Stables, and I seldom encountered anyone whose skin was different from my own, except for one middle-aged man named

Leopold Wolfchild, who, each Friday, walked from Lapwai to The Stables, a journey that brought him to that line separating his people from the people of Snake Junction.

The Stables was the checkpoint between the reservation and the town. If the high school served to unify the students into one large pep rally, The Stables offered a more adult respite from the confines of social life: attorneys danced with grocery clerks; farm-hands stomped their feet across the floor, high school teachers in tow; college men from the Palouse barked insults at long-haul truck drivers, fought in the parking lot, then hung on one another's shoulders like war buddies.

From his place at the bar, Wolfchild watched, knowing that for all the flirting and backslapping he witnessed as the night wore on, there was one line he dared not cross. Nothing, he knew, would bring the people who were not his people together more surely than the threat of who he was and was not. He did not ask a white woman to dance. He did not allow his eyes to linger on the stockinged legs or bare shoulders but kept his gaze fixed somewhere just above the stage. He'd stay for one set, pay for his two fingers of sweet vermouth, nod good night to Harvey, then take off back down the road for his long walk home.

I regarded Wolfchild with little more than dull curiosity and could not have dreamed how, over the next year, our lives would become entwined, what truths would be buried and resurrected in his name: even the chasteness of his vision would not be enough to save him.

In those months of not knowing, months I remember as a time when the world held still for me, I spent my hours at the river, skip-ping rocks, fishing for silver-bellied trout, so unlike the sluggish cat-fish and carp I'd dragged from the murky Oklahoma waters, meat tainted with silt. I walked farther into the terraced hills of basalt, came back smelling of piss pine, wild onion. The draws exploded the moment I entered them, grouse beating up from their nests, deer leaping from their lays, crashing through the tangle of trees.

I explored the feeding creeks, napped beneath cottonwoods lining the banks, waited for winter to force me inside. But the weather remained mild. No snow fell. Christmas, I returned from my hike to find Lee, Spud, and Harvey studding a doughnut with maraschino cherries.

"Jesus' birthday," Harvey said, then held up a cherry. "Ever had one of these?" He tongued the red fruit, laughed when I blushed.

"He's still young, Harv," Lee said. "Don't want to spoil him." He slapped down a ten-dollar bill. "Go buy yourself something," he said. "I don't know what you want anymore."

And a few days later I did—a pair of binoculars from Lolo Sporting Goods through which I could bring the saw-toothed horizon into focus. I watched bald eagles fall to the water talons first, struggle upward with their catch. As the weather warmed, the eagles left and the osprey came, building their crosshatched nests atop snags and telephone poles. I loved to watch them chevron above the river and wished for their eyes, even as my vision blurred from so many hours peering through the magnifying lenses. The afternoon I dropped the binoculars while scrambling up a steep slide of basalt, watched them skitter and disappear into the river, I sat down and willed myself not to cry. There was no sense in it. They were gone. That was all.

Spring came early and hard. By February, green shoots pushed through the remnants of eave-shadowed snow. "Watch out for rattlesnakes," Spud warned, and so I studied the ground at my feet until vertigo set in. I was wary but did not fear the snakes the way Lee did. I remembered the morning in Oklahoma when he had risen from bed to use the outhouse before school and we'd heard him screaming, found him backed against the kitchen wall, wet with his own urine, pointing to the door leading outside: along the upper threshold ran a thick golden ribbon. Our father was in the fields, but it was our mother we most trusted to destroy the serpent, and she did, sending me out through an open window to retrieve her hoe, hooking the snake down, hacking through flesh to wooden floor. For weeks, Lee couldn't eat in that room, believing he could still smell the vermin stink of the snake, the floorboards oiled with blood.

March brought snowmelt cascading down the gullies, bleeding through the fissured rock. Watercress greened the pools. In May, chokecherry bloomed white along the benchland. Eighty miles upriver, bulldozers pushed a winter's worth of felled trees into the swollen current. The Clearwater became a giant flume, channeling larch, hemlock, and fir toward the mill. Many of the company men signed on to work the log drive, craving the adventure, needing good pay. They rode herd in motorboats, roped wayward logs, seeded the giant tangles called deadheads with dynamite.

A celebratory crowd gathered just above the mill to welcome them at their journey's end. I stood on the bank and watched the men walk the rafts of loose logs, their spiked boots digging into the spongy wood like spurs. I'd heard of the dangers they faced—the yearly deaths that came when the jams broke loose without warning, the logs rolling, pinning—but I couldn't help wishing I were there with them, waving to the clutch of family and friends who threw kisses and clapped at their courage. I did not know that the rich moistness of spring would soon give way to one of the driest summers on record, that those same men I had watched step wet and shivering from the icy water would, in a matter of months, find themselves manning the fire lines, faces blistered by heat.

I tested myself not against water or fire but against the body of my brother. Afternoons we wrestled, scuffling across the empty dance floor while Harvey refereed from his place behind the bar. Bracing myself against Lee, I felt my legs and arms grow strong. But those lighthearted bouts came less and less often, Lee more inclined toward whiskey and women than sibling scraps.

Yet I did not think of myself as lonely. I don't remember that I ever wondered where I might go from that place, down what paths my life would lead me. I did not know who or what I wanted to be, except, perhaps, in the negative: not a drunk like my father, not a nightclub owner like Spud, not a bartender like Harvey, not a crooner like Lee. My world existed between the walls of The Stables, the walls of the canyon. Even then, some part of me must have wanted more, but I had no way to know what more I wanted.

Until Irene.

CHAPTER FOUR

I was sitting at the bar the first time I saw her. Harvey had let me come out of the back for the last set, worth the underage risk, he said, to have someone sober to talk to at night's end. He offered me the evening's mistakes: vodka tonic made with gin, martini with an olive instead of a twist. I'd drunk just enough to relax and listen, let my legs stop their twitching and even my hands, which wanted to tap, brush, and flick. *Nervous energy,* my mother called it. *Boy, quit that noise!*

When I saw Irene, I found myself gone still. She took her place in the line of men at the bar, sipped her drink, smoked—one sip, one drag—as though she hadn't noted Harvey's disapproval, hadn't heard him bellow, "Last call!" High heels, tight green skirt, coppery red hair rolled and tucked in against itself—later, I would learn the word for it, *chignon,* its sound alone enough to make my stomach tighten. Even though I was not near her, I thought I could smell her perfume, the scent of overturned rocks and cottonwood blossom, spring's last snow.

The nightclub echoed with the knock and click of metal as tables were cleared, chairs lifted. Harvey motioned me closer to where he worked, dipping glasses in hot water. He took my empty, tipped his head toward Irene.

"Nice-looking dame. Not from around here, bet your bottom dollar." He wrung a rag, slapped it over his shoulder. "My guess is that brother of yours will have his tags on her before the night's done."

Lee had already caught sight and was working fast to stow his equipment, but she paid him no more mind than she did the other men in the room. For a moment, her eyes settled on me, but if in my young man's ignorance I had hoped for a spark of interest, there was none, just the same cool observation with which she took in the waitresses tallying their tips, Harvey buffing the counter, the last of the drinkers stumbling against one another as they made for the door. She seemed possessed of a sense of space that had nothing to do with other people or time. Even then, I understood that no one would think to hurry her. She would sit at the bar for as long as she wanted, and we would let her because we suddenly could not imagine it otherwise, because there was something in the way she took us in that made us part of who she was.

Lee coiled cords, never turning his back, as if he feared she might disappear in his moment of not looking. When he jumped from the stage, his boots hit the floor with a sharp rap.

She was older than most I'd seen him take up with, *a grown woman,* my mother would have said, something in the phrase reminding me of ripe tomatoes hanging heavy on the vine. Lee paused to light a cigarette as he walked. No, he didn't walk. He loped, shoulders back, arms relaxed. Irene was not surprised, and in the way she held her place, not leaning forward or away, I saw something different. She didn't allow her knees to touch his but kept them together, canted to the side. She lifted her chin, let the smoke out easy. She'd been keeping her own company for a long time.

"Ma'am," Lee said, and dipped his head like he was tipping his hat. "These boys treating you all right?"

"Sir," she replied, "I'm being treated just fine."

"Harv, why don't you bring this lady another drink."

"No, thank you," Irene said. "I believe I'm done for the night."

"But the night ain't over." Lee motioned to Harvey, who stood halfway between the liquor shelf and the counter as though paralyzed. "The lady here will have another. I need a double." Lee sat down next to Irene, pulled out his smokes and lighter, put them on the bar like he meant to settle in for a while. Harvey made his move for the liquor.

"You'll want to save that drink for another time," Irene said, and swiveled her stool so that she faced the door instead of Lee.

Harvey hesitated, shrugged, grabbed the Jack Daniel's, poured Lee his double. "I wish to God someone around here would make up his mind."

"There ain't no doubt in my mind about nothin'." Lee leaned back, elbows propped on the counter, legs extended, ankles crossed. His boots shone like the wings of blackbirds. "Now, why would a beautiful gal like you be in such a hurry to leave a place like this? Hell, I could even play some more music, if that would make you happy."

"You want to make me happy?" Irene smiled just a little.

"Hell, yeah, I want to make you happy. I'm good at making people happy."

"And how long does that last?"

"Does what last?"

"This happiness that you bring to people."

Harvey raised his eyebrows, shot me a look. Lee took a swallow of whiskey. "Well, now, I guess that depends on who it is we're talking about here. There's some stay happier longer than others." He licked his lips, winked at Harvey.

"And who would that be?" Irene asked.

"You going to take down names?"

"I would think that one would do. One person you've made happy longer than a few hours."

Harvey's eyebrows arched higher.

Lee pulled himself straight. "You know, I'd never have guessed that you'd have such a rock in your craw. From up there onstage, you looked like a pretty nice girl."

"Distance can do a lot for people." Irene stood, laid a few bills on the bar. "It may be that I'll like you a whole lot better when I'm a few miles down the road."

Floyd's voice broke in, calling that it was time to load up. As much as I hated to miss any part of the conversation, I was quick to move to the stage, to help Laurette with her gear.

I carried the bass out to the Ford station wagon, stopped in the parking lot to feel the warm June wind off the Clearwater, let it catch in the arms of my shirt, cool the back of my neck. The river and its canyons seemed less threatening in the dark. Even the harsh geometry of the mill softened beneath the moon, its industrial thrum melding with the sounds of the river. I took a deep breath to clear my head, the sulfuric odor mixing with the camphor of sage and black locust.

As I walked back, I lit another Winston to steady the nervous flutter beneath my ribs. Just as I was reaching for the door, it swung open and there she stood, only inches away. I jumped back, flushed with surprise. At six-foot-three, Lee beat me by a thumb joint; Irene looked me square in the eye. I thought of her high heels, but even that wasn't enough to take her down to what I was used to in a woman. It was like seeing the canyon for the first time—the sudden disorientation, the shock of the unexpected.

She stopped long enough to open her purse beneath the light, and I saw that it held little other than the single key she pulled from its folds. Harvey and Lee came into focus behind her, and the three of us waited, mute and immobile, as the clasp clicked shut. She smiled at me, asked, "Would you mind walking me to my car?"

"No, ma'am," I said, but she'd already turned.

I wondered if I should cup her elbow, guide her across the gravel. She tipped her head my way so that what light the moon and stars allowed caught in her eyes.

"What's your name?" she asked, her voice sugared with a southern accent truer than my Oklahoma drawl.

"Buddy," I said. "Buddy Hope."

She stopped, turned full toward me, held out her hand. I pulled my right hand free of its pocket, felt the sweat in my palm, the nubbins of lint.

"I like your name, Buddy Hope. I'm Irene." She held my hand just long enough for me to take in a breath, then turned back to our invisible path.

Later, I would remember the unhurried pace of our walk toward her black Lincoln, the brush of her against my chest, the slide of her legs, the way the car made a smooth turn onto the highway. I'd remember how I stood there, Harvey and Lee behind me, how the small breeze seemed suddenly cooler, and we all shuffled inside to get warm.

Harvey started shutting down the lights, stopped long enough to look toward the door, shake his head.

"That one's trouble," he said.

Lee hunkered protectively over the last of his JD. "I don't know about trouble, but I can tell you one thing. She'd put ice in your deep freeze."

I thought of the warmth of her hand, the way her smile brought heat to my face. "She didn't seem that cold to me."

Harvey snorted. "Gal like that don't come in here for no reason."

"Aw now, Harv," Lee rolled his head, rubbed his neck. "A little stubborn maybe, but there's ways to work with that. Give me a few hours and I'll have her loosened right up."

Harvey ran the towel one last time across the bar, settled his weight on the heels of his hands. Light shone off the skin of his scalp, clean and polished as the counter he buffed. "What kind of automobile is that for a woman to be driving? Goddamn undertaker's car. And what's she doing in here by herself this time of night?" He straightened, the bulk of his belly a burden after so many hours upright.

"Maybe she's just lonely, Harv. Maybe she's an independent woman knows what she wants." Lee was gathering steam, and I didn't like the direction his train was headed. "And maybe," he went on, "what she wants is me. She just don't know it yet. Don't you think, baby brother?" He slapped me on the back in a way that made me want to knock him flat.

"Harv," he said. "I think our little brother here's in love."

"I ain't in love. I just don't see the need to talk about her that way."

Maybe it was his own hurt feelings that made Lee unwilling to leave it be. "He thinks he's going to have him a girlfriend. Thinks that redhead might make a pretty swell babysitter."

"Shut up, Lee."

Lee cocked his head; his smile tightened. "Now," he said, just as our father might have, a summation or warning. "Now, you don't want to talk that way, brother. You know I'm just ribbing you."

"I don't like it, that's all."

"What makes you think I give a good goddamn what you like?"

Harvey rapped the counter with the knuckles of one hand. "I'm ready to shut this place down. Why don't you boys call it a night." Not a request but a command. I held to my empty glass.

Lee drained his whiskey. "I can tell you this. If I can't get that redhead, no one can, especially not some snot-nosed kid mewling around for a titty to suck on."

My first punch caught him in the chest, bowled him to the floor, and I might have hit him again if I'd thought about what I was doing. His right fist struck me behind the ear, sent me tumbling. Glasses and ashtrays spun off the counter, shattered; chairs racketed across the floor. Lee pinned me facedown, jerked my arm between my shoulder blades. The pain stopped me cold.

"You little son of a bitch. Don't you *ever* hit me." Lee pressed harder, and I felt my shoulder pop and burn.

"Lee!" Harvey had him by the collar and was dragging him backward. "What in the hell!"

I rolled, held my injured arm to my chest. Lee stood over me, breathing fast, hair fallen across his forehead. "You want a fight, I'll give it to you, brother. But you better know what you're asking for." He wiped back his hair, ran a hand down his face. "Harvey, you make sure he's all right."

I watched Lee slam out the door, heard the chatter of gravel as he gunned from the lot. I pushed myself to my feet, slid onto a stool. Harvey poured a shot, sat it in front of me. "I'd say you'd best leave that redhead be. Hell, she's twiced your age. Nothing worth fighting over."

I drank the shot, nodded sullenly, then made my way down the narrow hall to my room, where I undressed, worked my shoulder until I could raise my arm and know it wasn't torn, begin to savor the small pain.

I lay in the dark, thought of Irene. I said her name, to myself at first, and then in a whisper, and in that moment I remembered that I'd once known another girl named Irene. She was the youngest of the Yorks, the family who raised broomcorn just down the road from our farm in Oklahoma. We'd played together in her father's barn, where she'd let me touch the cool buds of her breasts. Her parents last saw her the morning of her twelfth birthday, when they'd sent her out to gather eggs and feed the stock. Some believed a stranger had found her; others said she had fallen from the fence while feeding her family's hogs, the boars big enough to trample most men. We watched as they dredged the deep mud of the wallow, convinced they would find proof: a knob of bone; a rag of yellow dress. Hogs will eat anything.

And though they found nothing, I would sometimes stop at that pen, where the hogs grunted and fought over eggshells and melon rinds. There was a mystery beneath the cloven hooves, the pig shit and slop, trampled deep into the earth. I wondered how the Yorks could bear to keep those hogs, but the animals were what held the family just shy of starvation. When they butchered that fall, the air filled with rifle blasts and screams nearly human, the smell of singed hair, the rasp of skin being scraped clean. They offered hams and feet and heads in exchange for the help of friends; they ate the meat all winter long and were glad for it.

Irene. I repeated the name to myself until it became something new, pulled up from the mud, reborn.

CHAPTER FIVE

I woke the next morning to the roll of Spud's chair between desk and file cabinet, the smell of pipe tobacco like the drift from a fruitwood fire. I lay for a while, allowing my eyes to adjust to the sun that filtered through the single window. I stretched my arm slowly, rolled my shoulder a few times. Across from me, Lee lay on his back, blanket kicked to the bottom of the bed, one arm across his face. He'd always slept late, even on the farm, when my mother would roust me for chores and whisper, "Leave him be. He's got to sing tonight."

I rose quietly, pulled on my jeans and shirt, slipped out into the hall. I needed some time to myself, some room to sort through my dreams. All night, they had been about Irene—her hair, her smell, her voice. I needed coffee, the sun, and the river to bring me back, knock some rightful sense into me.

Before I could make for the door, Spud called from his office. He sat behind his desk, in snap-button shirt and pressed trousers, thinning hair parted and neatly combed, looking more like a banker than an old cowboy, only his boots and the gray Stetson hanging from its peg giving him away.

"Buddy, come in here. I got something to show you." Across his desk were scattered several ledgers, sheets of papers covered with numbers. He held up a sheaf of receipts between his forefinger and thumb. "You know what these are?"

I half shrugged, nodded.

"No you don't. You don't know what these are." He flapped the bundle at me. "You think it's just money. But it's more, kid. Money ain't never just money." He opened a ledger, ran his thumb down the outside column. His hands betrayed him, roughened by the ranch work he'd done as a young man. No matter how many pencils he pushed, his fingers remained barked with scars, knuckles ridged with old wounds. The last joint of his right index finger was missing, but he never spoke of the incident that had taken it. Some thought he had missed his dally while roping steers for old man Norris; some believed he'd lost it in the war. Harvey said it had been bitten off by a jealous husband, one of the many who had caught Spud in bed with their wives. It was easier for me to picture Spud dallying a rope than it was to imagine him dallying with women, but Harvey said he'd been a different man in his younger days, before the death of his daughter and wife in a house fire. Something had quit in him then, and now, at the age of fifty, he seemed resigned to a life of safe margins and controllable risk.

In his office, Spud was the owner of The Stables, all business and intent. "Here's what I'm telling you," he said. "I'm taking in

checks from as far away as Spokane, and Lee Hope is the reason."
He relit his pipe, swiveled his chair so that he faced the back wall
where a window might have been, but this was a bar and he'd
seen no reason, he said, to let in light. I watched him study the
wall as though he might find some validation of his thoughts
there, some message posted on the cinder-block grid.

"You know, Buddy, this place is all I've got. It's what I've put
my heart into." I stood with my back to the door, wishing I could
ease from the room, wishing I cared more than I did.

"It's been touch-and-go. Idaho's a hell of a place. Only so
many liquor licenses, and those to the highest bidder. They've got
you by the balls." Spud wasn't talking to me but to the air, to the
forces outside those four walls, the politicians, the bank, the
liquor inspector. "Had to borrow just to get started. Sometimes I
think I might as well be working in the mines like my old man."
He leaned forward against the weight of the memory. I settled
against the door jamb, surrendering my morning. I owed him that
at least.

"Christmas, Pop was laid up with a broken leg, infected."
Spud stood, paced a few steps forward, a few back. "Family had
nothing but a sack of potatoes sprouting eyes."

I crossed my arms, stifled a yawn.

"Heard a knock at the door. Nobody there, just three boxes
of groceries. Mother went right to the kitchen. Wasn't but about
an hour till I began to smell the turkey roasting. My brother and
I got new gloves and whistles. Pop got wool socks. My mother
opened her gift, held up a pretty pair of amber earrings. 'Now,'
she said, 'where am I supposed to wear these?' 'In your ears,
Gladys,' Pop said. 'In your ears.' Probably the last time I heard her
laugh."

Spud stopped his pacing. "She wore those earrings to his funeral. Those boxes kept coming until my brother and I joined the service."

I waited for the answer.

"Don't know." He shook his head. "Maybe Jew Ida."

"Jew Ida?"

"Owned the whorehouse top of the hill." Spud squinted, looked toward the ceiling, ran his tongue along his bottom teeth. "Wonder if she's still living?" He grimaced against a flake of tobacco. "Not many like that no more."

"Miss Kitty." I'd seen several episodes of *Gunsmoke* and had been coveting Matt Dillon's girlfriend for some time, almost as much as I did his buckskin stallion.

Spud looked at me in surprise. "Miss Kitty's a whore?"

"Well, there she is in the saloon all the time. I guess she's a whore. I mean, the right kind."

"Damn." Spud stared past me, allowing the news to settle, then laid his pipe in the ashtray, licked the stub of his finger, flipped through another pile of checks. "Here's how it is, Buddy. What you're seeing here means I can sleep at night. Means I don't have to sell out, find another job. If Lee stays, The Stables stays. That's all there is to it." He pulled a handkerchief from his back pocket, worked it across the neat trim of his moustache. He was not fat but thick through the middle, barrel-chested, the kind of man my lean father would have described as built low to the ground—so stout a tornado couldn't take him.

Lee hadn't said a word to me about any notion he might have of leaving Snake Junction. Perhaps he knew, as I did, that he had the talent to move on to bigger stages, bigger crowds, radio—it had been our mother's dream, the only way she could imagine us finding our way out of poverty. But Lee was a man of limited aspirations. He'd found his place of comfort.

"I don't think Lee's going anywhere, Spud. I think he's happy right here."

Spud bowed his head. "Yesterday, I got a call from the Palomino Club in L.A. Guy's heard about Lee. Said he might come up and take a look."

Spud's words didn't mean much to me. California was a place so distant and exotic that I could hardly conceive of it as real.

"I know I don't own Lee." Spud brought his face up, steadied his eyes on mine. "It's just that he's come to mean something to this town. He makes people feel good, like they can dance and laugh and forget for a few hours. Truth is, I can always find another band, but I don't think I'll ever be allowed another Lee Hope. It was like you and Lee just dropped in here out of nowhere. Like those boxes on the porch."

"Lee's still in bed." I dipped my head toward the door of our room. "It's his concern."

"What are you going to do if Lee leaves Snake Junction? You need to think about what you want to do with your life. There are possibilities here." Spud stood close enough for me to smell his Old Spice, a hint of rum. "Kid, what goes well for me can go well for you." He clapped me on the shoulder, walked out into the hall and toward the bar. I understood that I should follow.

Spud poured himself a finger of 151, handed me a bottle of Coca-Cola. The sweet soda hit my empty stomach, and I felt a momentary wave of nausea. What I wanted was bacon and eggs, my mother's sausage gravy, baking powder biscuits cooked in the heat of her wood-fired stove.

"The same road that brought me here brought you." Spud

drank his rum neat, taking it in between his teeth. "When I was just back from the war, I drove west all the way to the Pacific, turned around, drove east straight through Snake Junction and on into the Dakotas, St. Paul. I wanted to see what I'd been willing to kill for, but all I saw was everything green, then brown, then Detroit gray as an old nickel."

I tried to imagine doing such a thing, heading for nowhere in particular, looking not for work or family but for something less namable. Maybe war let you do things like that. I listened as Spud told me that he'd never felt so free, just him, his first Oldsmobile, and a carton of Pall Malls on the dash. He'd slept in his car, eaten pepperoni sticks and Moon Pies, stopped when he felt like it, and drunk what he wanted. It was the dark bars he associated with that freedom, he said, not the wide-open spaces of Montana, not Michigan, churning its waste into the Great Lakes. It was the familiar interiors of Custer's Last Stand and Louie's Bar and Grill, Buster's Tavern and Diamond Lil's Lounge. He'd listened, decided that this was where real life began and ended: not in the office buildings or even in the trenches, but where people met their wives and lost their husbands, broke out their sorrows and celebrated their blessings, where the cigars got passed around, where the gleam in the father's eye first sparked.

Spud saw all this and brought it home to Snake Junction. He wanted a wife and a house and a business. He got the wife first, worked odd jobs and saved until he could get the loan that would buy him the land and the license.

"And then," he said, "things kind of went to hell."

I waited. All I knew about the death of Spud's wife and daughter was that it was awful.

"Becky would have been about your age." Spud smiled a bit.

"She had Sunny's blond hair. I always said that when she got to be grown, I'd have to keep a rifle at the door." He leaned over his shot glass, swirled the rum. "Doc said the smoke got to them before the fire did, but I can't help but wonder."

I remembered my cousin Del, who'd doused a stubborn garbage fire with gasoline and had it blow back in his face. I'd heard the explosion, screaming, found him running in circles, his face red and hairless. I remembered the cloying smell of roasted meat, the surprise still in his eyes. I remembered my mother with her canister of lard, the skin sloughing beneath her fingers.

"I couldn't even afford to bury them right. Those stones that are on them now, they're recent. It's been almost ten years, Buddy. You'd think that some peace would come after a while. You'd think that."

I figured it was probably worse to have lost a wife and daughter than a mother and father, but I didn't care to spend much time weighing loss right then. What I felt more than anything was a need to leave the dark building and head for the river, escape into sun and wind and the feel of the perfect rock in my hand. I wanted to feel the strength in my own arm as I threw it, aiming for the distant bank. It was my daily goal—to throw that hard, that far—but each time I hit only water.

"I could use some help around here, things keep going the way they are." Spud grimaced through another swallow of rum. "What I'm trying to say, Buddy, is that you've got a home here. You're getting to know people. They like you."

They like Lee, I thought, but did not say so. Didn't have to.

Spud straightened. "Harv says you and Lee had a disagreement last night."

I dropped my eyes.

"One of the best things could happen would be for Lee to find a nice girl, settle down. And I'll tell you something else." He pointed the stub of his finger my way. "No good's going to come of letting a woman make a fool of you. Just keep your head on, okay?"

"Sure," I said. "Thanks for the Coke." I set my mouth in an encouraging smile.

Out in the parking lot, I inhaled, like a diver coming up for air. Lee could remain at The Stables. Spud could hand the night-club to him on a silver platter. There was nothing I could say that made any difference in any of it. All I wanted was to go out and throw rocks, to be left alone with my dreams of a woman whose smell was the river's clean current, the sun warming the loam.

I crossed the highway, followed the faint trail leading to the shore, where I searched for rocks worthy of flight—round or oval, thin and flat, sized to fit my palm. My first throw brought a bright shock of pain: I'd forgotten about my shoulder. I lessened my effort, spent several minutes on short, shallow tosses until I'd worked out the soreness, but I knew I wouldn't be able to make the far bank that day. I blamed Lee, though my anger eased with the ache in my arm. Only once before in those first months after leaving Oklahoma had things gone bad between us: I'd been wait-ing for Lee to emerge from a trailer just at the edge of Snake Junc-tion. After an hour, I'd exhausted ways to keep myself occupied. I'd considered knocking on the door, but I knew better. Instead, I slid across the seat and turned the key, made a wide sweep through town, past the Blue Hare and the Pair-A-Dice, their parking lots empty. I'd gotten back in plenty of time, but Lee had heard the engine ticking, felt its warmth through the thin floorboard.

"What'd you do?"

I'd pretended to sleep, my arms folded, my head against the side window.

"Did I say you could drive this car?" He punched my shoulder when I didn't answer.

"I needed some heat, that's all."

"You want heat, you're going to get it."

"All right, all right. I got tired of waiting, so I drove around the block."

Lee glared. "Nothing in what I've got to do for you says you can drive my car whenever you feel like it."

"You don't have to do shit for me. You didn't sign a contract, did you?"

"I should have just left you back in Oklahoma to rot. You don't feel a moment's gratitude for how hard I work to fill your belly."

"I see how hard you work. You're still sweating."

Lee ran a quick hand across his forehead. I knew he wanted to hit me then, and some part of me wanted him to, wanted it over and done with, but instead he did what was in his nature to do: he began to laugh.

"God damn you," he said. "I can tell you that it's not bad work. Not bad at all." He had turned the key, pulled onto the road. "One more year, and then you can do whatever you damn well please. We both can."

We had come to some kind of understanding, some place of repose. But now that calm had been broken. I pitched one last rock and was headed back to The Stables when Laurette pulled into the parking lot, her station wagon bumping across the gravel. It needed new springs, probably more, things that a man like Dean wasn't likely to provide.

She leaned out the window, face flushed, hair tangled by the inrushing air. "Lee up yet?"

"Not yet." I shielded my eyes, saw that she wore the same outfit she'd been in the night before. "Everything all right?"

She smoothed back her hair, looked toward The Stables. "Spud in there?"

I nodded. "Counting his money."

Her eyes were red, the hollows beneath smudged black. She moved her gaze slowly from one point to the next. I'd seen that look on my mother's face those times my father staggered home in spite of himself, cursing anyone and anything he found in his path: the last of the cats scurrying for cover; the pail of string beans just picked for our dinner; my mother; me. We held ourselves still, kept our eyes directed at the task in front of us. But always he found something not right: kindling stacked too close to the fire, wick left too long in its chimney. Sometimes he could be distracted by sweet cakes and coffee. Sometimes nothing would stop him from hurling the chairs against the wall, belting me with the razor strop he kept hung on a nail behind the kitchen door.

I knelt beside the station wagon. "Want to come on in and have a Coke?"

She smiled, shook her head. "Don't want to wake your brother. He needs his sleep."

I wanted to ask what rest she'd had, but knew it wasn't my place. I considered our options. "I'm just headed down to the river," I lied. "You can come on with me, if you want. Maybe Lee will be up by the time we get back."

She looked toward the water as though she'd forgotten it was there.

"Maybe that would be nice," she said.

I held her elbow as we crossed the highway, steadied her as we climbed down the rocky bank to the beach, where I led her to a large boulder shaded by locust. She sighed, pulled off her boots and socks, rolled her cuffs, dug her toes into the sand.

"I used to spend all my summer days at the river," she said. "Some of the sweetest memories."

"It's a good place to be." I gathered a few rocks, sent them skipping across the ripples, the soreness gone.

"Is it like this in Oklahoma?"

"You mean the water?"

She nodded, long hair catching in the downriver breeze.

"Not like this," I said. "Nothing this big and clear."

She closed her eyes, took a deep breath. "It smells like so many things."

"I've been trying to figure it myself. Like alfalfa."

She lifted her nose as an animal might, taking in the wind, the waft of the mill, the heavy sweetness of dogwood and syringa. "Horses," she said. "It smells like horses."

"It does." I was nervous there by myself with Laurette, as I would have been with any girl or woman. I felt she might need something from me, expect a certain action I didn't know how to give.

"Want a smoke?" I asked.

"No. Never took to it. Thanks." She seemed embarrassed. I quickly pocketed the pack I'd extended, tried to figure what to do with my empty hands, picked up another rock.

"Wish I could do that," she said, watching the long skip across water. "Never been able to."

"Ain't hard. Here." I held out a stone the size and shape of a silver dollar. Perfect.

"I don't know how to throw that thing." Her shyness made her seem younger than she was.

"It's easy. Just keep it flat to the river." I gave it a good throw, and we watched as it arced again and again, like a salmon jumping for home. I found another, placed it in her palm. "The secret's in keeping *this* finger *here*." I curled her long fingers around, aware of the faint but sharp scent of someone up all night crying. The child smell of Lee. "Now, pull your arm back, just a little at the shoulder, more at the elbow. Sling it out there."

She pursed her lips, concentrated. One skip, two, and then the rock disappeared.

"Hey," I said. "That ain't bad for a first try." I gathered several more, handed them to her one by one, until the last winged perfectly, slapping the water ten times before sinking.

She laughed, sat down, and leaned back with her face to the sun.

"My daddy took us to this river every weekend of the summer." She closed her eyes. "All us kids piled in the back of the station wagon with the dog and a cooler full of Shasta. Sounds good right now, don't it?"

"You want me to run back and get you a pop?"

"No, no. It's not that I'm thirsty. It's the memory that tastes good." She twisted her hair into a rope, laid it over one shoulder. "He taught us how to swim. Just threw us in and watched us thrash around until we figured it out. He believed strong swimmers could survive most anything." She took a deep breath, seemed to relax. "Taught me to dive off the biggest rocks. He'd get down below, tread water, tease me off the edge. Those holes"— she nodded to where the river darkened and pooled—"they're deep."

"He still alive?"

"My father?" She knitted her eyebrows as though suffering some pain, then nodded. "He's alive. I'm the one who's dead. To him, anyway."

I felt myself being pulled toward a place I wasn't sure I wanted to go. I stayed quiet, hoped she knew what came next.

"I got in trouble right out of high school." She looked at me quickly, made sure I understood, pulled her knees close to her chest. "He never forgave me that."

I had a sudden picture of Laurette, just about my age, beautiful, unmarried, and pregnant. "I'm sorry," I said.

"Me, too, Buddy. I've made a lot of mistakes in my life. Too many."

"Did you, I mean, the baby . . ." I swallowed hard, not sure what it was I wanted to ask.

"My parents sent me to a home down south of here. The nuns took the baby away soon as it was born. Never even told me if it was a boy or a girl."

Somewhere behind us, a magpie nagged. Light shot off the water, so bright I shielded my eyes. Laurette made little fan shapes in the sand with her heels. "'Like a knife through butter,' my father always said. Wasn't happy if we made a sound or ripple. Wanted the water left smooth as glass." She looked toward Spalding Bridge. Only days before, I'd spent hours watching Nez Perce boys climb the girders to the top, push off and out, diving for the blue below. I'd wanted to be up there with them, full of dread and excitement, but I never jumped or raced anymore. That part of me was gone, buried in Oklahoma.

Laurette touched her stomach with one hand, remembering, I imagined, that baby she'd lost. I wanted to ask whether she missed it, whether she'd have kept it if they'd let her. I wanted to share with her what I'd always wondered: What would my family's life have been like if I'd never been born? One less mouth to feed. One less burden weighing my mother down. "A mistake," I'd overheard my father telling the men who gathered around the scalding pot at butcher time, passing the bottle around. "Should have taken care of it early on." I'd been drawn forward by the sound of my name and had watched from my place behind the shed door as they wrestled the dead hog into the cauldron, then hooked it back out, steaming and blistered red.

"Maybe you'll have others," I said. "You and Dean."

She rested her forehead against her knees, choked out a little sound. Her shoulders hunched forward.

"Laurette? You okay?" I could have reached out, touched her, but I was afraid that the current of pain that ran through her body might enter me. I looked around for some help, came up with a speckled rock, oblong and flat.

"Here. Throw this on out there. Make a wish first."

She forced a smile, took the rock, lobbed it without intent or direction. It *spaloop*ed into the river, dead weight.

"That was *good*," I said. "That was *fine*."

She laughed through her nose, shook her head. She was older, in charge.

"You're a good guy, you know that? Lee's lucky to have you for a brother."

"I don't know about that. He might be a lot better off without me."

She looked at me, pressed her fingers against my skin. "Don't you ever think so. Lee's good at what he does. He knows music.

But he has no sense of how the world's got to work. He can't see outside the brightness of those lights." She pulled away, crossed her arms and shivered, even though the day was heading toward swelter. "He needs you, Buddy. You're all that keeps him grounded. He may not say so. You just got to believe it. He could really be something someday. But I'm not sure he can do it without you." She ran a finger beneath each eye. "I better get going. Dean's liable to wake up and wonder."

"I'll walk you." I stretched, felt my spine pop.

"No need," she said. "I can find my way." She slid into her boots, started up the embankment, turned. "You take care of yourself. Take care of Lee. You two, you got good things ahead." She worked her way to the top, waved, and was gone.

I listened for the sound of the car engine, but all I could hear was the blow of trucks and cars down the highway. I settled back on the rock, felt the heat soak through my shirt and into my skin.

I thought about what Laurette had said about Lee, as though she could see some part of him that I couldn't. Hard for me to believe that he needed me more than he needed anyone else—just somebody to tell him how good he was, make him feel bigger.

But Irene. She was more than somebody, and Lee knew it as surely as I did. In those few moments, I'd felt she'd *seen* me. Seen who I was apart from Lee, some promise that I myself was never sure I possessed. I became aware of possibility, of a world outside my experience. Perhaps, even then, I knew she was the one who could take me there.

I imagined her in town, buying a dress, or at the market, picking out plums. Or maybe she was somewhere along the river, shoulders bare. I could not stand to think she might be on the road, headed away. I had to believe that she was still near, some-where in the cleft of the valley. I had to believe that I would see her again.

I looked to the clear southern sky, remembered how my mother would gaze out over the parched fields. Sometimes she could see ahead for days, rain coming, or not. But there was no way she could make it happen. "Out of my hands," she'd say, and extend her palms like shallow bowls. "No use trying to figure." Wishing for rain, she said, was like wishing for the moon in a ma-son jar. But then, when the rains did come, or when the town grocer scooped an extra pound of sugar, no charge, or when she made Lee stop the pickup along the road home because the soles of her feet were itching, and there, just beneath the running board, a silver dollar—these things were fate, pure and simple. "Good things come knockin' at your door," she'd say, "you'd bet-ter have your travelin' hat on."

I pitched a willow stick into the current, watched it bob out of sight. Maybe what I was feeling about Irene was fate, a pull so hard and sure there was no turning away from it. Maybe there was nothing to figure. Maybe all I needed was to be ready.

I left the river, walked back across the sticky black highway. I'd take it a day at a time, just like Mama always said. One day at a time.

CHAPTER SIX

Even though I was leaning into the darkest corner, Harvey spied me where I sat at the end of the counter, listening to Lee sing "Tennessee Waltz" too fast for such a sorrowful tune. It needed to be sung slow to feel the glide, like the rise and fall of a child's swing the longest day of summer.

Harvey gave me a stern look, then shrugged. I stretched against the slump of my back, felt my skin itch and tingle. Sometimes my hide felt taut, like the shrunken pelts of the rabbits I'd skinned and hung on the barn door to cure in Oklahoma.

I hadn't seen her come in, but then her voice, slow as winter syrup.

"Mind if I join you?"

She looked at me as if she had all the time in the world to let me consider. I jumped to my feet, knocking my cigarette from its ashtray. Harvey caught it as it rolled across the counter, handed it to me butt first. Irene smiled and I saw her teeth for the first time, straight and white against her lips. Other men at the bar were watching, some beginning to smirk and chuckle. She lowered her eyelids, gave them a look that would take the wood out of any man.

"May I?"

"Yes, ma'am." I watched her slide onto the stool next to mine just like she had entered her car—knees together, tilted in.

"What'll it be, lady?" Harvey asked. I wondered what it was about her that galled him so.

"A gimlet, please."

Harvey pulled a martini glass from the shelf, reached for the usual bottle of gin.

"*Tanqueray,* please."

Harvey hesitated, hitched his shoulders, mixed the good gin with the Rose's lime, put down the napkin and then the drink.

"I'll be starting a tab." Irene turned her head so that Harvey found himself staring into the perfect whirl of her ear.

"Come next spring," she said, "we'll see what Harvey can do with good bourbon."

"Spring?" My voice sounded tinny, high-pitched. I cleared my throat, relieved to hear she had plans to stay in the area for a while.

"Have you ever tasted a mint julep, all frosty and sweet?"

"No, ma'am."

She pulled a cigarette from her purse, held it between her fingers. I slapped the pockets of my shirt before remembering that my Zippo lay between us. I thumbed it open, flicked once, twice. She inhaled deeply, never looking straight at me, her eyes like the

56

eyes of a resting cat, their movement from one object to the next calm but intent.

"Do you know anything about horses, Buddy?" Her questions came out of nowhere.

"I know how to ride," I said. "Had a horse back home."

"Home?"

"Oklahoma." Surely I could say more. "Where are you from?"

"Further away than you." She made a little laugh in the back of her throat. "Greener than this place, though I like this better." She waved her cigarette in a circle as though tracing the circumference of the valley's disappointments or pleasures. When Lee caught sight of us, he pointed, smiled, then wagged his finger. I lowered my head to keep her from seeing the schoolboy redness of my cheeks.

"I'm going to dedicate this next tune to a new friend of mine," Lee announced into the microphone. "It's called 'Blue Eyes Cryin' in the Rain.'" A sigh of approval went through the crowd. "Honey," he said, waving a hand toward Irene, "this one's for you."

I glanced at Irene, found her still focused on me, as if nothing had interrupted our conversation. "My father loved his horses," she said. "He started taking me to races when I was old enough to stand."

"Did he raise thoroughbreds?" I pictured white-fenced paddocks, airy stables, long-legged stallions nickering for their mares.

Irene laughed. "He *bet* on horses. His dying wish was to see one of his picks beat the field to the finish line."

"My mare's name was Pepper," I said.

"Tell me about your horse, Buddy."

I felt my jaw tighten against the sudden grief, surprising me with its sharpness. "She was a good horse."

"Tell me," she said again, and so I did—sitting at the bar, the music carrying on without us, I told her more than I thought I could ever tell anyone. I told her how the mare would never stand still for my father to tighten the girth, how she'd shy away, he'd hit her, she'd shy again. How the more he beat her, the worse it got. How, in the end, he killed her.

Irene never took her eyes from my face. She did not care that Lee was singing just for her. She was a part of my story now.

"And all I could do," I said, "was stand there. Took her forever to die."

Irene's fingers touched my knee. Her smell settled on me like smoke, permeating my hair, my skin. Dancers swept across the floor behind us, and I felt a pang of foolishness, talking about a horse as though she were more than she was.

"I've always wondered about that song," Irene said, contained, pulling us back from something awful. "Whose blue eyes do you think are doing all that crying?"

It came to me that her eyes were the color of the crystalline green marble I'd treasured as a young boy, a marble I had turned before the window like a kaleidoscope.

"Now," she said. "How about a *good* story."

I nodded, waited for her to begin.

"Not from me, Buddy. From you. Tell me a happy story. Tell me what makes you happy."

I'd never been asked such a thing. What made me happy? I thought of the evenings on the porch with my mother and father, felt that I could say those had been good times.

"Music, I guess, makes me happy."

"Then why aren't you up there with your brother?"

I glanced at the band. "I'd rather just keep the songs to myself."

"What songs?"

I shrugged.

Irene considered me for a moment. "Do you want me to stop asking questions?'

"No, ma'am. I don't guess I do."

"Stop calling me ma'am. I'm not your mother." She held her hand toward me. "How about dancing. Does dancing make you happy?"

"The young man has got to get busy and stock." Harvey moved closer, ran his towel around the rim of a glass, nodded toward the back room. He and Irene studied each other for a long second.

"Another time, then," she said, and laid a five on the counter. When Harvey went to give her change, she pushed it away, then turned to me. "You might tell that brother of yours that I'd much rather hear a song about blue*grass* than blue eyes."

We all watched her go—the drinkers at the bar, Lee on the stage, the other women craning to see who it was that their men were taking notice of—until the heavy door swung shut. I felt the impulse to run after her, catch her in the parking lot, walk her to her car, just to hear that sweet drawl a while longer, breathe in the air around her.

The Spurs were finishing the set, drums and strings coming together in a final, drawn-out lament. I made for the back room, wanting to be alone, to reason it out. No one had to tell me that my longing would turn me sick inside. I knew, too, that it would not be enough to keep me from her. Already, she possessed me in a way I could not explain, and I understood without question that what choices still existed were no longer mine.

I woke to Lee knocking against the foot of my bed as he fumbled his way through the room.

"Shit," he said. "Darker than three feet down a cow's throat in here." The springs of his bed creaked as he kicked off one boot, then the other. They'd be there in the morning, slumped and stepped on. One of my self-imposed chores was to set them upright and out of the way. Though he had worked long hours to buy them, Lee didn't seem to understand their care. A quick brush, a snap of a rag across the toes, was enough to satisfy him. When I could stand it no longer, I'd get out the polish, rub up a shine.

He settled onto his back, sighed. "Get anything new on that gal?"

"What gal?" I pushed my face deeper into the pillow.

"You know what gal. Don't be sore about it. I ain't mad no more."

I tapped the wall with the tips of my fingers, keeping rhythm with the tick of the alarm clock. "What time is it?"

"Time to tell me what you and Red got going. Come on, Buddy. I'm up there on the stage, working like a dog, and you're having tea with the queen."

His lighter clicked. A faint glow reflected off the wall. "How old you figure she is? Hard to say, ain't it?" He inhaled, and the glow grew brighter, then dimmed.

"I don't know. Thirty-five maybe."

"Really? That old, huh?"

"She ain't old." I drummed harder.

"One thing you can see, she knows her way around. Probably *been* around a time or two. Think?"

"I'm going back to sleep." I willed myself still.

"Yeah, you're right. Time to quit thinking and start dreaming." He chuckled, stubbed out his cigarette. Within a few minutes, his breathing evened, and I was glad to be by myself again.

I rolled to my back, my hands across my chest, remembered the simple words to the song my father always sang, drunk or sober, as he made his way in from the fields. I sang along to the memory, whispering the words to the dark: "Good night, Irene, I'll see you in my dreams."

Lee shifted, sighed heavily. He had never liked the song, the words, he said, too sorry, bound to make anyone feel bad. Better to keep people happy and moving across the floor.

I wondered what Lee knew of love. In Oklahoma, he'd dated every pretty girl in four counties. Only one girl had ever held him more than a few weeks: Pattianne Jacobson. Long blond hair. Kewpie-doll lips. He might have kept her had he not taken off and joined the service. He received her letter while refueling in Bemidji, on his last leg home. My mother found the scented sheet of stationery in the pocket of the flight jacket he'd thrown on the floor, read the message aloud, the only way she knew how, then placed it back in the pocket. That night, she made oven steak, mashed potatoes, brown gravy. She put extra sugar in his tea.

Lee never spoke a word of it, and I never asked. Our family wasn't given to talking about such things. What good would it do? Like opening a wound. Like asking someone to cut a vein, bleed himself dry.

But it had felt good to tell Irene about the mare. She hadn't scoffed at my sadness or tried to tease me out of my anger. She'd simply asked, and then listened.

And maybe that is what first seduced me: not her beauty, not the melt of her voice, but the way she drew me out of myself, made me someone other than Lee Hope's little brother, the drunk-ard's son.

I closed my eyes, listened to the flight of a nighthawk, the deep, booming whir of its wings catching air. In the canyon, we were sheltered from the harshest winds, though I thought an up-river breeze might be rising—a low whistle through the window screen, a light perfume off the ditch lilies bordering the highway. I decided it was a good place to be on a summer night, my sheets cooled just to the temperature of skin. There was pleasure in the sense of it, and I realized that something in me was beginning to let go, give up its vigil.

I opened my eyes to the dark, sure that I had been dreaming, but the pleasantness remained, the nighthawk rising, falling, ris-ing again, each time the same sound, like the thump of a far-off drum, or the strong, steady beat of my heart.

CHAPTER SEVEN

I sat at the edge of Prospect Park, above a cirque of lilacs and paradise trees that sheltered a long stairway leading to the east end of Main Street. The walk from The Stables to the park was a few miles—just far enough for me to feel that I was escaping, leaving something behind. From where I sat, cool beneath the canopy of maple and sycamore, I could look out over the traffic and commerce of the town.

Most days, the swing set and teeter-totter were overrun with children bawling "Dibs!" and "Firsties!" This day the park was empty except for two old women walking their poodles, the kind of dog my father called bear bait. I'd just begun to doze when I heard Irene's voice coming from somewhere above me. I opened my eyes to see her standing at my shoulder.

"You know," she said, stripping a length of grass between her fingers, "they called my uncle the Celery King." She pointed to a building of notched logs no bigger than a root cellar that sat at the park's north edge. "He built that little shack there. Who would have thought a man could make a living growing celery?"

I sat up straight, then stood, out of respect, but also because her towering over me made me feel small. I remember the thin straps of her sandals, her toenails painted red, her short pants, her blouse the color of buttercups.

"Is that why you're here in Snake Junction?" I asked. "Because of your uncle?"

"That and other things," she said. A sheer white scarf held her hair. "How's your brother?" I couldn't see her eyes behind the dark sunglasses, just her mouth, pleasant and encouraging.

"He's fine."

"Seems that everybody thinks so." She lowered herself to the ground, crossed her legs.

"Don't you think so?" I asked. "That he's fine, I mean?"

She smiled, turned her head toward the valley. "I wonder if the Nez Perce used to camp here. Bet they did."

I considered her question, then the place: flat, high enough to see for miles, easy walking distance to the river. "I guess if I'd been an Indian, I'd have camped here," I said. "Seems like a good enough place. Good place to grow corn."

"The Nez Perce didn't grow corn. They were hunters. The women gathered berries and roots. There wasn't a farmer among them until the missionaries came along."

I felt the blood come to my face. I didn't want to be the one needing lessons. "Well, seems all they do now is drink and take the working man's money." I'd heard Harvey say it, and Spud, too, along with most of the other men who sat at the bar.

Irene looked at me, cool and even. "Seems you know a lot about some things."

Whatever blood had risen in me receded the instant I sensed Irene's displeasure. "I just know that they drink too much, that's all."

"Like your daddy?"

"My father didn't drink on government money."

"I bet he drank the food right out of your mouth."

I could muster no meanness toward her, no defense. "I've got nothing against the Indians. I'm just saying what I heard."

"What you hear, Buddy, isn't always what's true."

"I know that."

"What else do you know?" She took off her sunglasses. "What else do you think you know? Sit down here and tell me." She patted the ground beside her, and I sat, running a quick inventory of my knowledge.

"I know how to milk a cow and turn a field," I said. She looked away, her interest drawn by a starling that flitted from branch to branch. Something more. "I know how to hot-wire a car."

She sighed. I thought more carefully, considering every comical, brutal, magical thing I could remember: none of it seemed enough. What had I learned since coming to Snake Junction? I looked toward the place where the two rivers converged.

"There's a place in the Clearwater where all the bones settle, a deep hole full of nothing but bones."

Irene's eyebrows rose a little, but she kept listening. I sat straighter so that I could see the river better, see the story.

"There's old bones down there, bones of dinosaurs and buffalo, bones of cavemen and Indians and gold miners." I did not dare look at her for fear it would all fall apart. I had to believe what I was saying, make her believe it with me.

"New bones, too, some washed from shore in spring, others fallen from the sky, like when an eagle drops the fish it carries, or a hawk drops a rabbit, or maybe . . . maybe the bird just dies there, mid-flight, and falls into the water. It dies and its wings fold up and the water sweeps it along and down into the pile of bones." We both considered the probabilities, allowed silently that it could happen, that I could go on.

"Sometimes a deer swims the river in the same place it has crossed before, but this time the undercurrent catches it, pulls it down. Sometimes a man fishing for salmon in winter leans too far over, falls in, weighed by heavy clothes and boots. Or a woman just walks in and doesn't stop. They're never found because their bones are down there, caught forever, swirling around with the fish spines and the goat heads. That's what it is—a big stew of skulls and skeletons." She was seeing it with me, hearing the muted clack of bone against bone.

"The Indians call it Wa-Wan-Ka-Gookey: Place Where All Bones Come Together. Sometimes, at night, under a full moon, they go there to sacrifice. . . ." I hesitated, imagining the possibilities. "They sacrifice a pure white horse to Wa-Wan-Sha-Whinny, god of the river."

"Buddy, you're so full of shit." Irene pulled a handful of grass, threw it in my face. I resisted the urge to tackle her, push her to the ground, kiss her before she knew it could happen. Instead, I snatched a few green blades and threw them back. She smiled. "There's no such place. None of that's true."

"You didn't say it had to be true."

Irene lifted her chin, a faint sign of approval. "Have you ever been to Paulie's?" she asked.

"Once. When we first came to Snake Junction. Spud took us there for spaghetti."

"Let's go there now."

I felt a moment's excitement, then remembered that I had only a quarter and a dime in my pocket.

"I'd best not," I said, but Irene was already walking. I shuffled after her, quickened my step to open her door. She slid all the way over to the passenger side, then handed me the key.

The car had collected the sun's heat, and I squirmed against the burn of black leather, touched the steering wheel gingerly, resisting the urge to lick my palms. Irene sat with her feet propped on the dashboard, her legs above the blistering seat, and for a moment I saw her as she might have been at sixteen, ponytailed and lithe, bored and ready for a ride. I wanted to ask her what her life had been made of before Snake Junction. I wanted to ask if she had ever been in love, for I could almost believe that she had come to me at the end of some quest—years of looking and not finding the man she would give herself to.

I idled the Lincoln onto the road, watched from the corner of my eye the way her hair moved in the wind, lifting and falling from her neck. That day, everything about her—the bareness of her arms, her hair loosening in the wind—spoke to me of free-dom. Already, I was beginning the story of where the days might take us, how I might turn the Lincoln east, leave The Stables and Snake Junction behind.

And what if I had? Would she have allowed me to keep on driving, perhaps even smiled at the surprise of me? Was it my greatest failure to have taken, as I did, the known road through town? That moment of possibility comes to me clearly now.

Perhaps Irene, as she handed me the key that day, had hoped I would find the courage to save her.

She did not indicate disappointment as we pulled into Paulie's. She seemed full of good spirit, and except for the anguish I was feeling over my state of impoverishment, I, too, felt as lighthearted as I had in years. The restaurant didn't look like much, just a squat concrete building painted bright green. Only one other car occupied the parking lot. Irene pulled out her compact, applied a quick stroke of red to her lips.

"Maybe I should just drop you off and walk from here," I said.

"Why?" She moved her lips together, then touched a finger to each corner of her mouth.

I was too embarrassed to tell her I had no money, and I could not imagine letting a woman pay for my meal. Irene knew all this without my having to speak it.

"Just pretend I'm your aunt Agatha. Aunties spoil their nephews, at least where I'm from."

"I don't have an Aunt Agatha."

She snapped shut her mirror, looked at me over the top of her sunglasses. "Buddy, do you intend to be difficult?"

"No. I just . . ."

"You just don't find me good company?"

"No, that's not it at all."

"Buddy"—she leaned toward me just enough to let me see that the green of her eyes was laced with brown—"are you shy?"

"No, I ain't shy."

"Are you afraid of me, then?"

"No." And this was another lie.

She stepped out into the parking lot, led me through the entryway with its trellised partition woven with plastic grapevines. I could smell her—buttered toast, summer wheat, peach jam spiked with cinnamon. I knew that if I were to reach out, slide my hand beneath her hair, it would be heavy and hot with sun.

Paulie stood behind the cash register, counting his lunchtime take. He had the look of an immigrant Swede, big-jowled and flushed. His last name was Gertonson, but he claimed to have learned to make lasagna from his Italian grandmother. He seemed to recognize Irene and smiled broadly, then directed us to a corner table spread with a red-and-white cloth, handed us each a menu bound in cracked vinyl.

"Our special today," he announced, rubbing his hands down the white apron tied high on the mound of his middle, "is *penne all'arrabbiata,* but it is not for the timid." He spoke like a man uncomfortable with English. He looked at Irene and then at me. "We also have fried chicken."

"Oh, heavens, no," Irene said. "I think we should go with the chef's recommendation. Don't you, Buddy?"

Paulie brightened.

I'd been keen on the fried chicken, which I hadn't had since leaving Oklahoma. There'd been great platters of it at the funeral, bowls of potato salad, baked beans and slaw. I'd thought my grief would disallow any pleasure, but I'd eaten with an appetite that seemed insatiable, clearing plate after plate until I'd sickened myself. Lee had found me retching behind the church, my mended suit stained with the mud I knelt in.

"What's the penny stuff got in it?" I asked.

"You'll like it, Buddy. And we need a bottle of wine. A good one."

Paulie's face grew even ruddier. "Yes, yes! Wait!" He held up a finger as though we might bolt, then disappeared through a narrow doorway. He returned with a bottle and two glasses, looked at me and winked. "In the old country," he said, "even the young drink wine with their meals." He made a quick cut with his knife, skewered the cork, then set it in front of me. "Smell it. Stick it right up to your nose."

I looked across the table at Irene, who raised her perfect dark eyebrows.

"Like this." Paulie plucked the cork back up, ran it beneath his large nostrils, inhaled deeply. "Ah! Now you."

I gave a quick sniff. Irene and Paulie laughed.

"Me," Irene said. She closed her eyes, opened her mouth, and breathed in. I had a memory of my father, letting his mouth drop open to better smell the wind, to trace the path of fire or the trail of a possum. When Irene opened her eyes, they were focused on me, and in them I could see her pleasure. I felt the muscles in my groin tighten.

Paulie touched the bottle to her glass, poured an inch, stepped back and waited. Irene swirled the wine, raised it to her nose, then her mouth. Paulie watched, as taken as I was.

"This is lovely," she said. "We should have some bread. And maybe some olives. Do you have olives, Paulie?"

Paulie nearly skipped to the kitchen. Irene filled my glass, then topped her own, raised it between us. "This," she said, "is to how little it takes to make life good."

I'd never tasted wine of any kind before, not even the fermented watermelon juice my uncle bottled every summer and swigged all winter long. I took a long drink and swallowed. Irene shook her head.

"Like this." I watched the delicate movement of her jaw. "Now you," she said.

I took a mouthful, swished it around.

"Don't you taste it?"

I didn't know what I was supposed to be checking for. Another drink, and I felt the warmth in my chest. We were alone except for the sad scratch of opera—the record Paulie had put on the hidden hi-fi—and I was glad that there was no one there to see me, working my mouth like a fish.

"Breathe through your nose," Irene said, and I did and thought I might taste something like dirt, which might be what she was looking for.

"How do you know all this?" I asked.

Irene shrugged, nodded toward the music. "This is Caruso singing Verdi. Opera is like wine—best when it's old. But then," she said, "maybe that's the very reason why you don't like it."

"I like it," I said, and I meant the music and maybe the wine, which was tasting better with every swallow, and I hoped that she knew I meant that her age was nothing but good to me. I knew how she must see me: a country boy, ignorant, crude. What she didn't know, what I was just beginning to understand, was how tired I was of having my life defined by nothing more than simple survival. I knew that there was a different kind of existence, but I could not imagine how I might cross over the boundary that separated my kind of people from the kind who kept books on their shelves, who listened to the music of composers with names like Verdi—people who understood that food could be for something other than filling your belly, and wine for something other than filling your head. Even the bread was different: tart and thick-crusted.

Paulie steamed toward us, platters lining each arm. I drank more wine. Irene refilled our glasses.

"Are your parents still in Oklahoma?"

"They're dead. Car wreck. My father . . ."

Irene nodded. "My father never drank. Horses seemed to be his only vice."

"Is he still alive?"

"No. He died when I was young. My mother, some years back." Irene pushed herself away from the table. "I've got to use the powder room. You keep eating."

I watched her move between the tables, watched her calves and her hips, the soft curve at the base of her spine.

"That hot enough for you?" Paulie stood over me. "You're not leaving much for the dogs." He seemed less Italian with Irene out of the room.

"It's good," I said.

"You like that wine?"

"Yes, sir."

"You'd better." Paulie lifted my plate. "You're one lucky SOB. Lots of guys would give their left nut to be in your place."

"Yes, sir," I said. "Irene's a nice girl."

Paulie snorted. "You better look again if you think that's a girl you been sitting across from."

Just then Irene came back into the room, and I could not help noticing the fullness of her breasts. She smiled at Paulie, laid her hand on his arm. "Paulie, I don't know when I've had better. You're a wonder." She kissed him lightly on the cheek. What passed across his face was a mix of oafish delight and pain—here, he knew, was a woman he would never have.

When we left the restaurant, I paused for a moment, breathing in the evening air, regaining my balance. I opened the driver's-side door, let Irene slide in and across. When we came to the stop sign, she pointed east with the tip of her cigarette. We passed The Stables, the mill, the small ranches, the cattle hunched tight behind barbed wire. We drove to Spalding, crossed the high-arched bridge spanning the river. Nearby was a weed-ridden cemetery full of dead missionaries and converted Indians, and next to that, two picnic tables, a plank-seated swing.

"Let's walk," Irene said. The bridge rose before us, silvering in the twilight. She stepped carefully over the round stones, didn't stop until she was beneath the bridge, and then she began to undress, first her sandals, then her blouse pulled over her head, the white moment of her bra. She worked pants and panties from her hips. There was the paleness of her stomach and breasts, and then she walked into the river until she disappeared in the black current.

I'd never treated my clothes so poorly. I shucked my way to the water, felt my scalp and scrotum tighten. When the current caught me at the knees, I buckled and swam toward where I'd last seen her. At first it was excitement that made my heart pound and breath shorten, but when, after several minutes, I hadn't found her, it was fear. I imagined her pulled down by an undertow, caught in a submerged root. I swam upriver against the water's flow, then let it carry me back down, then swam again, calling her name, the sound of my voice swallowed by the loud rush.

I willed myself to shore, crawled onto the pebbled sand, sat curled in against my knees. I was shaking, a bone-rattling tremble, my teeth grating.

"Do you know why I like it here?"

I turned and she was beside me.

She rested her hand on top of my head. I tensed against my desire to cling to her legs. She expected more of me.

"No."

"I like it here because I've always wanted to be near a clear river that I could ride my horse into, buck naked. I'd hang on to its mane, let the water float me up."

The moon was beginning to rise above the canyon's rim. There was enough light to see her teeth and the whites of her eyes, the shadow and glow of her. I realized as well that she could see me. I straightened my back, set my elbows atop my knees.

"Sometimes I wish that I could grow up all over again, here at the edge of this river. Be reborn, reincarnated."

"Reincarnated?" I worked to control the waver in my voice.

Irene's laugh was tender. She ran her fingers down my neck, traced the tops of my ears. I was warming now, the terror and chill leaving me in equal measure. There was in the air a peppery sweetness that reminded me of the meal we'd shared. I tried to keep my eyes on the river, but the moon gave more light as it came into the sky, and there was the dark of her nipples, the flare of her hips, the triangle of hair that she did not guard at all.

"Tell me, Buddy, why you think I'm here with you instead of Lee."

"I don't know. I wonder that, too."

"I never wonder. I never question the why of anything. Some things are just the way they are because they're meant to be." She knelt beside me, and I felt the brush of her against my shoulder. "I'm not looking for a man to belong to, Buddy." She ran a fingernail through the sand between us. "Lee couldn't give me what I want any more than I could give him what he'd want from me."

"I don't know about that."

"Yes, you do. You do know." She leaned against me. "What if all I want is an hour with you along this river? One hour. Will that be enough?"

What answer could I give her? To say yes seemed a betrayal. To say no would have been more than foolish. She took my face in her hands, kissed me.

"Tell me something, Buddy. One thing. Something true."

I lay back, daring to rest my hand on her thigh. She could see all of me now, my weakness and desire. I closed my eyes. "There was another Irene, a girl with red hair like you."

"Yes."

"She let me touch her."

"Where?"

"In the barn."

"No, Buddy. Where on her *body* did she let you touch her?"

"Her breasts. She let me touch her breasts."

"Did she let you touch her anywhere else?"

"No."

"Did you want to?"

"I don't remember that I knew there was anything else to want." I moved my fingers higher up the inside of her thigh, but her hand caught my arm.

"Tell me more."

"There is no more."

"About Irene."

"She disappeared one day. Maybe a stranger got her. Some said she fell off the fence into the hog yard and got ate. That's all."

I felt her pause a moment, but then she brought my hand around to the small of her back. "Poor girl," she said. "Poor Irene."

I moved my mouth to her shoulder and then to her breast. I tasted the river and the sage around us. I tasted the metallic air and the sand. I wanted to beg, to demand, and thought I might die if she denied me. A single touch would have been enough to finish it, but she kept her fingers light across my back, along my arms. I groaned, rolled to be on top of her, but she pressed me back.

"You're a boy," she said. "A very beautiful boy." She brushed the hair from my forehead, kissed above each of my eyes.

"I'm almost eighteen. I'm old enough." Please, I thought. Please.

"For what? What are you old enough for?"

"For this."

"For this," she whispered against my lips. Then she sat back, turned her face toward the river. "Should we swim some more?"

"I'm done swimming." I ran my hand beneath her hair.

"It's time to get you home." She stood, looked downriver as though taking her bearings.

"I don't have a home." It was the first time I'd let myself say it, and I felt a wash of self-pity. I thought to reach for her, talk her out of her judgment, but I feared she would turn away. I touched her leg. "What did I do wrong?"

"Nothing. That's the problem. There's so very little wrong about you."

She's wavering, I thought. Reconsidering.

"You're going to get hurt, Buddy."

"I can take care of myself."

"It would hurt you and Lee." She wasn't talking to me but to the moon, it seemed, casting her words toward its stony face.

"What's Lee got to do with this?" I felt my desire and frustration building toward anger.

She sighed. "In some ways, nothing. In other ways, everything."

"You're wanting him instead of me." I set my jaw, pulled my eyes away from her, contemplated the distant bank, pretending conviction.

Irene turned to me slowly. "Don't you think I know what I want?"

"You're making me wonder, that's all."

"Don't wonder. What I feel for you is something I'm not even sure *I* understand. What I know is that you're a good person, Buddy. We've got to take care of each other, and I'm not sure this is the right way to do it."

"It feels pretty right to me."

Irene laughed, touched my arm. "Come on. Let's find our clothes."

I didn't want to find my clothes. I didn't want to move from that spot with the shallow imprint of Irene's body next to me. I wanted to demand that she finish this thing she had begun. Instead, I stood, turned my back to her with exaggerated modesty, brushed the sand from my legs. I stepped into my pants, looked around to see her standing, feet apart, arms crossed, face raised to the dome of stars.

I wanted to tell her how beautiful she was, like ivory, I'd say, like marble. Already, I knew better than to offer her such easy praise. I shook the sand from my shirt.

"Irene?"

"Yes?"

"This didn't take up all of that hour, did it?"

She stepped closer, kissed me, began searching for her clothes. I watched her, feeling that I was floating, the river's current pulling me far from shore.

CHAPTER EIGHT

"You're headed places you ain't got no business going. You're headed for trouble."

Lee steered the Chevy south with one hand. I watched the speedometer hit seventy, then eighty. The sun had baked all the moisture from the air. Even with the breeze coming in off the fields, tasting of sweetgrass, we were both sweating, shirts unsnapped, collars laid open.

We were driving toward the small town of White Bird, where Lee and the band performed now and again as a favor to Hap, one of Spud's old drinking buddies. I loved the drive across high prairie, had come to accept the mountains in the distance, *true* mountains, ragged and abrupt in their rise, nothing like the worn-off hills of Oklahoma. There was little I missed about that place of high humidity, storm cellars, and scorpions. Unlike Lee,

I never yearned for the drone of cicadas filling the night. Times, I felt like a traitor.

Just before Lapwai, we passed Wolfchild. He walked straighter than any man I'd ever seen, braids hanging down like plumb bobs.

"Friday," Lee said, and hit the horn as we sailed past. Wolfchild gave a slight nod of recognition.

"Old boy's going to be disappointed to find we ain't there." Lee smiled a little, then got back to business. "That Harvey's got you thinking you're older than you are. You should be studying history, playing ball." He scratched the back of his neck, raked a fingernail across the wale of his slacks, lit another cigarette but didn't offer me one, and I knew better than to ask.

Paulie had stopped by The Stables, mentioned to Harvey that he'd seen me with Irene. Harvey told Lee, who'd done little more than bellow that come hell or high water, I was headed back to school and that he'd damn sure see me there. It was an idle threat: we both knew he had neither the will nor the discipline to monitor my movements, chart my daily progress.

But I wasn't thinking about school or playing ball—I was thinking about Irene, how we'd agreed to meet again beneath the bridge Saturday morning, only one long night away. Nothing Lee could say would shake the pleasure of that. I let his words blow past me, out the open window.

"God damn it, Buddy. What's happening here? Everything was going great, and now we can't hardly be civil. It's her fault. She knows what she's doing, you can bet your ass." Lee spat out the window, wiped his mouth with the back of his hand. "What I can't figure out is why. What's she after, Buddy? What's she doing this to us for?"

I laid my head back, lidded my eyes against the hot light. "I don't think she's doing anything. Why is it so hard to believe that she might just like being around me?"

"Shit, Buddy, can't you see? I don't mean for this to sound wrong, but, hell, why would she, I mean . . ."

"Want to be with me when she could be with you instead." I didn't look at him but at the mountains in the distance.

"Okay. Okay. Let's say that's just what I mean. It's not about you, Buddy. Not *you*." Lee opened his palm toward me. "You're just a kid. If she was twenty, I could understand it. Lord, Buddy, she looks good, but she's damn near too old for *me*."

"Then what are you worried about?"

Lee's lips tightened. "You listen to me. There are some things you just don't know yet. There ain't nothing wrong with you wanting a girlfriend, but you need to find a girl your own age. A girl who won't mess up your mind. Besides"—he turned his head, spat again—"ain't no way you can handle a woman like that."

I wanted to tell him I'd lain with Irene on the bank of the river, touched her breasts, but I knew it was weak brag. I took a sidelong measure of Lee's height and weight. It wouldn't be long before I caught up with him, maybe even grew past him, and then the pecking order would come down to something other than size. I closed my eyes slowly, opened them again.

Lee snorted. "You're right. What in the hell am I worried about? You wouldn't know what to do even if you had that gal naked on the bed in front of you."

He gave himself over to the delightful obviousness of his statement, began to hum a little. He took the cutoff at Grangeville that dissected the just-mown fields. Idaho farmers had it good, he said, no matter how much they grumbled about lack of rain. Let them try raising broomcorn and cotton for a season or two. Let them plant their seeds in broken clay, watch the dust rise up and the locusts come down, not grasshoppers but *locusts,* swarms of them, so hungry they ate the feathers right off the chickens.

"Sissy farmers," Lee pronounced. "Catholic boys, whining about how bad they got it. They don't know what bad is." Our family had never had any use for Catholics, eating fish on Friday and praying to idols on the Sabbath, all of them sprinkled with water and thinking that meant they were baptized. Believers in Oklahoma knew what it meant to be washed free of sin: full immersion in the brown creeks, cottonmouth nests downstream and up but not in that place that was marked and prayed over and kept free of limbs and cast-off twists of bailing wire. I looked out the window to where the green and gold gave way to charcoal blue, the canyon. Rivers ran through Idaho like veins through a hand.

We stopped at the top of White Bird Grade, took in without comment the enormous sweep of open country, the battleground where the Nez Perce had fought and destroyed most of the First Cavalry. Lee pissed on a clump of sagebrush. In the valley below, the scattered ranches and buildings squatted beneath a light haze of harvest dust.

"You want me to drive on in?" I don't know why I asked. Maybe it seemed an easy distraction.

"Hell, no. We're there, for God's sakes." Lee mouthed a smoke, stuck his hands in his front pants pockets, tipped his head back, looked at the sky. His black hair hung thick against the collar of his shirt, and I recalled what my mother often said, that you'd think a squaw had birthed him. I remembered an old sepia-colored photograph, a brown-skinned woman with sad dark eyes.

When I'd asked who it was, my mother had said it was our great-grandmother. "But she married an Englishman," she added, "and that blood's been washed clean." I'd studied the photograph a long time, understanding that the eyes I looked into were the same color as my own.

"God's country," Lee said. "That's what Spud thinks. You think so?"

"Guess it could be."

Lee cocked one eyebrow at the basalt and blown sage, laced his fingers and stretched, his knuckles popping. "Maybe I'll let you drive home tonight. I could use a little extra sleep."

An uneasy truce hung between us. I felt the need to offer some other token of goodwill, but I couldn't think of what it might be.

"Christ, Buddy." Lee brushed his fingers toward me. "I don't care nothing about that redhead. Hell. She don't know who she's messing with." He feigned a punch. I pretended defense, hunched and fisted. He laughed, clapped me on the shoulder. "There's plenty of fish in the ocean, baby brother. We might just catch us a few right down there." Lee pointed toward the town. I thought of the women I'd seen in White Bird, knew that none of them could be anything like Irene.

Lee dropped the Bel Air into low, took the switchbacks easy. "Did she say where she's from?"

"Somewhere down south, I guess. Kentucky." I felt Lee gathering himself for another question, and then I remembered the one thing I felt I could give up without feeling robbed. "She said that she'd like to hear you singing about blue*grass* instead of blue *eyes*."

Lee considered this for a moment, then laughed. "Hell," he said. "If that's all it takes, I'm shittin' in tall cotton." He picked up the refrain of "My Old Kentucky Home" without a hitch as we pulled up in front of Hap's Saloon. It was as though Lee had been born with all the words and melodies of every song in his head. The old country ballads, the new tunes by Elvis, Fats Domino, Pat Boone. The songs the old women wanted to hear and the ones the young men requested, scrappy in their dress boots and wanting to shine. I'd heard talk of the Holy Rollers speaking in tongues, and I thought it must feel the same: just open your mouth and the soul of the song was there.

Lee sang louder as he stepped out into the last wedge of sun the mountains allowed. A dog took up barking, and then others down the street, Lee's clear and vibrant tenor filling the narrow corridor between hillside and hillside, drifting down toward the rough water of the Salmon River, so that even old man Bilson, homesteaded below the bluff, might have heard it above the mewl of his peacocks and the constant haw of his own failing lungs. He'd be there at the bar, and Mrs. Bilson, too, and most folks from miles around.

Tina and Todd Carlisle brought their five-year-old twin boys, settled them beneath their table to play with toy cars and suck on dill pickles from the big jar by the cash register. No liquor inspector was ambitious enough to take on Hap. People in White Bird savored their isolation, their self-regulation, and the law they'd hired: Emery Hewitt sat across the table from Mr. and Mrs. Bilson, still wearing his badge but holding himself to coffee, passing the few hours until ten, when his shift would end.

When the rest of the band arrived, I watched Dean shake Emery's hand, rub the twin heads that bobbed at his knees. I noticed something different right away: too much cheerfulness, a slide in his words. Laurette smiled at me tightly, her face pale against the dark frame of her hair. It was her silence and averted eyes that made me realize Dean was drunk.

Floyd concentrated on setting up his steel. He'd been in the station wagon with them, two hours of who knew what kind of meanness.

"Hey, Buddy." Dean snaked toward me, bumped me with his belly. He ordered a Jack Daniel's, then stuck his hand deep into the murky jar Hap kept next to the dills, stuffed a pickled egg into his mouth, and grinned at himself in the mirror behind the bar, nearly choking on his own laughter. He raised his drink in the air. "Here's to one-eyed jacks and anything red." He threw back the shot, set the glass down hard, wiped his mouth, staggered to the stage, collapsed on his stool. He was sweating, his hair fallen down from its backward sweep, making him look greasy and old.

The good feeling of the evening was gone, replaced by memories of my father, those nights we'd forgotten to miss him, surprised at first and then saddened by his reappearance. Those were the times, after the quiet hours spent with my mother, that I wished my father dead.

I felt a sudden loathing for Dean in his weakness. I hated Floyd, who glowered like a troll and plucked at the strings of his steel. I looked around the room, saw that I hated wheezing Mr. Bilson, his wife who sat like a lump of manure beside him, her mouth red as a monkey's ass. I hated the bloated lawman with his holster and gun, the young couple sucking on their cigarettes, kicking at their sons under the table. I thought I might hate the little boys, too, though in them I could see some remembered part of myself. I hated that no one in that room would ever move beyond what was held within its walls: the beer and whiskey, the stinking jar of eggs and hillbilly tunes. I thought of good wine and Verdi. I thought of all that Irene had spoken of that night after we left the river, when we'd driven the back roads for hours, and I had listened to her talk about Shangri-la; butter made from the milk of mares; the miracle of Michelangelo, how he worked on his back atop a scaffold until his death, and this she had been reminded of by the ceiling of stars that turned above us. She had opened me up, gutted me, begun to fill me again. I was hungrier than I had ever been, and I could not separate my hunger for her from my appetite for the new world.

Lee picked up his Gibson, ran his fingers down the strings, said, "I'm Lee Hope, and this here's the Golden Spurs. Let's do it!" He dipped hard into "Hound Dog," caught Laurette and the others by surprise, forced them to follow. He played loud and sang louder, stomped his foot, urged people to the floor with a long swing of his arm. He made eyes at Tina and winked at Todd. He puckered his lips at Mrs. Bilson, who ducked her head and covered her mouth with one fat hand. He led into "Jailhouse Rock" without a break, pointed his finger like a gun. "Almost ten, Emery. Better start lining them up."

Emery laughed and nodded. Dean worked the drums, wiped the sweat from his eyes. Lee moved in front of him and smiled down, said loud enough for everyone to hear, "You're *workin'*, ain't you, brother? You're going to *work* tonight."

They played two hours without a break. Emery tapped his thick fingers on the table. Mr. and Mrs. Bilson sat and listened and drank themselves into a deeper state of idiocy. Hap made his rounds, glad to have Lee onstage and more people coming through the door.

Lee took his hand from the strings long enough to hold up two fingers. In another minute, he had a double Jack and was drinking it down, another on the way. I could see how the liquor flowed through his fingers and into the music, out the door opened to the air, out into the night to mingle with the dogs' baying.

It was a while before I noticed the two men who came in late and stood at the bar instead of sitting. Greasy caps, shirts with ragged armholes where the sleeves had been cut away to ease the heat. Farmhands, I guessed, just off the fields. They watched the dancers without interest, drank their shots quick. I could hear them talking to Hap, sizing up the season's crop, reciting a litany of broken tractor parts.

The taller man was fit, tanned. White teeth, dark eyes—the one girls would think was handsome, except for his missing lower right arm. The hook didn't surprise me. Pickers, tillers, thrashers—all could crush a hand, shred it to pieces. I felt a moment's luck to have escaped that life whole.

And then I saw the short one, face red beneath the dirt, point at the stage, saw his friend laugh, Hap draw back a little. Shorty, for surely that was his name, gave a high whistle, clapped and stomped his foot against the bar rail. I followed his gaze and saw that it was Laurette his attention had settled on. He licked his lips, nudged his friend, ordered another beer. I felt the hair on the back of my neck prickle.

When the band finally took a break, I silently willed Laurette to stay onstage, but like everyone else, she needed some air. She worked her way through the crowd, eyes down, was almost past when the tall man grabbed her with his good left hand.

"Buy you a drink?"

She shook her head, cast a quick look toward Dean. But

Dean had collapsed against the wall, wiping his forehead with the tail of his shirt. It was Lee who caught her eyes, walked to where she stood. I pushed away from the table. Emery had checked his watch at ten and was out the door before the two men arrived. I felt we were about to miss him.

"Come on. Just a drink." The man pulled at her wrist, tipped Laurette against his chest. Shorty laughed.

"Listen," Hap said. "The lady needs some air." He set down two beers. "You might be off the job, but she's still got work to do."

"And what kind of work's that? Anything I might be willing to pay for?" The tall man tried to draw her closer, but she struggled away, knocking his cap to the floor. The top of his head was bald as a baby's behind. A few people laughed. He snatched up the cap, glared his friend silent. Laurette took two steps toward the door before he reached for her, catching her hair in his fist, pulling her backward onto his lap.

I was a running leap ahead of Lee. It didn't take much to throw Shorty to the floor, but then I stopped, not sure how to get at the tall one without hurting Laurette. Lee stood behind me, pointed his finger.

"Mister, if you know what's good for you, you'll let her go."

The man smiled, took another twist of hair. He opened the hook, pinched it around the neck of his beer bottle. Laurette closed her eyes, braced herself against the man's body.

Shorty was hauling himself to a stand. He raised both hands, backed away. Floyd moved next to him, nodded at Lee.

I reached out a hand to Laurette, but the man yanked her sideways. "She's that good, huh?" He looked from Lee to me.

"Let her go." Lee's eyes never left the man's face.

Hap didn't see it coming, and neither did we. The man busted the beer bottle against the bar. Brown shards flew across the room. Mrs. Bilson screamed and shoved out the door.

"Now," he said to Lee. "Who gets cut? You"—he moved the jagged glass to Laurette's cheek—"or this sweet thing?" He was sweating, older than I'd first thought. The low lights had hidden the oily creases of his face, the puffiness beneath his eyes.

"Get the rest of them out, Floyd." Lee held the man's eyes as Floyd shuffled Shorty and the others out the door. "Hap, you best stay as witness."

Hap grunted, took a few steps back.

"Dean," Lee called over his shoulder. "You still here?"

I looked, saw Dean's place was empty, shook my head.

"Now, what you got here," Lee told the man, "is two against one. Maybe that ain't quite fair. You let the girl go. You want to fight after that, you pick." Lee moved his finger between us. "Me, or my little brother. The other won't interfere."

I blinked, swallowed hard.

The man raised one side of his mouth, snorted.

"There's one thing I can guarantee you," Lee said. "You ain't going to hurt that gal and live to tell of it, so you might as well take your chances right now. But fair. No cuttin'."

"And what do I get out of this deal?" The man grimaced a smile.

"You get to keep your balls, pal. And you get the chance to prove that plowboys can do something more than finger their own assholes, which must have been just how you lost that hand of yours."

The man's smile faded. He dropped the broken bottle behind

the bar, looked at me. "Your brother always get you into this kind of trouble?"

"What trouble?" I gave him my best Marshal Dillon grin.

He unwound Laurette's hair, pushed her to the floor. "Okay," he said. "You and me, little brother." He straightened, and I saw he had me by a good thirty pounds.

Lee nodded once, moved a few feet off. I took three steps back, raised my fists.

"Take off the hat," Lee said, and pointed to the man's head. "Fella can't fight with his hat on."

The man gritted his teeth, threw down his cap. Lee snickered.

"Shut up, God damn it. Shut the hell up." The man turned his angry eyes on me. "I hope it's something good you owe him for, 'cause you're sure as hell going to pay."

He lunged beneath my arms. I brought my knee up, caught him square in the throat. He rolled to his back, clutching his windpipe. I stared down at him, fists still raised. I couldn't believe my luck.

I waited a few seconds, then called over my shoulder to Lee. "Should I hit him again?"

Lee sauntered closer, lighting a cigarette as he came. "Kick him once."

The man gasped for air, eyes wide. I gave him a light tap in the ribs.

"That should do." Lee looked toward the door. "I'm going to check on Laurette, drag the band back in. We got songs to play."

The man's face had paled some. I extended my hand, but he shook his head and rolled away. I shrugged, walked to the counter. "Guess I'll have a whiskey, Hap." I was about to bust with pride.

Hap turned to get the JD, and when he came back around I saw him startle. I had just enough sense to raise my shoulder before the chair caught me across the middle, knocked me to the floor. I rolled, saw the boot coming for my head, reached out blind, brought him down on top of me. We scrambled apart, stood, circled once before the man reached in his pocket and pulled out a penknife.

"No knives," Hap demanded. "No cutting."

"Not my rules," the man said, and made a swipe across my belly. I jumped back, felt the short blade catch a button.

"What we got here, Hap?" Lee stood in the doorway, faces peering in behind him.

"Looks like this fella don't like your rules."

"Wants different rules, huh?"

The man whipped his knife in Lee's direction, then directed it back at me. I grabbed a tray, held it like a shield.

"What say, Buddy?" Lee asked. "Figure that blade's about the size of his dick?"

"Figure." I coughed to catch my breath.

"Your little brother here ain't going to have a dick once I get done with him." The man took another swing. I deflected with the tray. He came up and around, knife aimed at my ribs. I brought my elbow down, clipped his wrist, jumped back, felt the table against my legs just as I fell, my stomach exposed, the tray clattering to the floor. But then Lee was on him, one arm around his neck, dragging him backward. The man dropped the knife, clawed at Lee's arm, eyes bulging.

"Help me out here, will you, Hap?" Lee motioned with his head toward the man's hook.

Hap looked around quickly, then heeled off one boot, slipped it over the clacking pincers.

"Got the pig-sticker, Buddy?"

I nodded, came up with the knife.

"Ready?"

"I'm ready." I wasn't sure for what.

"Floyd, move those ladies back. This ain't going to be pretty. Buddy, take off his belt."

The man let out a little scream.

I worked loose the buckle, not at all comfortable with the intimacy of the act.

"Zipper."

I hesitated.

"Just unzip it. Ain't no different than yours. Now pull them down."

The man kicked, but Lee held fast until pants and underwear lay accordioned on the floor.

"He as bald down there as he is on top?"

"Not quite, I guess."

"Better shave him, then. Think?"

"Don't really want to get that close," I said.

"Just take a few swaths. Don't have to be neat."

I stepped forward. The man bucked and squealed.

"What?" Lee said. "You don't like these rules?"

The man shook his head.

"Think you'd rather go home?"

I moved the knife a little closer. The man nodded.

"Take off his shoes, Buddy. Hand them to Hap. Britches, too." I tossed the bundle to Hap. "Bet you got a burn barrel, don't you, Hap?"

Hap smiled. "Just getting ready to light it."

"Don't forget this," I said, and floated the cap his way.

"Now, I want all the ladies out there to close their eyes. This man's got to get home before he catches cold." Lee gave the man an elbow toward the door. "Someone get on the horn and tell Emery the moon came out early tonight."

Floyd stayed outside long enough to see the two men pull away, took down make and model in case Emery wanted to investigate. When he came back in, Lee was already on the bandstand, retuning his guitar.

I folded the penknife into my pocket, scratched behind my ear. "I don't know whether to say thanks or be pissed."

"Might as well be both. Keeps things interesting." We watched as Laurette ducked beneath the strap of her bass, then rubbed her neck. "You want to take a rest?" Lee asked her. "You going to be all right?"

She nodded, shook the hair from her face, straightened the lapels of her fitted turquoise jacket.

"Next time," I said to Lee, "let me volunteer my own fight."

"Guy was a sucker," Lee said. "Should have known I wouldn't let nothing happen to you. Brothers got their own rules." He scuffed my head. "You sure laid him out that first time. Looks like you finally learned something. Where's that goddamn Dean?"

Floyd went out again, then came through the door, pushing Dean ahead, and got him positioned behind his drums. The Spurs finished two more sets before Lee called it quits, but by then he'd drunk his way through a pint of JD.

I helped Laurette break down the drums, load the gear in the station wagon. "Looks like I'll be driving," she said. Her rhinestone collar shone like ice beneath the cool stars.

"You want me to ride with you?" I didn't really want to be in the same space with Dean, but I knew it was right that I offer.

"No, Buddy. You need to drive Lee. Floyd will be with us. I'll be okay."

With Hap's help, we wrangled Dean out the door and into the wagon. He was feeling less jolly now, starting to come down. Lee, Floyd, and I stood by the car, waiting for Laurette to find her keys.

Floyd took a long last drag off his smoke. "Guess I better stay with these two." I stepped back from the car, saw Lee walk Laurette a few yards away, bend to hear what she whispered. I couldn't make out what words they exchanged, tried not to notice, but I could see that Laurette was crying. I knew that Lee was good with women at such times, a comfort, my mother always said, to have such a man to lean on. He gave Laurette his handkerchief, put his arm around her shoulders, led her back to the car.

We watched them pull away, then gathered the last of the gear. I took the wheel, followed the long highway back toward Snake Junction, half expecting to see the station wagon pulled over alongside the road.

Lee was coming down himself, sulled up like a possum. I knew he was still thinking about the fight. He felt protective of all women, but I thought I might have detected something else in his mood that night, some special tenderness toward Laurette. I let him be, figuring he'd talk when he was ready. I was willing to let the night slip by and away, to feel the steadiness of the wheel in my hands.

When we got to The Stables, Dean was lying on the hood of Floyd's Buick, his arm crossed behind his head, refusing to go home. Laurette remained in the Ford, looking drawn and tired in the dirty light from the mill. Floyd shrugged. "Dean wants another drink," he said. "I'm afraid he's going to get ornery about it."

Lee cursed under his breath, looked toward Laurette. "You all right, darlin'?" She nodded. "Okay, Floyd, here's what you do. Tell the old boy you're taking him for a nightcap. Get him to The Ramrod. He'll be hungry once he smells food."

Floyd heeled a divot of gravel. "I know what to do. Only thing is, I'm dead broke."

Lee looked from Floyd to Laurette and back. He reached in his pocket, pulled out a ten.

"Not really what I had in mind for tonight," Floyd complained. I remembered that he'd been dating Beverly, one of the waitresses from The Stables, a woman with the whitest skin I had ever seen. "She only comes out at night," Floyd had said, "and that's just fine by me."

Lee held out another ten. Floyd took the money, turned toward Dean. "Come on, you sack of shit." He hesitated, said to Lee in a low voice, "Couple of hours enough?"

Lee scowled, cast a quick look my way, nodded. We watched Floyd's Buick pull from the lot, then walked to the station wagon. Laurette had let her head fall back, her eyes closed. She'd draped a pale pink sweater over her shoulders, something a girl might wear to school on a spring day.

Lee reached in the window, squeezed her arm. "You want to come in and have a cup of coffee with me and Buddy? You hungry?"

She lifted her head to gaze at Lee. There was something she wanted to say, something she might have said if Lee hadn't stepped away from the car.

"Probably best we all hit the hay. I got some early business to attend to tomorrow." I looked at him quickly, knew it was a lie.

"Why don't you just go on home and get some rest, doll. You worked hard tonight."

She lowered her eyes, nodded slowly. Lee and I walked toward the door of The Stables. When I turned, she was still there, the engine idling. I remember the mill's big lights staining the fog, casting a jaundiced glow across the parking lot. I remember Laurette sitting immobile behind the wheel, looking toward town as if she had forgotten why she might go there.

I followed Lee down the hall, watched him pull off his boots, cast them aside. "I'm beat," he said. He unsnapped his shirt, lay down, closed his eyes.

"Aren't you worried about Laurette?"

Lee's voice was nearly a whisper. "She'll be all right."

"I'm not sure about leaving her like that."

He didn't respond, and I thought he'd already dozed off, but then he let out a long breath. "Sometimes," he said, "there ain't no way of being sure about anything."

By the time I got back from the bathroom, he was asleep, arms crossed over his chest, mouth open. It wasn't just the whiskey that made it easy for him. He could fall asleep anywhere, as though he believed nothing that mattered could take place without him, as though he believed the world would wait.

I listened to his regular breathing, heard the moths batter the screen. For me, it took time. I would angle my pillow, lie on my right side, count to one hundred, then roll to the wall and begin the count over, a routine I repeated each night like an equation whose answer was sleep. But this night was different. Maybe it was all that had gone on, the long drive home. Maybe it was that I could now make that shorter count of hours until I'd be with

Irene. I closed my eyes, imagined the bridge, felt the warm current of sleep, the last hush of air.

The next morning, I rose early, stomach growling. I'd go to The Ramrod, have steak and eggs. And then I would meet Irene at the bridge.

It was all I could do not to whistle as I washed myself in the men's room, lathering my hair with hand soap, straddling the sink to get at my crotch. On my way outside, I grabbed a fistful of maraschino cherries from the cooler, and popped them in my mouth as I stepped into the summer heat.

The station wagon was still there. I walked to the driver's side, saw that the door was open, Laurette gone. I stood for what seemed a long time, considering.

I thought of my breakfast, of meeting Irene. I thought of walking away. And then I saw the keys still in the ignition, the light switch pulled out. The car had died when it ran out of gas; the battery had lasted a little longer.

I turned off the key, shut the door, looked east to where Spalding Bridge shimmered above the river. I had no way to reach Irene, no address, no phone. How long would she wait?

The sour-sweet taste of the cherries was still in my mouth as I crossed back to the building, where I would wake Lee, who would begin the calls and then the search. Irene would not wait long at the bridge but would come to find me at The Stables, praise me for doing the right thing, and we would drive the highway for miles, searching the ditches for a glint of rhinestone, asking people along the way if they'd seen a woman dressed in turquoise who looked like the queen of the rodeo.

CHAPTER NINE

They found the pink sweater three days later, floating in the mill pond like a lily, its soft color catching the eye of a log scaler as he went for a second cup of coffee.

Word spread fast, and soon Snake Junction was thick with rumors: she'd been kidnapped, raped, murdered. When questioned, Dean allowed he remembered little, but Floyd told how he'd hauled Dean to his own apartment that night rather than dump him at the trailer with Laurette. They'd drunk and played blackjack until dawn, then fallen asleep in the same bed.

Even the man who'd mauled Laurette in White Bird had an alibi: he'd left the bar, driven the half-hour south to his sister's house in Riggins, where the county sheriff later found him bedded with the local health department nurse, who swore he had been with her overnight and hadn't left her arms except to grab a loaf of bread and bologna from the kitchen.

"I just can't see it," Harvey said. "Things like this happen in some big city, maybe. But not here." He moved slowly behind the bar, weighed down with bad feelings. I sat with Spud and Lee, drinking beer, smoking. The sun hung brightly at the door, wedged open an inch for air.

"Maybe she just took a powder," Spud offered. "Finally had enough and walked on out."

Harvey shook his head. "That'd be a dangerous thing to do."

Lee sat quietly. He'd taken to talking in a low monotone, forcing a smile edged with pain, strangely subdued. He hadn't vowed injury to whoever might have harmed Laurette, nor did he rant against Dean, whose meanness had precipitated her misery, but he'd made one thing clear and absolute: he would not perform until they found Laurette; and though The Stables remained open, the customers came in quiet and left early.

"I'll tell you this," Harvey said. "It wouldn't take much to convince me that bastard Dean's behind this whole thing."

"You mean you think he killed her?" I couldn't keep the wonder from my voice.

"I'm surprised she wasn't dead already." Harvey gave his bar towel an extra twist, slapped it over his shoulder.

Lee, who had been staring blankly at his glass, straightened. "She ain't dead, Harv. She just got smart and left. That's all." He pushed himself from the bar. "I'm tired of all this. I'm going on back to take a nap. Buddy, let me sleep for a while, will you? Stay here and keep these two out of trouble." His voice was strained, his humor weak. I knew he was hurting like we all were, maybe more.

"You'd almost think he loved that gal." Harvey cocked his head, sucked on the end of a plastic toothpick.

"Maybe he did. Maybe we all did." Spud rubbed his forehead.

Harvey threw the toothpick toward the garbage can, shifted gears. "Looks like Patterson might hold on to his title for a while. That kid Rademacher from over by Grandview put him down in the second but couldn't finish him. White boys ain't got the staying power. Now, Marciano could take and give, but those black boys"—Harvey shook his head—"they just keep coming back for more."

"Joe Louis," I said. "He was my father's favorite." I remembered listening to Louis's last fight, huddled on the porch around the new Motorola, pulling in the count from a station in Tulsa. No one was happy to see the Brown Bomber beaten, even if he was a black man. It was Louis who'd won the war, Louis who'd knocked down the big German and sent him home to Hitler.

"I've got office work to do." Spud drained his beer. "Folks will be coming pretty soon." He walked away stiff-legged, his back bent slightly, a man much older than his years.

"Everyone's so goddamn gloomy. Maybe if they'd given more of a shit before now, Laurette would still be here." Harvey's good spirits were gone. "This kind of stuff happens. You got to keep going, that's all."

"I wish she'd just come on back. Things would get back to normal." I peeled the label from my bottle.

"Ain't nothing normal around here. Not with Laurette and that redhead you're doggin'."

"I ain't dogging her."

"Okay, then. She's doggin' you."

"Nobody's dogging nobody."

"That so?"

"It's so."

Harvey grunted. "World would be a better place without women, I can tell you that."

"What about you, Harv? What about you and women?"

"Had 'em."

"I mean, why aren't you married now?"

"Why should I be?"

"Don't you get lonely sometimes?"

"Not as often as I'd need to make it worth taking on a woman. Never met a woman who didn't want to fight."

"Maybe you should join the priesthood."

Harvey snorted. "Never said I didn't want to get laid again. What could possess a man to swear off that? Ain't natural. Just like it ain't natural for that gal to be doggin' you."

I scowled, looked toward the door. "I sure as hell wish everyone would just mind their own business."

"Don't be getting your dick in a kink. I'm just joshing you. Everyone's so goddamn pissy." Harvey studied the clarity of a shot glass, gave it another rub.

"Guess I'm going to go on out, get some air."

"You do that, kid. Bring me back a *Tribune*." Harvey opened the register, flipped me a dime.

The sun had bled everything of color. I blinked slowly, already wishing for cooler nights, the first smell of woodsmoke. I hadn't seen Irene since the day we spent looking for Laurette. It was as though she, too, had taken a powder. But I didn't believe that. I felt I'd know if she were to leave, that her going would wake me from sleep, that some visceral part of me would tear away with her.

Lee's Chevy gleamed. I ran a finger along the fender, began walking toward town, past the marginal farms, Blaston's Dairy, Whistler's Fruit Stand, where I stopped and bought a large peach and a smaller red apple with Harvey's dime. I took off my shirt, tied it at my waist, ate the peach as I walked, licking the juice from my hand and arm. Just before Paulie's, a weedy pasture held a black-and-white billy goat and a palomino gelding. The horse nickered his way toward me, laid his ears back when the goat tried to follow.

There is something completely satisfying about feeding a horse an apple. I held my palm flat, the apple balanced at its center, felt the whiskered lips, suede-soft, the teeth just grazing my skin. The horse's mouth, large enough to take a man's arm to the elbow, seemed unable to command the entire apple; half of it fell to the ground. The gelding waited patiently for me to retrieve each dropped section. When he snuffled for more, I gently blew into his nostril, felt the return exhalation. I rubbed his muzzle, whispered to him as I might have to my old mare Pepper, who knew more of the world's misery than most. I longed to pull myself onto the gelding's back, wrap my legs around his barrel, lean into his neck, smell the grass and dung, the bark and pitch of trees he had rubbed against, the cedar scent of fence posts.

The goat crowded in, eating dirt in his bid for crumbs. The gelding let him, having known the apple when it was whole. When the heavy head came up, ears pricked forward, I followed his stare, saw the sheriff's boat working upstream. They were dragging the river for Laurette.

"Easy, fella. Just a boat, that's all." I scratched along the horse's jaw. He shook his head, shagged the goat out of the way, then turned to the business of grass.

Three cars at Paulie's, none of them Irene's. I kept walking, sweating now, glad for the hard climb up the hill toward the park, where I sat for an hour, then two, waiting for the sound of her Lincoln, the suddenness of her near me. Perhaps I thought my wish alone was enough to summon her. Maybe I believed that she could feel my need, that she could be prayed into existence.

From my place above town, I could see the length of the river's curve. I could see the mill. I could see the pasture, the two moving things that were the horse and the goat. I could see Paulie's and The Stables, the sheriff's boat and several others. I could see east to Lapwai. Directly below me were the department store, the jewelry shop, the stationer with its candy counter that sold caramel corn and red rope licorice; the Silver Dollar Tavern, the Corner Club, John Smith's with its card tables in back, where old men gathered to smoke cigars and bemoan the state of the nation. To the west, the blue roan hills of Washington humped toward the Pacific.

How was it, I wondered, that I could see so much and not see Irene? I knew that she would tell me to quit wondering, but how could I? My head was full of questions, and I believed that she could answer them all, if only she would.

"Irene?" I asked of the trees, the air. "Irene?"

A squirrel chucked, trapezed from one limb to the next. A few blocks away, a dog barked twice, then stopped. Children prattled over swings and teeter-totters, their voices strange to me. I stood, walked toward the play area. Two small girls in matching dresses chased each other around the sliding board, screaming. A few yards away, a young mother and her toddler squatted by a large black beetle, which the child desperately wanted to pluck up and put into his mouth. "No," the mother warned. "Don't touch."

I had a sudden awareness of how shut-off my life had become, how I'd aged behind the doors of The Stables, become more like Harvey and Spud than the seventeen-year-old boy I was. I pulled my hands from my pockets and stretched. I had a strong urge to climb the slide, whirl myself sick on the merry-go-round. I knew then that Irene was somewhere close, or I would not be feeling such things. I searched the streets, the benches, the windows of nearby houses.

"Buddy!"

The voice spun me around.

"Buddy!"

The mother, having turned away to give the girls a push in their swings, called again to her runaway son, who shrieked with delight and headed straight for the street behind me.

I reached down as he gamboled by, grabbed him beneath the arms, swung him up. He kicked to be let go, then lunged for his mother, who scolded him and thanked me until I grew red with embarrassment.

As I watched them walk back to their picnic blanket, I wondered at the strength I had sensed in the boy, his small body like a coiled spring. I rubbed my hands down the legs of my jeans, but it was still in my palms—a hum of muscle and will. I felt the vibration travel up my arms and into my chest, a tremor that made me want to leap, yelp, and holler.

As I walked toward Main Street, my hands came free. I began to run. I was not running toward something or away. I was simply running for the sheer joy of it. Because I was seventeen and alive and had good legs beneath me.

Because I could.

CHAPTER TEN

It was a fisherman casting for trout who found the body. At first he thought it was the carcass of a deer, pushed up against a back-eddy dam of cottonwood branches. But then he saw the long black hair, the pale arm weaving the water's surface. He stared for a long time, he said, unable to make sense of what he was seeing among the flotsam of bark, before finally reeling in and going for help.

By the time the sheriff arrived, Spud, Harvey, Lee, and I had already heard and crossed the highway to the river. We watched as they pulled at her with hooked poles, unknotted her from the tangle of roots and limbs. Five days in the water had bleached her skin of color, the gash of her mouth a thin line. We helped the deputies cover her with blankets, then lit our cigarettes to mask the stench and looked off to the horizon, as though unaware of the woman who lay between us, warming in the sun.

"You think somebody killed her?" Spud asked the sheriff, a thin man of about thirty named Grady Westin whose left arm was sun-baked to the color of jerky while his right arm remained freckled and pale.

Westin shrugged, chewed at a sprig of rye grass. All the hair on his head, even his brows and lashes, was the same bleached yellow as the straw he worked from one side of his mouth to the other.

"Hard to say. Coroner will have to be judge. Clothes gone. Then, too, a hard current could do that."

I imagined Laurette's body spinning, torn and battered.

"You boys will have to come in for some more questions. Might as well follow me on back. I'll radio Walter to pick up Dean." The sheriff started toward his car, then stopped. "Anyone else we might want to talk to? Acting suspicious? Hanging around the place? Anyone along the road?"

Lee ran his fingers through his hair. "Passed that Indian Wolfchild on the way out of town. Only one I can remember."

"Wolfchild?" Westin flipped open his notepad. "Ever been trouble?"

Harvey shook his head. "Never seen him drunk. Never seen him offer a fight. He just comes in, has a drink, then leaves."

"Ever hear him talk about Mrs. Fletcher?" It was the first time I'd heard Laurette referred to in that way.

"Never heard him talk about nothin'," Harvey said. "He's a real quiet Indian."

Westin pinched one eye closed, scratched his head, checked beneath his nails.

Harvey sucked the inside of his cheek. "Do have to say, he seemed to kind of keep his sights on Laurette. Never thought much of it."

"Seen him since the night of the disappearance?"

Harvey thought. "No, guess I haven't. But he only comes in on Fridays."

"*Every* Friday?"

Harvey nodded.

"How long's he been doing that?"

"Hell, I don't know. Couple of years, maybe. Since the Spurs been playing, I'd say."

Westin looked toward the river. "Well, we might should call the tribe, bring him in. Can't hurt."

We stepped back to make way for the coroner, then followed Westin to the sheriff's office. There wasn't much that hadn't already been asked and answered. I repeated my statement, signed several papers.

Afterward Lee leaned against the Chevy, lit a cigarette. "What do you think, Buddy?"

"I think we shouldn't have left her alone like that."

"No."

"I can't stand to think about someone getting her."

"Yeah."

"We might have been able to help her."

"Yeah."

"Is that all you got to say? 'No' and 'Yeah'?" I was tired of Lee acting like this was about him somehow, tired of all his moping around.

"What the hell else do you want me to say?" Lee flipped his cigarette.

"I guess I'd hoped for something more, like '*Hell,* yes' or '*Shit,* no.' Something that showed a little more feeling."

He turned full on me, gritted his teeth. "What do you want me to do? Blubber around? Kill somebody?" He held out both hands with exaggerated sincerity. "What the hell do you want me to do?"

I spat in the gravel. "I want you to get the hell away from me, that's what."

"You got it, mister." He roared from the parking lot, the Chevy kicking up gravel and a heavy cloud of dust. I looked east, wondered at my anger. One thing my parents' death had taught me was that each man grieves his own way: some take it out on their dogs, the animals cowering with dread; some hole up and drink themselves into oblivion; some stay sober for years, then go out one day for cigarettes and never return.

Westin stepped from the building. "You without a ride?" He squinted my way, rubbed his sunglasses against his stomach.

"Guess so."

"I'm headed out to Lapwai. Want me to drop you?"

I weighed my need for solitude against the heat ribboning up off the asphalt. "Sure," I said. "Thanks."

The inside of the car smelled sharp and metallic, like strong coffee and sweat. Westin steered with his right hand, settled his left elbow on the opened window. "You know, now, that no one thinks you and Lee had anything to do with this."

"Yes, sir."

"You boys do all right here, and Spud's glad to have you. You never finished school, though, did you?"

"No, sir."

"Have you tried to get on at the mill?"

"No, sir."

"Young man like you needs to work. Keep busy. There's plenty of jobs to be had around here. Don't want to spend all your time mooning over the girls. Want to stay away from the beer."

"Yes, sir."

Westin turned the dark lenses of his glasses toward me. "You got any more words in you besides 'Yes, sir' and 'No, sir'?"

I looked to where the plume of smoke rose and settled above the river. Sometimes I couldn't even smell the mill anymore. You get used to it, people said. Like any other smell. Give it time. "I'm just not sure what else to say, I guess."

"Say you'll find something else to do with yourself besides hang around The Stables." Westin settled back in his seat. "Anything you want to do for a living? Anything grab you?"

I thought longer than was comfortable for either of us.

He shook his head. "This gal you've taken up with. Where's she from?"

I'd begun to hate the way news traveled in Snake Junction, the nightclub a center for communications, connecting millworkers and housewives, drunks and weekend partiers, lawyers and the law.

"Kentucky somewhere. That's about all I know."

"I hear she's a real looker." Westin cast a sidelong glance my way as we pulled into the Stables parking lot. The Lincoln was the only car there. I felt a rush of simultaneous excitement and dread.

"That hers?"

I didn't answer.

Westin scribbled on his notepad, slipped it back into his pocket. "Well," he said, "don't do anything I wouldn't do."

My anger disappeared as he pulled from the lot, headed

toward Lapwai. I smoothed my hair, dusted my jeans. When I opened the heavy door, I stood blinking in the dark.

Irene and Spud were leaning toward each other over the bar, talking, sipping rum. I understood immediately that Spud's car was parked around back, and I felt an overwhelming sense of betrayal, as though they were both trying to hide something from me.

"Hey, Buddy." Spud moved slowly to look at me, spoke with exaggerated care. He'd been at the rum for a while, probably since leaving the river.

He motioned me over. "You could probably use a drink, too. How about a Coke?" He opened a bottle and set it on the counter.

Irene tipped her head sideways. "Spud told me about Laurette. I'm so sorry." She wore black pants, a white top that showed her arms. "Come and sit down with us, Buddy." She patted the stool beside her.

I remained where I was. It was like coming into a room and finding the adults in secretive conversation. I couldn't shake the feeling that they were talking about me.

"Buddy? Are you okay?" Irene looked from me to Spud, then back.

"I think I'm just going to go rest for a while." I slapped the counter as I went by.

Spud shrugged. "Suit yourself."

I was halfway down the hall when I heard her following. I kept walking until I got to the door of my room, then turned.

She stopped a few feet away. Her hair was combed straight back, held by a black band.

"What's wrong, Buddy? What is it?"

"I guess it's been a long day."

"That's not what I'm asking. Why are you acting this way?"

"What way?"

She lifted her chin. Her face took on a hardness I had not seen before. "I don't play these games. We can either talk this out, or I can turn around and leave."

I could smell her now. My pulse quickened. "I don't want you to leave."

"Then act like it." The hardness around her eyes softened. She stepped toward me, took my face in her hands.

"Don't ever think you know something about me without asking." She whispered as though she were giving me words of love.

Spud must have known, having watched her go down the hall and not come back. I heard a door close, the start of his car engine.

"You're going to be all right," she said. "Everything's going to be all right." She ran her hand down my chest, pressed her thumb to each rib. "These things are hard, especially when you're so new to everything. So new to this world."

I leaned my face into her hair. "I only feel new when I'm with you."

She took my hand, walked me through the door of my room. I stood while she unbuttoned and pulled off my shirt, gently, as if she were dressing a wound. She kissed her way down my chest. I jumped and moaned like I was hooked to a charged wire. I pulled at her hair, brought her mouth to mine, terrified I would ruin this, end it too soon. She had to know that I could not stand another moment of waiting.

I meant to tell her this, to whisper it to her, let her lead me through this thing I'd dreamed and never had. But then I felt the tip of her tongue tracing my lips, and her breath came into me like fire. I pushed her to the bed.

"Wait," she whispered. She flinched but did not resist as I pulled her pants from her hips, wedged one knee between her legs. She didn't utter a sound but kept her hands resting lightly on my shoulders as I forced myself into her and was done. Only after the blood-rush had cleared my ears did I hear the silence, the slow breath of her disappointment.

"I'm sorry. I've never . . . I'm sorry." I sat up, laid my face in my hands.

She traced a slow circle between my shoulder blades. "It's my fault, Buddy."

"No, don't say that. It's awful."

"No, it's not awful. Our hour isn't up."

I turned and looked at her in the dim light.

"Sometimes," she said, "being new to something just means you've got to keep at it until you get it right."

I shook my head. I was a child again, shamed, wanting a place to hide. "Shit," I said. "I hate it."

"What?"

"Being who I am, what I am."

"A boy."

"I'm not a boy, Irene. Please, quit saying that."

"I will. Come here." She pulled me down beside her, and I could feel the softness of her breasts against my back. I could hardly believe that I had forgotten to touch them.

"I'm sorry that you were there after they found Laurette. You didn't need to see that."

I felt a hurt well up in my chest, choked it back down. "Have you ever seen anyone like that before? Someone who's been in the water for a long time?"

"I'm not sure how to tell you about some of the things I've seen." She reached to the floor, pulled a cigarette from my shirt pocket, struck one of the kitchen matches I kept by the bed. "Sometimes I'm not even sure what I've seen and what I've dreamed. Like I've lived other lives."

"Do you know what happened to Laurette?"

"I think I do."

"Tell me."

There was a long silence. She was gathering the words and images, bringing them into focus.

"Close your eyes, Buddy." Her palm brushed across my face, like the hand of a magician. "Now imagine that you're Laurette. Imagine yourself there in that car. Imagine how tired you are. Imagine that all you've got to look forward to is a man you know will hurt you bad, if not tonight, then tomorrow, and that nothing in your life is ever going to change." I remembered the slump of Laurette's shoulders, the pleading look she'd given Lee. "Are you afraid? Are you afraid to go home? Do you feel anything at all?"

"All I feel is mad. I feel like I want to beat the shit out of Dean."

"Then you're not her." I heard Irene let out a long breath. "I can see the parking lot and the dark bar. I can hear the mill rumbling. The night's hot, but I'm cold, like fever." I felt Irene shudder. "I know that all I have to do is drive on home. That's all I have to do."

I could feel the heaviness come into Irene's body, like she was sinking, dying beside me. "Don't," I said. "Irene. Don't."

"Listen."

I lifted my head, heard only the silence, and then the quick beat of my own heart. "What? What do you hear?" She did not answer. "Irene?" I shook her shoulder, gently at first, then harder.

"What, Buddy?" Her voice was calm, as though nothing had happened.

"What are you doing? Don't do that."

"I'm not doing anything. I'm just thinking. Remembering."

"What are you remembering?"

"Too much."

I sank back onto the bed. "Jesus, Irene. Why can't you just say something straight? Why can't you just tell me *real* things?"

"Like what? What's real to you, Buddy?"

"Like why you're here. Like what made you come to Snake Junction."

"Nothing made me come to Snake Junction. I came because I wanted to."

I heard Harvey's words in my head—*Gal like that don't come in here for no reason.*

"I don't believe that's much of a reason," I said.

"What good does it do me to tell you something if you're not going to believe it?"

"You're not telling me anything. I don't even know where you're from."

"You do."

"Okay. I know you're from Kentucky. But that's a whole goddamn state, Irene." I could hear my voice rising, feel the muscles tensing in my neck and shoulders.

"Ashland. That's east. My father was a coal miner. Died of black lung. After a while, my mother remarried. I left home and never went back."

"How old were you?"

"I was young."

I waited. "Is that all you're going to tell me?"

Silence.

I rolled to face her. "Irene."

"Yes."

"Tell me something I don't know. Something true. Something I'll never forget."

"Ah"—a short laugh, a note of approval. I reached out, touched the lobe of her ear, smoothed the fine hair at the nape of her neck. She was coming back. I had not lost her.

She blinked slowly, let the smile fade from her face. "I know what it's like to lie in the dark, waiting for a man you hate. I know what it's like to smell the stink of him come to the bed."

I let my hand rest against her cheek, my thumb stroke the fine bone toward her ear. "I didn't know you'd been married. It doesn't matter. I just didn't know."

"I never said I was married."

"Well, that doesn't matter to me, either."

"It was my stepfather."

My hand went still.

"I don't blame you for feeling disgusted. I can hardly bear it myself sometimes. It's like I carry the smell of that man with me wherever I go. It's like he will never die."

"Is he? Is he dead?"

"Yes, he's dead."

I rolled to my back, felt my fists clench. "It's a damned good thing, because if he wasn't, I'd kill him."

"He's dead."

"I hope the bastard suffered."

Irene's only answer was a long exhalation of smoke.

The rage made me want to lash out, cause pain, but it was her soft warmth beside me that made me remember how badly I wanted to touch her, remember who she had been only minutes before. I buried my nose in the silk of her hair, drew my hand to her breast.

"You don't have to keep on if you don't want to," she said.

"I do."

She brought her hand to my face. "I could tell you were different, Buddy. It's because you're so new."

"I don't want you to say that anymore. It makes me feel funny inside."

She smiled, closed her eyes, opened them again. "Maybe it's me, then. If you don't want to be new, I do. That's how you make me feel. Like I'm starting all over again." She traced each of my eyebrows, ran a finger across my lips. Already, I was moving against her, pushing between her legs.

"Wait," she said, and this time I willed myself to stop, pulled her to me. She felt smaller somehow, fragile, her head nestled beneath my chin. I began to discover the secrets of her, softly touching the bones of her shoulders, touching each hip point and vertebra. I kissed the hollow of her jaw, the pulse of her throat, the skin beneath each breast. I kissed the bends of her elbows, traced the small, shallow bowl of her navel. The musky sweetness drew me down, and I kissed there and the insides of her thighs, her knees, her ankles. I kissed and caressed until I could stand it no longer.

We began to move together then, and I was lost to everything but the ache and spasm of my own release. Only after I rested my head against hers did I feel the dampness on her cheek.

"It's okay," I said. "It's okay."

We lay for a long time, drifting toward sleep. When I woke, she was gone. I had no idea where she lived, how I might find her. Without her having said so, I'd come to understand that these were questions I should not ask. What existed between the two of us came on Irene's terms. I was well over my allotted hour, I knew. All I could do was remain where she could find me, and wait.

I turned on the lamp, pulled on my jeans. I gathered the sheets from the bed, carried them to the men's room, washed them in quarter sections at the sink, hung them across the tops of the stalls to dry. I walked down the hall to the bar, poured myself a shot of Jack Daniel's, drank it standing, then poured another, took it back to the room. I lay on the bare mattress and sipped my whiskey. I didn't know where Lee was, and I didn't care.

It took me a while to realize the building's silence, and to remember why: The Stables was closed until after the funeral. Irene had never finished telling me what had happened to Laurette, and I felt a pang of guilt for feeling as good as I did. I knew that I'd experienced more joy in the last few hours than Laurette had felt in years. I wondered if she had known such pleasure when she was young, in that short time before the trouble brought her down. I remembered the way she had laughed when the stone she threw broke over the water, trailing rainbows of light. Maybe even then I was beginning to imagine her perfect dive off rock to the water below, where her father had once waited, arms upheld. The will it took to not fight, not swim, not breathe.

I remembered the way her hair had swirled around her as they pulled her from the river, the leached putty of her skin.

"No more," I said. I closed my eyes, wished myself back into the arms of Irene, whose body remained whole, molded to mine.

CHAPTER ELEVEN

Leopold Wolfchild admitted one thing: he'd come to The Stables all those Friday nights for one reason, and that reason was to see Laurette.

He'd had his eye on her since that September ten years before, when she'd entered the rodeo arena, black hair flying out behind her, legs tight around the Appaloosa's barrel, saluting the crowd—two fingers at the brim of her powder-blue Stetson. There was something in the details Wolfchild recited that riled the readers of the article about his arrest in the *Snake Junction Tribune*—the careful way he described her hair, the glittering tiara circling the crown of her hat, her boots the color of morning cream.

He'd been a younger man then, hunted elk, trapped muskrat, worked sometimes for Okie Richardson, who ran the dairy just west of town; he figured he might have made her a good husband. But that night, after the broncs and the bulls and the men who rode them had gone to the bell or failed, with the smell of beer, cotton candy, and manure still thick in the air, he'd stepped from behind the loading chute to say something to her, what, he wasn't sure, but something that would tell her how he'd fallen in love that moment she swept past him. Instead of bending to listen, she'd startled back into the arms of the cowboy who shadowed her, who then pulled her to his side, told Wolfchild to quit sneaking around like some kind of spook, and guided Laurette toward the carnival lights.

And that was the closest Wolfchild had come to Laurette in his life, the years since spent longing from a distance, and then from his place at the bar, where he could watch her and hear her voice and believe that the songs of love she sang might be meant for him.

When asked where he had been the night she disappeared, he hung his head. "On the road. Just walking." It was enough to convince the judge that he should be held, enough to convince the people of Snake Junction that Leopold Wolfchild was guilty of murder.

When word came from the coroner that Laurette had been four months pregnant, Wolfchild was moved to solitary, away from other inmates who might find themselves suddenly righteous. Whatever lines had divided Snake Junction were erased by the town's unifying hatred; Wolfchild's trespass whetted an old grudge. Every injustice, every wrong—price of bread gone up a nickel at Hughes's IGA; Johnson's dead collie found along the railroad tracks just south of the mill; the Varley boy's fall from the back of the pickup as his father swerved to miss a deer that ran into the road in broad daylight; the way the boy's head wouldn't heal but oozed and festered for weeks—all of it because of Wolfchild's dark spirit.

When I stepped into the bank's cool interior with the pouch of cash and checks Spud had sent me to deposit, the president, Chaz Hunt, stood with me in line at the teller window to get my take on things.

"He must have been waiting for just the right time." Hunt's breathy voice belied his burly build, heavy jowls, thick fingers. He limped beside me, the gout he suffered reason for the gin I'd heard he kept cool in the walk-in safe. "Just like an Indian to sneak up on her like that."

Orville, the butcher at M&R Market, where I was sent to purchase a new jar of brined sausages for Harvey, spat into the bloody sawdust at his feet, guided the saw through a fat leg of beef. "Best thing they can do is make an example. Indians been getting too much. Makes them think they deserve. Makes them think they can take whatever they want, just the way they take game anytime of year, when the rest of us got to wait for season." I felt my teeth go sharp as the blade buried itself, throwing bone grit and fine bits of muscle.

"Life would be a whole lot better without a one of them," Curly Lind said as he reamed a tractor tire off its rim, the only man at Valley Ranch Supply big enough to do it solo. "Stand back in case it blows." Lee had awakened in the middle of the night, remembered he hadn't checked the spare since leaving Oklahoma, jumped up, came back in and shined the flashlight in my face. "Knew it," he'd said. "Flat as a pancake. First thing in the morning, you take it in. One flat tire brings on another. I'll give you a buck for lunch at the A&W."

I'd eaten the Coney dog and fries first, stood sipping my root beer, belching onions. Curly grunted the tire off the stand, thumbed one nostril and blew hard, landing a wad of snot just shy of the trashcan. The second nostril produced nothing but a watery spray.

"My sister tried to date one back in high school. Only took me and Bickford one night to make that Indian understand some blood don't mix." I studied the calendar, wondering what Miss July had tucked in the cleavage she fingered so shyly. As he wrote me a receipt, I shifted my gaze to Curly, his broad shoulders and thick neck, the way his skull narrowed at the top, a sure sign, my mother would have said, of too quick a birth.

I smoothed my hair at the crown. Maybe some part of me was ashamed to stand by so dumbly, offering neither agreement nor quarrel. Maybe some part of me knew that things had gone wrong, floated off the bubble, like the bad tire atop Curly's balancing stand, wobbling and in need of a steadying weight.

Laurette's funeral drew a surprising number of people, many of them regulars from The Stables, others who hadn't thought of her since her days as rodeo queen, who had put her out of their minds years before, when she'd turned up pregnant with the cowboy's child. No reason, they said, why she couldn't have gone on to nationals, taken her shining tiara and her black-and-white horse and the proud name of Snake Junction with her. Instead, her parents had moved south to Bliss to escape the shame, dropped her at St. Anthony's, the home for unwed mothers, the orphanage next door.

Dean was all but forgotten. He seldom appeared outside his stinking trailer except to pawn his possessions, piece by piece—

his bowling trophies and Ludwig drums; Laurette's boots, buckles, and bass—until all that was left was the ruined chair he slept in and the station wagon full of empty bottles. A few days after the funeral, the landlady came to collect the rent and found him on the steps unconscious, one leg oddly angled, femur broken. They carted him off to the VA in Walla Walla. It took several weeks for word to reach town that he'd died during surgery, poisoned by his own blood.

Lee hired a man without wife or children to take over on drums, found another young bachelor with a pockmarked face and a pronounced Adam's apple to play bass. He wasn't pretty, Lee said, but he could sing, and you hardly had to look at him anyway, since he, like Laurette, kept to the shadows. The two men took their place beside Floyd, who spoke even less than he had before. Maybe he believed people blamed him for what had happened to Laurette; maybe, Harvey suggested, he knew something more than the rest of us did, and if so, it would come out soon enough. Best to leave him be.

Laurette's death had taken the fight out of all of us. Lee hardly noticed my presence, didn't ask where I'd been. He kept the crowds dancing, had started to drink right along with them, from beginning to end, and no longer cared which woman waited for him. He was often asleep at the bar before Harvey switched off the lights and sent him to bed. But once there, he'd lie staring at the ceiling, or only pretend to sleep. His humming turned to a kind of moan, each breath the same note.

I found it easy to leave the dreary rooms and sour breath of The Stables behind. The moment the sun touched the window, I'd be up and moving, cleaned, dressed, and waiting. Whatever might bedevil the world, there was this one sure thing: Irene would come for me, and nothing would keep me from sliding in beside her, hungry for the day's first kiss, the road that would lead us away.

"They'll kill him," Irene said.

I looked out the window of the Lincoln, unable to argue or agree, as we passed a freshly mown field ten miles south of Snake Junction. I never asked anymore where we were going. Sometimes we drove for hours along the narrow highways, through the tight box canyons, across the ridges and down into the draws, passing through sun and shadow, the air cooling as we gained elevation, warming again as we dropped down into the valley. We stopped at every café and bar along the way, not always to eat and seldom to drink, but just so that Irene could step inside and know something about the people there, about the place, not judging but evaluating, like an animal sensing the coming cold, questing for its winter den. Other times we followed the logging roads deep into the woods, searching for huckleberries. Irene could smell them. One afternoon, she parked at the edge of a dirt bank, which we climbed to a waist-high grove of berry-laden branches. We lay in the late heat of high altitude, and I licked the juice from Irene's lips, sucked the bruise-colored mound of each finger. Another day, another highway, we stopped at a roadhouse set deep in the north canyon, where the owners kept a caged cougar just outside the door, pacing, spitting, spraying its urine so that every corner of the place smelled dankly of musk, and even as we ate our thick burgers and drank our beer, the wild scent came in around us and I felt the hair rise at my neck and the stirring that meant I would take Irene before we'd gone a mile down the road, pulled over next to a trough of spring water and rutting in the backseat while cars sped by, their passengers thinking us only thirsty.

"They will," Irene insisted. "Because he's what they got."

I heard the conviction in her voice, her belief that Wolfchild would hang, but I will say right now that my mind was not on crime or punishment that day, not even on justice, but on Irene, her bare arms honeyed by sun, the hem of her cotton dress riding high. I could feel the Lincoln building speed, the town falling away behind us.

"I want to show you something," Irene said.

We followed 95 south into Lapwai. Main Street was a slow quarter-mile, grain elevator to the left, Mike's General Store on the right, where we stopped for two strawberry sodas and cigarettes. A dozen low-roofed dwellings bunched behind the store; other townspeople had chosen to cast farther out, seeding the draws with their farmhouses, barns, and sheds.

We circled a clump of small houses, all painted the same faded yellow. No yards, just patches of sun-bleached thistle. A few bicycles, drying racks, an old Ford pickup foddering into grass, and to the back of one house, a canvas tepee. Irene drove on, past the houses and back onto the highway, then turned left onto a dirt road that followed a narrow creek lined with cottonwood and plum. The dust rose around us, the rank odor of wild fruit gone to rot. Grasshoppers ratcheted off the windshield, dun and rust, the colors of autumn leaves.

The draw we followed narrowed, blocking the light, cooling the air. Irene guided the Lincoln along what was now not a road but a path, the barrows and loose rock jolting us from side to side. Blackberry canes scraped our doors. Birds that nested in the brambles flitted up in a whir of distress. I thought we would come to a clearing, but what we entered instead was a woven cavern of hawthorn, elderberry, chokecherry, sumac, a gray cedar shack at its center.

"Here," Irene said. She took off her sunglasses, smoothed her hair.

"Here what?"

"Come on."

A few steps toward the shack, we flushed two whitetail, watched them pogo deeper into the thicket. All around us, the shadows chicked and whispered; a hummingbird trilled past, then darted back, drawn by the red of Irene's hair.

The door opened easily, and we stepped into the pleasant dusk of the single room. To the left sat a thin double bed on metal legs; across from it, an oilcloth-covered table and two wooden chairs painted white. There was an enameled sink, two rough pine cupboards, a wood-fired cookstove, an apple crate full of good kindling. A faded quilt, a kerosene lantern, a row of sixteen-penny nails, one still hung with a green chamois shirt. Floors swept, cobwebs dusted. No rodent droppings; no flies along the sash. In the south window, a gallon jar of tea brewed amber.

"Someone live here?" I asked.

"Someone." Irene walked to the sink, turned the single handle, cupped her hand and drank.

"Is this going to be another riddle?"

She straightened, wiped her mouth with the tips of her fingers, ran the wetness through her hair. "No riddle. I lived here one summer when I was twelve."

Finally. Some sense of why she'd chosen Snake Junction, some connection to the secrets of her life. I pulled out a chair, motioned her toward it, but she shook her head, walked to the window.

"I stayed here with my grandma, mother's side."

"She's dead?" I swung the chair around, straddled it backward.

"Some time ago. My uncle called to tell me."

"The one who grew celery?"

Irene nodded. "Uncle Lou. He married a Nez Perce woman named Esther. After my grandfather passed away, they went to Kentucky and brought my grandmother here. She didn't want to live next to a bunch of other folk. She'd always loved the tules back home." Irene ran her hand across the bedstead, sat on the quilt-covered mattress. "Gram and I slept here that summer, windows open, moths flying through, crickets going on and on. You've never known air so sweet. All day, I'd wade the creek, sit for hours beneath the cottonwoods and read. She found me books at the library, borrowed them from the schoolteacher. She wanted me to learn something. And I guess I did."

I was getting sleepy, lulled by Irene's voice, the rustle of leaves.

"Every afternoon, Uncle Lou would take us to the river. Gram loved to fish more than anybody I know. Fried trout and eggs for breakfast, cold trout and cornbread for lunch, trout and fried potatoes for dinner. So good just pulled from the water." Irene closed her eyes with the memory, and for a moment we were both dreaming. "Good things are hard to make last."

I stirred, willed my eyes open. I didn't want to hear the resignation in her voice. "Some things are meant to last longer than others," I said.

She tucked a strand of hair behind her ear. "Someone else will be here soon."

"Who?" I could not imagine who might be drawn or called to this secret place.

"Aunt Esther." Irene rose, opened the cupboard, took out a cloth and a bar of soap. "I'm going to wash up before she gets here."

I could see now that the shelves contained a towel, a comb and brush, a small toiletry bag, a few books, several rows of jars. I watched Irene run the rag across her face, beneath her hair. She unbuttoned her blouse, pulled it from her shoulders, walked over and knelt down beside me. I reached for her, but she shook her head, then pulled a suitcase from beneath the bed. Stockings, slips, panties, brassieres, blouses neatly folded. She shook out a light cotton sweater sewn with pearly beads.

"*You* live here? You live *here*?"

Irene smiled, stepped from her skirt. "Go out to the Lincoln," she said. "I need something from the trunk."

All her dresses were there, laid out on one white bedsheet, covered with another.

"Bring me the blue skirt. The full one." She stood at the doorway, smiling in her top and panties.

I ruffled through the fine clothing, made a mess of it before finding the skirt. When I closed the trunk, dust clouded up. "It'll shake out," Irene said. "Bring it on in before I get arrested for indecency."

"I don't know who'd be doing the arresting way back here."

"Sheriff Westin, perhaps. He seems inclined." Irene stepped into the skirt, brushed it clean.

"Why here? What brought you back to Snake Junction? I mean, I'm glad. You know I am."

She went to the table, pulled cigarettes from her purse. I lit hers, then mine, waited as I so often did, learning patience.

"I don't know that I can say for sure what brought me back. Maybe memory. Maybe hope."

"What were you hoping for?"

"Less than I got." She smiled at me. "Hoping for change, something different, some way out."

"Out of what?"

She touched my cheek, a sudden sadness in her eyes. She turned just as quickly. "This place gave me respite for a while. It still feels that way to me. Safe."

"Nothing's going to hurt you. I'm here now."

"I know," she said. "I know you'd do most anything for me."

"I would."

"Esther can't know what's between us. You've got to be someone else while she's here. Do you understand?"

I did, but I hated it anyway. "Who should I be, then?"

Irene contemplated, looked at me like she was seeing me for the first time. "Well, let's have you be who you are. You're Lee Hope's younger brother. I've told her about Lee." I raised my head. "What a good singer he is, that's all. It won't hurt for her to think I might be friendly with Lee. Aunt Esther's not the kind I usually feel the need to lie to. But this . . ." She shook her head, stepped outside, came back in with a fistful of aster and fireweed. "I'm not sure she'd understand this at all."

"*This* meaning me."

"*This* meaning *us*." She filled a jar with water. I was mesmerized by her actions, the ease with which she went about such small domestic tasks. "Whether you want to believe it or not, I could get in trouble for *this*."

"What trouble?"

Irene stripped the leaves from the ends of the stalks.

"You think they care how old I am? Jealous, sure. But they're not going to do anything like that."

Irene concentrated on the flowers, trimming them to height. "Not unless they believe they've got other reason."

"Like what?"

Irene shrugged one shoulder.

"This thing that happened to Laurette. It's got you scared." I walked to where she stood, laid my hand between her shoulder blades. "If Wolfchild didn't do it, they'll let him go."

"Listen," she said, then seemed to catch herself. "Why don't you go to the creek and wash up. I've got a comb if you need it."

"Just because we're going to pretend you're my nanny doesn't mean you have to act like one." I slicked a palm across the top of my head.

"It's hot, that's all. Take this jar of tea down with you and set it in the water. Best we can do with no ice."

I followed the path, tea sloshing in the crook of my arm. The afternoon was quiet except for the drone of bees and the chatter of birds. When I squatted at the water's edge, a school of minnows darted from beneath my shadow. I laid the jar against a mossy cottonwood root that extended into the creek, dipped my hands and rinsed my face, patted the back of my neck. Some part of me must have known that Wolfchild had washed his hands in this same stream that flowed toward the Clearwater, that he had cleansed the summer dust from his face, looked to the same sun to gauge the hour. But I could think only of the time before me, the next hour, and the next: nothing but more of Irene.

By the time I got back, Aunt Esther had arrived, having walked, I guessed, for there was no other car in the narrow drive. I patted my hair, wiped my palms down the legs of my jeans.

They were at the table, Aunt Esther fanning her face with an envelope.

"Buddy, this is Aunt Esther."

"Pleased to meet you." Maybe I could think of it as a game we were playing, a joke between us.

"Buddy, would you be so kind as to fetch the iced tea? Esther's thirsty, I'm sure." Irene widened her eyes at me, made a funny gesture across her face.

I stiffened. Chore boy. That's how she saw me. "Sure. Ain't iced, though. Probably ain't even cooled."

"I'm sure it's fine." Irene raised her eyebrows.

I retrieved the jar, which came up from the water impossibly cold. I thought for a moment to let it warm in the sun, just out of orneriness, but I knew that was the child in me, and that was not who I wanted to be.

I pulled several smaller jars from the cupboard, poured us each one full. Irene and Esther talked quietly. The older woman, small but stout, skin the color of nutmeg, wore her graying black hair in two braids wrapped about her head like a turban. She accepted the tea, fingers burled with arthritis.

"Sugar?" she queried.

Back to the cupboard, where I found sugar cubes. I watched Esther pinch six, then seven into her cup. Her skin wrinkled across her cheekbones and the bony backs of her hands, but her shoulders were straight beneath her faded housedress. She kept both of her sturdy brown oxfords flat on the floor as she drank and studied me.

"Your husband was the Celery King," I said.

She grinned, showing straight white teeth. "Ayee," she answered, and I thought she must mean yes.

"Must have raised a lot of celery."

"Ayee." Her grin grew larger. I looked at Irene, who looked back at me with great amusement.

"What's so funny?"

The two women looked at each other, then burst into laughter. I sat straight and silent, afraid to move.

"Buddy." Irene could hardly speak. "You need to go wash up some more."

They broke into another gale. Esther covered her mouth with her palm.

"Gosh dang it. What?"

"Use the car's rearview," Irene said.

I hurried outside, my ears burning. In the mirror, I saw my face, the dust washed away from my cheeks and forehead, dark streaks of it beneath my eyes, under my nose, a strip down my chin. "Well, shit." I looked around, found one of Irene's white handkerchiefs in the glove box, hesitated, then spat and began rubbing. I stepped back into the room, my face the color of rhubarb.

But Irene and Esther didn't notice. They were talking harder now, in lower tones, Irene's forehead arched with seriousness. I sat on the bed, an outsider. When Esther finally rose, I stood, too. She was a foot and a half shorter than I was, but she raised her face and set her eyes on mine.

"The Celery King," she said. "He was a good man." She tapped my arm with one crooked finger, then moved toward the door.

"I'm going to drive Aunt Esther home," Irene said.

"I can walk." Esther turned to face us both, her handbag held waist high, like a shield.

"I know you can," Irene said, "but I need to pick up a few things." She cast a conspiratorial look my way. "Lee might come for dinner."

Esther nodded, turned toward the car. I opened the door for her. "I can walk," she repeated, then slipped nimbly into the passenger seat, snatching her purse close, as though she thought I might steal it.

I backed away from the rooster tail of dust, gave a final wave. I sat on the bed, smoked, got up, sat back down, reached under and pulled out the suitcase. Beneath the satin folds of Irene's clothing, I found a thin sheaf of folded papers bound tight with blue ribbon. I looked up the narrow drive, began reading:

May 22, 1958

Irene,

Danny died yesterday just after lunch. It wasn't as bad as it could have been. We'll bury him in the Protestant patch without a funeral, like he wanted, though it doesn't sit with me. I had Loren Slickpoo come in and burn some sweetgrass. I don't know what you'll think of that, but it seemed the right thing.

Love,
Aunt Esther

Dear Irene,

Guess you know things don't look good for me. Esther can't keep her mouth shut. She's been real good to me.

Irene, you've got to find someplace and stop for a while. I'd sure like to see you one more time. Come on out here, spend some time by the river. The old house is empty except for hornets and mice, but that's nothing to deal with. I go up there sometimes and just sit. It's peaceful. Folks around here all leave it alone, like it's haunted or something, or maybe it's just respect for the dead. We could talk there, have some time alone. I still dream about you.

I know you don't need me to take care of you. When I'm drunk, I think it's me who needs you. But I'm sober now and I'm saying that you need to find someplace and settle down, even if all you're going to do is turn into a sour old woman off by herself in the woods. There's worse things.

OK. I'm done. I get real tired. Gives me excuse to sit by the river. I can still knock hell out of the fish.

All my love,
Danny

There were more, but I feared Irene would return and catch me going through her past, unfolding the secrets she was keeping. I stacked the letters just like I'd found them, tied the ribbon, slid the suitcase back. I paced the room, glared at the bed, imagining Irene atop the quilt, Danny beside her.

"I hope you suffered, you son of a bitch," I whispered, my jealousy surprising me with its venom.

When I heard the Lincoln, I stepped quickly to the door. Irene didn't get out of the car but motioned me forward.

"Another ride?" I asked.

"I'm taking you back. I've got things I need to get done."

"Things?" I could not hide the sharpness in my voice.

"Matters to settle," she said, and her words were final.

CHAPTER TWELVE

I waited until Lee's breathing smoothed, then counted to one hundred, lifted his keys from the wooden box we'd upended for a nightstand. Once outside, I sat on the steps, pulled on my boots. No cars in the lot except Lee's.

Pull out slow, or hit it hard? I chose slow, the speedometer hardly registering as I rolled out of the lot and onto the highway. Three a.m. I might be too early, or too late. I knew so little about her, where she began her days, ended her nights. Like a cat. "They'll sneak in and steal the very air you breathe," my father would say. He searched each new litter for the occasional black kitten still slick with mucus and blood, dragged it from its teat, tossed it over the fence to the chickens.

Just past where the rutted road to the cabin met 95, I made a

U-turn, idled in close against a hedge of serviceberry, killed the engine. The glove box held not one but two half-empty pints of Jack Daniel's. I rolled down the window, heard the *spee-ik* of nighthawks, knew that I could wait for as long as I had to.

Four a.m., I crawled out the passenger door, peed into the dense brush, a little dizzy from the whiskey but still awake. I finished off one bottle, considered the other. Sun brewed the sky violet, then gold. I closed my eyes against the glare, opened them to see the Lincoln nose onto the highway and head toward Snake Junction.

She would recognize the car, I knew, and I felt the hair rise on my arms at the thought of her sensing my presence behind her, aware of my intent. I eased back, then panicked and sped forward, saw her take the short bridge into Snake Junction. Few other cars traveled the roads—too early for bankers, too late for workers leaving their graveyard shift at the mill.

At the courthouse, the Lincoln swung a smooth arc. I chose the alley behind the fire station, watched Irene take the steps, ring the buzzer. When the deputy came, she entered without hesitation, and I caught a quick glimpse of the canvas bag swinging heavily from her wrist. Twenty minutes later, she walked out, the bag weightless, floating in the early-morning air. She stopped for a moment, looked to where I hunkered, but then she let her gaze touch the valley all around, and I saw that it was the horizon she was seeing, the day's light just coming on, and I knew she was marking its beauty.

We retraced our route, came into Lapwai, hooked a left onto a short gravel street. The small house she entered was nipped into neatness: a frugal border of flowers; a single wooden chair on the tilted porch. "Aunt Esther's," I said aloud. Ten minutes later, Irene was back in the car.

Home now, I thought. Go home. I knew that Lee could wake to find his car gone, and the thought of his anger filled me with dread. *You go home, I'll go home.* But the Lincoln had disappeared. I crossed the next intersection, looking one way, then the other. I sped up and reached the road she had to cross to get back on the highway. I looked in the rearview, sure she was behind me, but all I saw were houses and a few white hens pecking at the roadside.

I screwed down my courage and made for the shack, bumping along the path, worrying that I might bring Lee's car back minus its muffler. The Lincoln wasn't there. I threw the Chevy into reverse, zigzagging across the ruts, bouncing the glove box open, bottles and papers and empty cigarette packs falling to the floor.

I hit seventy, then eighty, furious with frustration and a gnawing in my gut that would not be soothed with food or more whiskey. But whiskey is what I had. I reached toward the floorboard, felt the car swerve, pulled it back, snagged the bottle before it slid farther away. I drank until my eyes watered, took a breath and drank some more.

The Chevy felt strong and solid beneath me. I pushed harder. One hundred. Now the wind was whistling in at a higher pitch, the road coming faster. A good road. A straight road. Empty.

And then the stock truck pulling out from nowhere, the startled face of the rancher. I jerked the steering wheel to the left, felt the car heave and lift. I closed my eyes, straightened the wheel, pressed the accelerator to the floor. I was flying. When I opened my eyes, the truck was small and still in my rearview, miraculously whole.

I coasted down to sixty, pulled into The Stables, not bothering to position the car as it had been hours before. I didn't care that Lee might discover my trespass. Let him. I shivered with adrenaline. My head pounded. I left the keys in the ignition, found my way to the door, clattered down the hall, and fell into bed. Lee and I both slept then, each oblivious to the other.

I had not marked the clouds boiling up from the peaks of the Seven Devils, the sky gone gunmetal gray. I slept on, even as thunder boomed and echoed across the canyon, not knowing I had seen the last clear sunrise of summer, that I would awaken to air thick with smoke, the lightning-struck mountains ablaze. They would burn until October snow, even as the canyon cooled and the sap of maple and sycamore receded, brilliant leaves strewing the streets of Snake Junction.

It wasn't the thunder or the gathering smoke that woke me, but Lee, hauling me from bed feet-first.

"Get up, you little bastard! I should have known I couldn't trust you." He kicked my legs.

I pulled myself straight, stood, staggered, realized I was still wearing my shirt and jeans but only a single boot. I scrabbled through the bedding, looking for its mate. Lee hoisted me upright, shook me. Sharp wedges of pain settled at my temples.

"Let me go, Lee. Jesus, I'm sick."

"You don't know what sick is, mister." He dragged me into the bathroom, stuck my head beneath the faucet, turned on the cold water. I howled and sputtered until he wrenched my head back. "Take a good one, 'cause you're going down again."

The water filled my mouth, poured up my nose. Lee dropped me to the floor, where I lay choking, soaked to my ankles. I made one weak move toward the toilet before I vomited, a yellowish pool spreading across the tile.

"Now you're something, ain't you? Now you're a big man. You best not be drinking liquor you can't handle. And I'll tell you something else"—he leaned over me—"you keep your stinking hands off my car."

He grabbed one of the laundered rags that Harvey kept stacked on top of the water heater. "Here. Clean yourself. We got business, and you sure as hell better look prettier in fifteen minutes than you do right now."

I listened to Lee stomp down the hall, pushed myself up, felt the bile rise in my throat. I heaved, but my stomach was empty. I didn't think I could walk but I did, retching as I wiped the floor and rinsed the rag. I stripped, rolled my soiled clothes into a ball, then pulled the sheets from my bed and bundled them all together. I couldn't stand the smell of myself, so I stood at the sink and scrubbed with a bar of Lava. Only then, catching my own eyes in the mirror, did I remember the rancher, his fear-stricken face framed in the truck's window. I felt the closeness of my father's life, and his death.

When Lee returned, I was dry-eyed and combed.

"You're green," he said.

I gave a shallow nod, looked away.

"Come on. There's someone out here you need to meet."

I followed Lee down the hall, trying to soften the painful jolt of my steps.

Spud stood behind the counter. At the bar sat a middle-aged man, legs crossed, drinking a martini. Buckskin Stetson he hadn't deigned to remove, ironed shirt, pants sharply creased—I disliked him immediately.

"This the boy?" He leaned toward me without uncrossing his legs, and I felt a wave of revulsion. Blond hair winged back under his hat. Square jaw, pale blue eyes, tanned skin. There was something overdone about him, like a bed tucked too tight. I looked to Spud, who was sucking the pulp from last night's orange slices, a napkin dimpled in the V of his vest.

"This here's my brother," Lee said. No "little." He was putting me up equal, the two of us together. In this, there was no room for his anger toward me; he'd come back on me later, when there was nothing more important that demanded his attention. "Buddy, this here's Raimey."

Raimey stuck out his hand, offered a wide grin, like a dog that might beg or bite. I stepped forward, gave a quick, hard shake.

Spud cleared his throat, swiped the napkin across his mouth. "Now, listen," he said. "I don't need to tell you boys how I feel about this, but Raimey's got an honest proposition, and it wouldn't be right of me to stand in the way. Hear what he's got to offer. Make up your own mind." He jabbed one thumb at the cash register, took out a twenty. "Harvey'll be here anytime. I'm headed into town. Need anything?"

Lee and I both shook our heads.

"I'm gone."

"You all hear about the wildfires?" Raimey swiveled to face the dance floor, leaned back, his elbows on the bar, cigarette between his teeth. He pinched one eye shut against the smoke that furled beneath the brim of his hat. "Burning right up to the road."

"That's the problem with all these damn trees," Lee said. "You might get a bad field fire down in Oklahoma, but the whole goddamn place ain't going to burn down."

Raimey smiled, motioned toward the stools. "Sit. Let me buy you boys a drink."

The thought of whiskey made my knees quiver.

"Spud keeps us supplied," Lee said.

"Sounds like Spud's pretty darn good to you."

Lee nodded, stayed standing.

"How about the boy here? You want something to drink?"

Lee saw that I'd paled considerably. "Buddy, fetch me and you a ginger ale. That'll hold us for a while."

I fumbled ice into two tall glasses, decked each with cherries and orange slices, felt my mouth water with nausea or hunger.

"Spud tells me that Tennessee came through while back," Raimey said.

"Didn't like him." Lee didn't say that Tennessee Ernie Ford had offered him a year's contract. I remembered the way Ford had sniffed the air of The Stables as if he might be standing in horse shit. I'd hated the dark-haired man's pencil-thin moustache, the way he combed his hair into a slick part. When Lee told him no, he'd taken a final sniff, then given a backward wave of his hand as he stepped into his blueberry-colored bus.

Raimey snorted into his martini. "You made the right decision there. Truth is, he's an asshole. Had him in once. Never again."

"In where?" The soda had revived me enough to speak.

"Raimey's a scout for the Palomino Club," Lee said.

I felt my heart lurch sideways.

"What do you think, son? Think you'd like to spend some time in L.A.? Lots of pretty girls." He winked, licked the rim of his glass. "Six-month contract," Raimey told Lee. "Month's salary up front. We'd find work for your brother here." He turned and looked at me more fully. "You sing?"

Lee raised his eyebrows my way, but I shook my head. Sometimes I felt that I no longer had a voice, that Lee had melded my song to his.

"Guess not," Lee said.

Raimey relaxed back into his casual slump. "Too bad. Give those Everly boys a run for their money. Got to have the voices, though."

"Didn't say he don't have the voice. Got other prospects, that's all." Lee's words had taken on an edge, but Raimey seemed not to notice.

"The Hope Brothers." Raimey rolled it around. "Exposure. More than you'll ever get playing this joint." He raised his hand before Lee or I could protest. "At the Palomino, you get seen by people who matter. Record company folks."

I was only half listening to Raimey's pitch. My eye had been caught by the large gold ring he wore—a horseshoe with diamonds that flicked and fired beneath the lights.

"Tell you what, Raimey," Lee said. "Get us something in writing, and we'll get back to you."

Raimey's smile thinned against his teeth. "These chances don't come along every day. I made this one trip up here. I won't be back." Raimey looked at me. "You better have a powwow with your brother." The ring sparked. "You don't want to spend the rest of your life in this Indian camp, do you?"

"That ring from L.A.?" I surprised myself. Wristwatches made me feel like a dandy. But that ring—love, luck, and money rolled into one.

Raimey lifted his hand. "You like this?" He slipped the ring from his finger, laid it on the counter. "Signing bonus."

"We don't want no ring, Raimey. We'll decide this thing. Us and the band." Lee set his jaw.

"Well, now, that's something else I've been meaning to mention." Raimey scooted the ring an inch closer to me, tried to catch my eye. "You come on down, we'll get you set up with one of the best backups around."

"I don't work without the Spurs."

Raimey nodded. Sure, sure, he understood. "Wasn't there a gal? Bass player?"

Lee and I looked at each other. Lee worked his glass in a circle. "She passed away a while back."

"I'm sorry to hear that," Raimey said. "Bet you hated to lose her. Band gets to be like family." He lowered his head, pursed his lips in feigned distress at the shame of it all, then rapped his knuckles against the counter, turned his eyes on the empty stage. "But that sound you got going. We can fine-tune it a bit, get you pickers who know how to jazz things up. I got a bass player worked with Elvis. Fit your style just right. But"—Raimey held up both hands, shrugged—"you're the boss. You just got to understand that *you're* the one I want. This offer I'm making"— he tapped his chest, pulled a folded piece of paper from inside his jacket—"this offer's for you, Lee. The band can come, but I can't guarantee anything. They'd have to audition, just like the rest."

Raimey put the paper down next to the ring. "I'm staying at Charbonneau's in town. I won't consider any answer final until tomorrow at noon. I'll be back here then."

"Take the ring." Lee gestured toward the counter.

Raimey looked at me. "I said this ring would be part of the deal. You sign this contract, Buddy here gets the ring." He stood, shorter than I thought he would be, threw a twenty on the counter. "I'll get you down there. Then it's up to you." He stopped in the doorway, eyes shielded against the sun, said over his shoulder, "Hotter than a popcorn fart," and was gone.

"Asshole." Lee dumped the ginger ale, poured a shot of JD. "I don't give a shit about no Palomino Club." He knocked back the whiskey, poured another. I turned so I didn't have to watch, took another sip of my soda, ate a few more cherries and oranges. "Thinks he can come in here and tell me what I'd best do. Bad-mouths this place. I should have knocked his teeth out." Another shot and the bottle was empty. Lee perused the shelf, pulled down a bottle of Black Velvet. No need for a glass now. He was sailing.

"I don't need no fancy-ass telling me I can sing." He nodded in agreement with himself. "What's California got that we ain't got? Bunch of backstabbing muckamucks, that's what. Right here's good enough for me. Yes, sir. Right here."

I kept quiet while Lee paced, swore his disdain until he'd exhausted his defense and slouched against the counter. He raised his head, his brow furrowed. "But then there's you."

"I'm fine. Do what you want."

"We're in this together, ain't we? Hell, I could stay right here, die with my boots on, tits up on that stage." He held out his hand toward the empty floor. "What good's that to you?" He ran his fingers through his hair, turned a half-circle, turned back, sat down. "Hey," he said, eyes widening. "Maybe *you* could do something in L.A., take movie star lessons."

I snorted. "I ain't no actor."

"School, then. You could be a . . ." Lee stopped, blinked several times. "Hell, I don't know."

I chewed the inside of one cheek, lowered my head. Lee leaned close, gave the back of my neck a rough rub.

"That gal of yours. She's something. How'd you do that?"

I shook my head.

"I'm jealous as hell. Never get to look at her anymore. You two are always gone off somewhere. Can't say as I blame you."

I thought I might tell Lee everything—about the cougar in its cage, the little house in the draw, the letters I'd found—but his head doddered, and I knew I'd be speaking only to myself.

"What's she like?"

"Irene?"

"Yeah, dipshit. Irene."

I thought for a moment, trying to find the few words that might contain her.

"Never mind," Lee said. "I don't want to hear it. Just makes it worse." His chin rested against his chest.

"Maybe you should go lie down for a while. Take a nap."

"Shit, Buddy. I ain't going nowhere." He laid his forehead on the counter and was asleep.

I waited only a minute before reaching for the ring. I put it first in one pocket and then another. Finally, I slipped it on my finger, felt the surprise of its weight.

As I walked toward Lapwai, I flashed the ring this way, then that, like a beacon in the fog. Even the haze from the distant fires wasn't enough to muddy its shine. The mountains were enshrouded. The cars passing by me flashed their lights; I was nearly invisible in the ashy air.

I felt better outside the building, felt my appetite returning. I pulled off my shirt, tied it at my waist. She was there now, I was almost sure. Maybe she would feed me lunch.

I smiled, lit a cigarette, and kept walking.

CHAPTER THIRTEEN

The macadam was oily with the heat it had absorbed over days of one hundred–plus. My feet stuck and slapped, and I hummed along in easy rhythm. I'd tied my bandanna around my head, and still the sweat poured—all that poison working its way out.

I quieted when I reached the shack, saw the Lincoln. I took off the ring, pushed it to the bottom of my watch pocket. Through the window, I could see Irene at the table, reading a newspaper. When I tapped, she spun around, and I saw that she was wearing glasses.

"I didn't know you wore those," I hollered and pointed two fingers.

She looked at me over the rims, and for a second I saw her as a schoolmarm, hair pulled up, no makeup, a severe look in her eyes as she came to the door.

"What are you doing here, Buddy?" She folded the glasses into her hand.

"I got something for you." On the table behind her, I could see the *Tribune*'s front page, the now familiar photo of Laurette—the honest smile, the dark hair in a bun at the base of her neck, the tiara half-circling the crown of her cowboy hat—and underneath, "Royalty, 1948." Her life, like her death, seemed old news.

Irene crossed her arms, leaned against the door frame. "I really don't want you coming here uninvited."

"Invite me." I stepped forward, brushed my lips across hers. "Invite me," I whispered.

Irene pulled away. I walked in, sat on the bed. "Come here."

"I'm not up for this, Buddy. I've got things to do today."

"Didn't get them all done this morning?" I kicked back, folded my arms under my head. Irene studied me, seeing something different. I flexed the muscles in my arms, sucked in my stomach.

"Shoes off the quilt," she said.

I snubbed the heel of each boot, pulled my socked feet back onto the bed, smiled. I felt lean and able, fit for a fight.

"What's this all about?" Irene kept her arms crossed. I rolled forward, made a grab, but she was too quick. She kept backing, one hand held out to stop me. "Buddy, I'm not kidding. This isn't the time or the place. . . ."

I lunged, caught her around the waist, dropped her to the bed. I was laughing and giddy, nipping her neck, pushing myself against her. My weight alone was enough to keep her there.

But she wasn't fighting. She lay still beneath me, head turned away, eyes closed.

"Come on," I said, and danced my fingers along the softness beneath her ribs. I pushed the heels of my hands into the mattress on either side of her, bounced her up and down.

"Come on, Irene. Let's have some fun." I blew across her face, gently placed one finger against her right eyelid, playing the child's game. "Eye-winker." Then I touched her left eye. "Tom-tinker. Nose-dropper." Then her lips. "Mouth-eater, chin-chopper, *throat-cutter!*"

The second my fingers touched her neck, Irene went wild, raking, kicking. Her glasses hit the wall. I held up my arms, took a heel in the crotch, fell to the floor, ginger ale brewing in my throat. She was out the door before I could stop her.

I caught my breath, rolled to my back. It had been a long time since I'd felt so beaten. I cupped myself, felt the ring in my pocket, remembered why I was there.

I found her sitting at the creek, knees snugged, dress pulled to her ankles, face hidden in the folds of her arms. I dipped a handful of water, rinsed my mouth, spat.

"You can't do that to me," she said.

"Couldn't be clearer."

"Are you okay?"

"Will be."

She rubbed her lips against her forearm. "Do I need to tell you why?"

"Nope. Just a little surprised, that's all." I walked several yards up to where the water stilled and deepened. "Can rattlesnakes swim?" I asked.

"Some say so." Irene let her legs relax, leaned back, watched me as I shed my clothes, stepped into the water, dog-paddled the pool's circumference. "You sure you want to leave your clothes there?" she asked.

"Why not?"

"Just wondered." She stood, unbuttoned her dress, let it drop from her shoulders.

Nothing. Nothing on underneath that dress.

I cannot tell you how beautiful she was, the muscles of her legs tensing against the water's flow as she waded toward me. I felt the warmth of her skin, ankles to shoulders, her mouth on mine not just warm but hot. Her hands moved down my chest and stomach to the place between my legs.

"Still hurt?" She held me gently, and I thought I might float away.

"A little."

She pressed harder, and I felt my scrotum tighten.

"Careful," I said.

I felt the pressure of each finger, the muscle of her palm. She massaged, then gave a serious squeeze. "Do you trust me?"

"Jesus, Irene." I was on my tiptoes, holding to her shoulders.

She ran the nails of her free hand down my back, and I arched toward her.

"God*dam*mit!"

"We don't want to play these games, Buddy. You got questions, ask." She let go, started to turn away, but I grabbed her by the wrist.

"Wait. Isn't there a good way to finish this?"

She smiled a little, pulled free, made her way back down the creek. "It's not going to be a good day for you, Buddy."

"You could make it better."

"Come by later tonight. I'll have something for you."

"What'll I do till then?"

"Go see Aunt Esther." She had stepped into the flower of her dress, pulled it up around her. "You know where she lives."

I started to protest, then didn't, watched her disappear up the trail. I lay back in the water, felt the sun on my belly, the hollowness at my center, and realized that I was starving. My clothes pulled up from the green creek bank smelled of sage and clover. I used my shirt as a towel, wiped my face, the back of my neck, between my legs, decided to carry my boots, feel the moss-covered trail beneath my feet.

"Irene," I hollered. "Can I take the Lincoln?"

The screen door opened. Out flew the keys.

I finger-combed my hair, checked my face in the rearview for dust streaks. Aunt Esther's house was less than a mile away—not a long walk, even for an old woman. When I pulled up in front, she waved me in. The rooms smelled of bacon, pepper, parsley. My stomach clinched and growled.

"Sit down here." Aunt Esther pointed to a place at the table, already set with two plates, tumblers of iced tea.

"I don't mean to intrude. Looks like you got company coming." Something boiled on the stove. The kitchen was hot with cooking. My mouth watered.

"Got *you* coming." She bunched the hem of her apron, pulled a sheet of biscuits from the oven.

"Irene called?"

"You see a telephone?"

I surveyed the walls. "I just . . . I'm . . ."

"You're hungry, that's what." A skillet of fried potatoes and onions, bacon kept warm on the back burner. I watched as she broke six eggs, whipped them into froth. "My girls got to lay more. This heat puts 'em down."

I thought of the white hens along the road. "My mother used to keep leghorns. Good layers."

"Barred rock are better," she said. "I'll can these come fall, get some fresh for next year. Can't keep a rooster around this damn place. Get them raised just where they can cover the hens, then they disappear. Always getting picked off by coyotes. Damn fools don't know when to quit strutting and take cover." She spooned the eggs onto my plate, forked several strips of bacon alongside, went back to the stove to add more pepper to the gravy. "Eat. Ain't nothing keeping you."

I swallowed the scrambled eggs without chewing. The bacon was just like my mother's—sweet and crisp. Esther took my plate, replaced it with a platter of biscuits and gravy, another raft of bacon. When my tea glass was empty, she refilled it. She sat across from me, eating a single biscuit, one piece of bacon. I might have been embarrassed except I recognized the look on her face: like my mother, she took pleasure in feeding the hungry.

I leaned away from the table, took the toothpick she offered. "Best meal I've had since leaving Oklahoma." I felt the drowsiness coming on, an overwhelming need to find a flat space to lie down.

"Your folks still there?" Esther worried a bit of bacon from between her teeth.

"Both dead. That's why we came here. To find work." I nodded a fly away, too weary to lift my hand.

"But you ain't working." She looked at me with her head tilted back, appraising.

"I help out around The Stables. I got work to do."

"Hmph." She rose, began clearing the dishes.

"Let me help," I offered, though I could hardly rise.

"You go on in the front room there and take a nap. You need to rest up. All that work you do."

I slumped onto the rough brown couch, meaning to sit there only a minute, but then I was stretched out and asleep.

When I woke, it was to the sound of Aunt Esther tuning in the radio.

"What time is it?" I asked, searching the dark room for a clock. My back itched from sun and the prickly couch.

"Still early. News is just coming on. You hungry?"

I shook my head. Even my arms were crawling, scaled with dried creek water. I went into the kitchen, scratching my sides, my back, my chest.

Esther pointed a long fork toward my place at the table. "That Arkansas thing's still a mess, ain't it?"

I struggled to clear my thoughts. "Arkansas?"

"That desdridation, or whatever. I'm not sure I see the sense in it."

"Desedridation," I said. "Desegration. Shoot," I whispered. "Do you have any coffee?"

"Brewing."

I heard the chuff of the percolator. Then I could smell it, strong and smoky.

"Now here, they just put us right in regular school. Wasn't no difference. We all had to talk the same way, write the same way, pray the same way, Indians and whites alike. Some of those farm kids worse off than we was. Some didn't even know their alphabet." Esther shook her head, still in wonder at the thought. "Them priests come right at you, boy, you didn't know your letters."

Oklahoma was Indian Territory, but the only Indians I ever saw were at the county fair, dressed in native garb and posed for photos, tomahawks held high. Aunt Esther was the first I'd known up close, but I didn't think of her that way. She was Aunt Esther.

"Got some biscuits left. Got some Karo," she said.

"Guess I'd have some." I rubbed the back of my neck, felt the welts rise beneath my fingernails.

"Good." She was quick in her brown oxfords, heating the syrup, smearing the biscuits with butter. She sat, held a sugar cube between her front teeth, sucked her coffee through. The news droned on behind us. "You hear about Lana Turner's daughter?"

"No, can't say as I have."

"Know who she is?"

"Actress?"

"A good one. Not very smart, though. Took up with a gangster. You know he beat her." Esther leaned in close, sharing a secret. "You *know* he did."

"Shouldn't happen." I pursed my lips to keep from blowing biscuit crumbs across the table, resisted the urge to dig at my crotch, which was itching like mad, along with every other part of me.

"But he learned his lesson, I tell you." Esther eyed my twitching. "You got bugs?"

"No! Sorry. Went for a swim in the creek earlier."

She went on. "Lana's daughter kilt him deader than a doornail. Only fourteen years old. Stabbed him to death. Got off, too. And that's just as it should be." She looked out the window into the dark. "Lord knows what he was doing to that little girl."

I stopped chewing, but Esther kept her eyes on the window. I forced down a large bite. "Could you tell me something?"

"Won't know till you ask."

"I was wondering about Danny."

"What do you want to know?" Esther looked at me directly, nothing to hide.

"How'd he die?"

She searched the window. "He died slow, Buddy. Real slow."

"Irene . . . is that why she came back here?"

"She could have come back sooner. Wouldn't have done no good, though." Esther shook her head. "He left what he had to her, which was right. Had a policy he'd taken out. Like he knew he'd be dying and it was all he had to offer her." She pushed back her shoulders, and I heard the pop of vertebrae. "Them two. Always one step ahead or one step behind. Born too early or too late. Hard to say."

I wiped my mouth, drained my cup. "I need to get going," I said. I felt I was being eaten by ants, crawling up my legs, down my shirt, through the fly of my underwear.

"Tell Irene she missed some good cooking. Maybe next time, you both can stop by." Esther was folding biscuits into a clean tea towel. "Take these to her. She doesn't eat enough."

I moved toward the door, but Esther caught my sleeve. "Listen. That girl needs somebody to take care of her for a while. You aren't what I had in mind, but you might be just the thing. For now, anyway." She gave my arm a hard tug. "And don't think I don't know what's going on. The Celery King was younger than me by twelve years." She winked. "Young roosters are the best."

But then she turned serious. "Irene's always had the weight of the world on her shoulders. Bears everyone's burdens. I worry about that girl." She looked up, tightened her mouth. "Irene says that woman they found in the river was a friend of yours. I'm sorry for that."

"Me, too."

"Something like this happens, people are quick to blame." She let go of my arm, stepped back, and I felt a line being drawn. "Easy for them to come looking among us."

I wanted to reassure her, say that Wolfchild was innocent until proven guilty, that he'd be judged with the same fairness as any man. But I'd seen the hunts in Oklahoma, heard the stories of black men dragged from their houses, the lynchings and burnings. I could have said what I sensed down deep inside—that Wolfchild had not killed Laurette—but nothing mattered to me. Not the fate of Wolfchild. Not the role I might play in his judgment. Nothing but making my way back to Irene.

And I was consumed with another need: I had to scratch. I thanked Aunt Esther, left her standing cross-armed on the porch. Once in the car and down the block, I pulled over and went at it, rubbing my back against the car seat like a cow against a fence post, scraping my shoulders bloody. I unzipped my jeans, plucked at my underwear, sure, now, that I was harboring fleas, maybe from Aunt Esther's couch, though her house had seemed clean enough, and I hadn't seen a dog or a cat. I was nearly out of my mind by the time I got to Irene's.

"Jesus, Irene, I'm itching to death."

She pulled me into the room, sat me down at the table, held up a mirror. My face and neck were blotched and swollen.

"What in the hell?"

"Go out on the porch and take off the rest of your clothes. Boots, too. Leave them in a pile."

I came back in, shivering, miserable. "It's everywhere."

Irene kept her eyes down, smiled.

"Why the hell do you think this is so funny?"

"I said I'd have something for you when you got back." She opened the cupboard, took out a large bottle of pinkish liquid. "Here it is. First we need to get you scrubbed off."

Back down to the creek, where she took a rough bar of brown soap, splashed me with water, rubbed me down like a horse. I didn't know whether to moan with pleasure or scream with pain—the two seemed one and the same. Under my arms, between my legs, my scalp—I was glad for the darkness, glad she couldn't see the tears welling up. She worked the lather in, then commanded me to walk upstream to the deeper pool and rinse.

I started my trek along the bank.

"I wouldn't go that way. Stay in the water."

"Why?" I could barely see her in the dark.

"Poison ivy."

I stopped, turned to face her, the drying soap and cool air raising every hair on my body. "*Poison ivy?* Why didn't you tell me that before?"

"You didn't seem to want to listen to anything I had to say before."

"Goddammit, Irene. This ain't funny. I'm going to have scabs from my ears to my ass."

She nodded with mock gravity. "When you're done, come on back to the cabin."

I floated in the pool, the cold water soothing the rash. Irene was waiting for me at the door.

"On the bed." She'd covered the quilt with a clean sheet. I lay on my back, spread out like I'd been crucified. She shook the bottle of pink liquid, began at my forehead, a film across my nose and cheeks, down my throat.

"My armpits," I said.

"I'll get to them." Slowly, a patch of skin at a time, she covered me. A thin coat spread gently across my genitals, soft and compliant. Between my toes, along the soles of my feet. And then she blew her breath all down the front of me, and I could feel the lotion dry, sucking the moisture from my skin, absorbing the poison.

"Roll over."

The backs of my ears, the small of my back. Her fingers parted the crack of my ass, a light slip of lotion, then the backs of my legs and ankles, the cool of her breath.

"Irene? You got to tell me something."

"Don't be so sure."

"I mean it. One thing."

"One thing."

"Danny."

She capped the bottle, wiped her hands on the sheet.

"I just need to know what was between you. I know he's dead. I know it don't matter anymore. I just need to hear what he was to you."

She clasped her hands, looked to the dark square of window. "He was everything to me for a long time."

I checked the skip of my heart, weighed my presence there against the sadness in her voice. She caught my hand when I began to scratch.

"You'll make it spread."

"What about it getting on you? Maybe you shouldn't touch me."

"Never had it, though I've been in it enough. Must be immune."

"How long will it last?"

Irene looked at me with a kind of tenderness I hadn't seen before. Maybe, I thought, this will be worth it.

"Awhile. The worst should be over in a week."

I groaned.

"I should burn your clothes. I can scrub off your boots."

"What in the hell am I going to wear?"

"I'll get some old clothes from Aunt Esther. Did she feed you good?"

"Too much." I touched the fullness below my ribs. "She knows about us."

Irene narrowed her eyes.

"I didn't tell her. She just knows. Said young roosters are the best."

Irene turned her head to keep me from seeing her smile. "You need anything else?"

"Glass of water, maybe."

I watched Irene's dark silhouette through the door as she poured kerosene. She came back in, laid a few coins and the penknife on the table. It was then that I remembered.

I jumped up. "Where's the ring?"

"What ring?"

I ran outside, grabbed a stick, dragged what remained of my jeans from the flames. Nothing but seams and ashes.

"Get me some water!"

I doused the fire, stirred the cinders. "Can you bring the lantern?"

Irene didn't ask any questions but held the light while I sifted the remnants of cloth. I spied the ring, picked it up, dropped it, my fingers seared. Irene snapped a twig from a nearby bush. I threaded the ring, carried it before me into the house, slid it onto the table.

"That ring must mean something to you." Irene brought me a wet rag, a sliver of soap.

"It means I'm going to get killed tomorrow." I began working away the soot, saw that two diamonds were missing.

Irene folded her arms, leaned against the sink. "I kind of like you sitting there at my table, naked as a jaybird."

I pulled the sheet from the bed, wrapped it around my waist, went back to work.

"Don't suppose you want to tell me what this is all about."

"Not right now, I don't."

"Fair enough." Irene tapped salt and baking soda into a jar, added some vinegar. "Drop it in here."

"It was supposed to be for you." I did as she told me, then fished the ring from the mix, wiped it with the rag. Its shine was streaked, its diamonds dull, the two holes like empty eye sockets.

Irene reached out, held it in her palm. "This is *your* ring?"

I felt too miserable and defeated to even attempt a lie. "No, it ain't my ring. Not yet, anyway."

"Now who's talking in riddles?'

I made my way to the bed, dragging my sheet along with me. "It's Raimey's ring. Guy come up from Los Angeles to hire Lee."

"Los Angeles?" Irene sat at the edge of the mattress, more interested than I wanted her to be.

"Palomino Club. Wants Lee to sign a contract. If he does, ring's a bonus. Got until tomorrow noon to decide." I rolled to my side. "Scratch my back, blow on it, something." Irene rose, returned with the newspaper, began fanning. I shivered.

"You've talked about it. You and Lee."

"What's there to talk about? Lee don't want to go to L.A., and neither do I."

"Why?"

I turned toward her. "Because I want to be here with you."

"What about Lee? Why doesn't he want to go to L.A.?"

"Is that more important to you?" My irritation was building. "Why don't *you* go to L.A. with Lee? You two just go on and have a good ol' time. There won't be much you got to teach him at all. God *damn!*" I threw off the sheet, began raking the insides of my thighs. "I guess that's the best part of all this: you got someone to keep you amused. Don't seem to bother you much at all to watch someone suffer."

"Stop it." She grabbed my wrists. I jerked away, dragged my fingernails down the sides of my neck.

"Stop! You'll scratch yourself bloody."

It felt too good to stop, too good to watch her face, see fear. I clawed at my chest, dug in hard, felt the skin rupture and tear.

"Buddy!" She pulled at my arms, threw her weight against me, but I pushed her away, my hands fisted. I was stronger, and it was that realization, that awareness that I could hurt her, that made me go still. She fell against me and we lay there, her fingers still clutching, blood oozing from the welts I'd given myself.

"Why do you give a shit, Irene? You're the one who made this happen."

"I didn't ask you to come here."

"No, but you sure as hell made it hard for me to stay away." I rolled to face the wall. "I just don't know what you expect of me."

"I didn't expect a diamond ring." She touched my spine; I felt

161

a whisper across my shoulder, her breath at the base of my skull, a flutter across my ribs. I twitched like a colt.

"Sometimes I'm afraid this will all end bad," she said, "afraid that what you need is to get away from me."

"Maybe I do." Her fingers went still. I waited in the silence, trying hard to believe that I didn't care.

She drew herself away, rose slowly, as though she were moving against water. "You should go."

"You going to make me walk back like this?" I looked like a cadaver, pasty white, bloody stripes congealing.

"I don't mean home. I mean to Los Angeles." She picked up the ring, worked her nails precisely around the stones. "My daddy had a ring. Won it in a poker game. Wore it to the track for luck."

"Did he win?"

"Not enough." She licked a thumb, rubbed the horseshoe. "Omega," she said.

"What?"

"Alpha and omega. The beginning and the end. This shape is omega."

"And omega means the end?"

She nodded.

"You trying to tell me something?"

Irene filled a jar with water, drank it standing, looking out into the moonless thicket. She blew out the lantern, and I heard the shush of her dress on the floor.

"Can I touch you?" She placed three fingers against my collarbone.

"Can't hurt."

"Might." She tested her palm against my thigh. "Okay?"

"I can stand it."

"You'll be blistered tomorrow."

"Can't wait."

She took in a breath. "I don't want you to go. I'm afraid. Afraid for myself. For you."

"Irene." I rolled her to her back, let the fever of my stomach rest against the cool of her. "I trust you." Her hands trailed the rails of my ribs, lingering where the skin puckered. "I don't feel so new anymore, do I?"

She laughed, then laid her face against my arm. "You see, I'm already wearing you out."

"Breaking me in. Just breaking me in." I traced the fine arch of her eyebrows. "Irene, I want to be with you. Here, L.A., I don't care. There's no reason why we can't be together."

"None of our own making."

"Who's to stop us?"

"Anybody. Everybody."

"Nobody." I kissed her carefully. "I'm sorry about earlier." She gave a small shrug. "But I have to ask you. About Wolfchild. About you going to the courthouse."

Irene brought her hand to my face, touched my eyes, my ears, my mouth. "You see too much, hear too much, ask too many questions."

"You said we can't play games."

"This isn't a game. Maybe for some people. Not for others." She rested her hand against the side of my face. "You've got too much life ahead of you. I can't let you get caught up in this."

"In what?"

"It's for your own good."

"That's what Daddy said before he whipped us."

"But it was, wasn't it? For your own good?"

I thought of my last whipping, my father strapping me with the horse reins he'd found dropped carelessly in a corner of the barn. I'd heard a huff and thump, turned to see Lee standing over him, the reins in his hand. My father looked at us both as if he might hate us, rose and walked straight to the pickup, then disappeared down the road in a red cloud of dust. The next morning, he came dragging home, the back of his shirt in tatters. Cut with a linoleum knife fighting over moonshine. Our mother was furious, less at his drunkenness than at the fact that one of his best work shirts was beyond her ability to mend. Two more nights and they were both dead, the bleached shirt still hanging from the knob of the pantry door, riven with stitches.

"This is something I have to do on my own, Buddy. That's all."

I didn't want anything to take Irene's attention away from me. "Aunt Esther and I are worried," I said.

"You two are quite the pair." Irene pressed one thigh between my legs. "Maybe you'd rather go spend the night at her house, let *her* rub you down with calamine."

"That need's been taken care of."

"Got any others?"

"Just the one."

We made love in a quiet way, fearing that too quick or rough a touch might tear what held between us. Afterward, as we lay in the dark, listening to nothing but the wind through the cracked window, I began to hum, and then to sing the words like a lullaby: "Good night, Irene, I'll see you in my dreams."

"That's the only hopeful part of that song," she whispered. "The rest is too sad not to be true."

"But it's someone else's story." I spooned around her, knees, hips, my arm draping hers. "We can make our own story." I nuzzled her neck, inhaled deeply. "Let's talk about what happens next," I said, but she was already sleeping, taking my dreams with her.

I lay awake for a long time, imagining the next morning, afternoon, evening. It was a happy ending, I told myself. All I had to do was get the ring back before noon. I thought to look again for the missing diamonds, but I didn't want to wake Irene.

Tomorrow, I thought. Soon enough.

CHAPTER FOURTEEN

"Damn, that boy can play," Harvey announced as I walked into The Stables. He was in early for lack of anything better to do. He tapped his fingers along the lip of the counter, keeping rhythm.

Irene had dropped me off before nine, having already gone to Aunt Esther's for clothes, picked the missing diamonds from the dead fire and glued them back in. I was surprised to see Lee onstage, tuning and retuning, playing bits and snatches of songs in the near-dark, the only light filtering in from the open door.

Harvey was too caught up in the music to notice my borrowed trousers or the way my eyes had puffed almost closed. In the back room, I changed into jeans, then looked for Raimey's contract, found it on the floor, half covered by Lee's thrown-off undershirt. I didn't expect to see a signature, and there wasn't one, only a few stains and a swipe of ash. I smoothed it with my hand, set it atop the nightstand.

I took the ring from my pocket as I walked back to the bar, slid it across the counter toward Harvey. It would take a discerning eye to see the damage. "Found this in the parking lot. Think it belongs to that guy from L.A."

In the pinch of Harvey's fingers, the ring looked small, nothing special. He snugged it onto his pinkie.

"Lee ain't said much. Any clues?"

"Nope."

He looked at me close for the first time. "Jesus, what happened to you?"

"Went fishing and got into some poison ivy."

"I *bet* you was fishing."

I shrugged, acted like I, too, was caught up in Lee's song, began bopping down the bar. I wanted to join in, but I'd been quiet so long, singing would seem like surrender.

Harvey smiled, wagged his head. I reached toward him, grabbed the thick of his wrist, batted my eyelashes as Lee sang, "For you, pretty baby, I'd even die."

"Shit." Harvey almost blushed, pulled away. He opened a Coke, sat it on the bar. "One thing for sure: I'd rather see you happy and rambling through poison ivy than moping around here. Glad that gal's good for something other than stirring up trouble."

I stopped jigging, took a casual drink of the soda, resisted the urge to take up the scratching that had occupied me most of the morning. "She ain't causing any trouble. Lee's laid off that."

"I don't mean with Lee. I mean with the sheriff."

"Guess I haven't heard." I pretended nonchalance, kept my fingers tapping.

"Doesn't surprise me." Harvey worked his rag down to the end of the bar, took his time coming back.

"What trouble?"

"Now, if I tell you, you're going to get mad, and then I'm going to be the one to blame."

"I'm already mad. Tell me." But I didn't want to know. I concentrated on breathing even, quelling the fear.

"I'll tell you because I think it's for your own good. She's been going to the courthouse."

"I know that."

"Yeah?"

"Yeah. Let me have a JD."

He filled a shot glass full of whiskey, set the bottle beside it. "You know what she's doing there?"

"Selling eggs."

"What?"

"Selling her aunt Esther's eggs."

"The hell she is. She's going there every day to visit that Indian. Takes him muffins and jam. Sits there with him and feeds him with her fingers, then licks the sticky off his mouth. She's got the damned deputy so stirred up he can't say her name without stuttering." Harvey tipped back his head, pointed his nose, flapped his lower jaw like a circus seal. "I-I-I-I-rene." He slapped the bar with his rag. "Eggs my ass. You're the egg, egghead."

I sipped the whiskey, felt the tremor of uncertainty in my chest. "If she's going there, she's got good reason."

"Sure, she's got good reason. He's about so tall and has hair longer than hers. You'd think any woman would rather spit on him as to look at him, after what he done to Laurette. But not your gal. She's bringing him tea and crumpets."

"She's not my gal."

"I'm glad to hear it."

"I mean she don't belong to me. She's free to do whatever the hell she wants, and if what she wants is to help Wolfchild, that's fine by me." I finished the shot, poured another, told myself it would help the itching. "I don't believe he did it, anyway."

"You mean *she* don't believe he did it. Hell, Buddy, what do you think she was hunting for, coming in here alone like that? With you, she's got herself a young buck who can keep her going all night long, with Wolfchild, a righteous cause for the daytime. That'd keep any woman happy."

I tried to erase the image Harvey had painted in my head: Irene sitting next to the Indian, holding food to his lips, leaning to kiss him. Was that why she didn't want me following her? Was that the secret mission she was on, the thing she must do on her own? I should have known, should have listened to the voice in my head whispering a truth I didn't want to hear.

"Little brother," Lee called. "Quit flirting with Harvey and get up here."

I looked at Harvey, worked my jaw to stay calm. "Why?" I called back.

"'Cause I said so, that's why. Get your ass up here."

I set the shot glass down hard, walked grudgingly to the stage.

"What are you so owly about this morning? Been *workin'* too hard?"

"Shut up."

Lee laughed, in high spirits, feeling too good to let me get in the way.

"What do you want me to do?" I looked around at the equipment, waiting for orders, anything to take my mind off Irene and Wolfchild.

"I need some harmony. You know the tune." Lee hit a chord, began crooning: "Well, a hard-headed woman, a soft-hearted man . . ."

"I ain't singing that."

"Come on, fool. It ain't about you. No more than it's about any of us." Lee moved the microphone toward me. "What in the hell happened to your face?"

"Poison ivy. Went fishing yesterday." I let the lie steady me, as though I could remake the past hours.

"Jesus Christ. What'd you try to do? Eat it?"

I started from the stage.

"Just wait. When was the last time I asked you to help me out with a song?"

"Can't remember."

"And now you're saying no."

"I just don't feel like singing, that's all."

"That's the problem, Buddy. You never feel like singing no more. Singing always makes you feel better, and this here's a good song." He poked me in the ribs with the head of his guitar. "Come on," he said. "Sing."

I wanted to snatch the Gibson from his hands, turn it against him. I wanted to scream that I didn't have a song anymore, that he'd drained all the music from my bones, took it with him onto the stage, bled it out to strangers—people who had never lain awake at night to hear him crying.

But I had. I'd been there at the beginning, when the songs were nobody's but ours, there on the porch with the sun finally down and the cool coming on like a blessing. I wanted to hate him for giving it away, handing it out so easily, as if it weren't the very food from our mouths, the only water we had to drink.

I took a hard breath. Lee stopped his playing. "It's all here, Buddy," he said. "Just you and me and this guitar. Don't need nothing nor nobody else." He gave my shoulder a rough squeeze, shook me, and I felt my anger starting to loosen, the liquor and Lee working their magic.

I dropped my head, wiped my nose. "Okay, okay," I said.

Lee smiled, nodded, picked up where he'd left off. When I tested my way into the verse, Lee stopped again. "You call that singing? You sound like a sick dog."

"I'm leaving." I made for the steps.

"You're too damned serious. Get over here." He gave me a poke. "Back, mule, back!" I grinned in spite of myself. "That's better. Let's go with Samson."

We sang about Eve and Delilah and every other woman who had ever been a thorn in the side of man, which, Harvey pronounced loudly from across the room, was just about all of them. Harvey and Lee seemed to have something going between them, each ribbing the other, both urging me toward another drink. It felt good to let the seriousness slip away. It felt right, standing there beside Lee. I looked sideways, saw his eyes wrinkle in a broad smile, and my heart felt suddenly emptied and light. He'd fed me, sang me through those long nights on the road when all I'd wanted to do was curl into myself and die. I needed to get my head straight, see things for what they were. Lee and Harvey were right: since Irene had come to The Stables, awful things had happened.

But then she was there, walking through the door, standing at the bar. Lee and I both throttled down. The easy feeling was gone. Lee took a quick look at Harvey, stepped off the stage. "You comin'?"

I followed, though I wanted to bolt for the back room or the river, anywhere but where I was headed.

"Harv, give me the same as what she's drinking." Lee pointed three fingers at Irene like a Boy Scout salute.

"Gin. *Tanqueray,*" Harvey added quickly.

Lee raised his eyebrows my way.

"A beer." Anyone could hear the misery in my voice.

"I'm just having the one." Irene spoke quietly. Her hair was loosely gathered at the nape of her neck. I'd never seen her in jeans. When she pulled a ten from her pocket, Lee reared back.

"Whoa! Things ain't so bad we got to let a woman pay. Harv, put this on my bill."

Harvey sucked in his cheeks. "Sure," he said. "No problem, Mr. Hope."

"Here." Lee gestured toward a table. "Let's take a load off." He sauntered across the floor, martini glass held high between finger and thumb.

We took our chairs across from one another. I wouldn't look at either of them. Irene tipped her head toward me, and I knew she could sense the change. When I looked at her, all I could see was Wolfchild. I didn't care what news she brought or what need she had. She'd been lying to me, all the time acting like she was answering a higher calling. I gulped my beer, wiped foam from my lip.

"Hot out there, ain't it?" Lee took a dainty sip of his gin.

"I like heat." Irene moved her hand beneath her hair. "It's the cold I can't stand."

"You'd probably like Oklahoma, then. Might should try it sometime." Lee's voice remained pleasant.

"It's dry heat I like. Not humidity." She looked at me, but I pretended fascination with my cocktail napkin, tearing it, wadding it into balls. We could hear Harvey grunting as he unloaded liquor boxes, checked the seals.

Lee gave up pretense, drained his glass.

Irene touched my knee under the table. "Buddy, I'd like to talk to you. Maybe outside?" I twitched away like I'd been stung.

"He's a little testy today. Noticed it myself." Lee tipped back his chair, lit a cigarette, blew the smoke straight up. "Needs food in his stomach. What say we all go grab some early lunch?"

"I ain't hungry." I couldn't look at either one of them.

"Food always helps," Irene said. "Where should we go?" She rolled the sleeves of her white cotton shirt. Except for the sandals on her feet, she looked like a ranch girl ready for chores.

Lee twisted his mouth in thought. "Paulie slings a good hash."

"No." It came out of me like a bark.

"Paulie's is good," Irene said. "But maybe Buddy would rather have a hamburger."

They were talking like I wasn't there, like I was too young to be burdened with an adult decision.

"I ain't hungry," I said again. I sat up straight, looked at Irene. "You and Lee go on ahead. I've got some things I need to get done."

"Like what?" Lee came down on the chair's front legs. "What do you got to do that's more important than being with this pretty gal?"

"It's okay," Irene said. "Another time, maybe." She pushed her glass to the table's center.

"The hell. If it's money you two are worried about, I'm buying. Let's go to Paulie's." Lee scooted back, suppressing a belch.

"What about Raimey?" I said.

"Shit." Lee settled back down in his chair. "About forgot."

"It's exciting," Irene said. "L.A."

Lee acted surprised that she knew, motioned Harvey for another round. I shook my head but got a beer anyway. "Maybe you should come on down with us." Lee leaned toward her. "I bet you sing."

Irene smiled. "Not for anyone but myself."

"Who says we're going?" I'd pushed the wads of torn napkin into a miniature pyramid.

"No one says. I'm just saying *if*," Lee said.

Irene checked her watch. "Don't have long to make up your mind." I remembered how I could encircle her wrist between thumb and finger, how fragile it felt, like the hollow bones of a bird.

"I like to just let things happen," Lee said. "Don't go in much for long-term planning."

I wanted to say that maybe they should run off together, being as they were so alike. I wanted to tell them both to go to hell. Instead, I shoved away from the table. "Let me know what you decide."

Lee drummed his fingers once. "What's eating you?"

I glared.

He turned a chummy smile on Irene, jabbed toward me with his thumb. "Must have to go do his laundry, huh? Maybe wash his golden locks. To hell with him and Raimey. Let's me and you go eat us some Italian."

I got in a good left cut beneath his chin, all my weight coming up from my toes, brought my right fist against his ear as he tipped backward. Before I could jump away, I felt his grip at my ankles, and then I was flat, my head bouncing off the wood like a bowling ball. In that split second of darkness, I heard Harvey holler, Irene say something I couldn't understand. I rolled, sucking air, saw him coming at me, dumped a chair between us, enough time to get myself up and steadied.

We faced off, either side of the table. I'd opened the skin; blood purled out, trickled onto the collar of his shirt. I wished I'd had on the ring, torn him even more, left a mark he'd remember.

"No! Please!" Irene bent forward as though she might throw herself between us, but Harvey had her by the arm.

Lee wiped the back of his hand beneath his chin, worked his jaw. "Shit," he said. He licked his lips, looked at Irene and Harvey. "Damn."

I tensed, ready for the charge, sure, now, that I wanted to kill him, sure that I could.

Instead of coming at me, he picked up a napkin, held it against his chin. "Well, all right," he said, then half grinned at me. "All right, then." He fisted my beer, let it spill out the sides of his mouth as he drank.

Harvey looked at me. "Where'd that punch come from?" I blinked, shook my head. He gripped Lee's shoulder. "You okay?"

Lee nodded, took his seat. "Taught him everything he knows, Harv." He popped a palm against his ear. "Damn near deaf." He looked up at me, bellowed, "Sit down and I'll buy you another beer," but I remained standing, waiting for Irene to say my name or touch me, waiting for her approval or her blame.

She stepped backward, said, "I'm sorry," and walked quickly out the door.

"Women," Harvey said, laying down fresh napkins. "Think everything can be solved with talk. Don't understand that sometimes a man just has to take action, do something, even if it means he'll regret it later." He went behind the bar, came back with ice wrapped in a fresh rag. "Hold this on there for a while." He pressed it against Lee's chin. "Going to swell."

Lee winced. "Better bring me a painkiller, Harv."

"Gin?"

"Hell, no."

Harvey laughed. "Dr. Daniel's, then."

"Sit down." Lee motioned toward my chair.

"I'm not sure I want to."

"Don't be pissy. I'm the one hurtin' here."

I sat stiff at the seat's edge. Harvey gave me the same "Be nice" look my mother used to give. Lee took the double shot he offered, propped one foot against the table. "Bet you a bucket of worms it wasn't you she was coming to see."

I stood, slapped the table with the flat of my hand. "I'm tired of listening to this shit. I'm the one, Lee. This time, it's *me*."

"What makes you so sure, little brother? There's a lot you don't know. A whole *helluva* lot."

I looked at his face, saw not my brother but a man more like my father, jaw gone slack, eyes heavy, fighting to focus. It was the liquor talking now, my mother would have said, but I had come to understand that such talk was as true as any other.

"What you're doing ain't right, Lee. You know it ain't right."

I glared at Harvey, who refused to look my way. "You ask me what I want. I'll tell you. I don't want you and your stinking songs. I don't want L.A. or even this sorry place. All I want is Irene." I leaned toward him. "Can't you see she's what makes me happy? Why would you want to take that away from me?" I hit the table. "Why?" I slid back down in my chair, my anger suddenly gone, leaving me weak and exhausted.

Lee lowered his eyes. We sat in silence. Harvey had stopped his cleaning.

"Truth is"—Lee took a deep breath, nodded slowly—"I'm scared you might find something better."

I rubbed the back of my head, beginning to the feel the ache. "Jesus, Lee. You're the one's got the offer to go to L.A. You're the one they want."

Lee's eyes settled to half-mast; his jowls sagged. "I ain't talking about a *place,* Buddy. I mean"—he held up his hand, fingers limply pointed toward some unseeable destination—"I mean . . . aw, hell." He gave a little wave. "I don't know what I mean." He made a huffing sound like laughter or crying. "Hell, Buddy, what'd you expect? Irene's the best thing's ever walked in here, and I'm not supposed to even try? Just want me to roll over and die like some old dog? Hard enough to have her turn cold on me, but then when she takes up with you . . ." He raised one hand. "Not because you ain't something to have, that's not what I mean." He wiped his nose, looked sideways. "It's just that I ain't you. That's all. I just ain't you."

"You got plenty of girls."

"But I ain't got *that* one," he said, pointing to the door. "And that makes me twice sorry." He sat up slowly, shifted his shoulders. "What time is it, Harv?"

"Ten-twenty a.m., bar time."

Lee stood, braced himself with one hand. "Just enough time for a nap before Raimey stinks up the place." He stretched, worked each elbow, twisted his head this way and that, took a few steps toward the stage. "Can't remember the name of that other song I wanted you to help me with. Maybe it'll come to me." He shuffled a turn, walked down the hall.

"That brother of yours," Harvey said, "doesn't know what he wants."

"Did you?" I straddled a stool, surveyed the rows of neatly aligned bottles, pointed to the coffeepot. I wanted my head to clear so that I could think about what came next.

"Never gave it much thought. When you got a war going on, that's what you know. Not much else matters except when you go in and what girl you got waiting when it's over."

"You had a girl? Waiting, I mean?" I blew on my coffee, resisted the urge to add sugar.

"Want Irish?"

I shook my head.

"Yeah, I had a girl. Wrote her every chance I got. Said I'd marry her. When I got back, she'd gotten knocked up by the preacher's son, already gone down the aisle. Guess you got to have the right girl waiting."

"How do you know when she's the right one?"

"Hell, I'm the wrong hombre to ask. Like I said. She didn't hold." He lifted my cup, swiped the bar with his rag.

"You think anybody really knows what he wants? Ever?"

Harvey straightened against the ache in his back. "Spud knew. Drew a straight line right through his life, like he was marking a map. But that goes to show you. Knowing what you want doesn't guarantee a goddamn thing. Maybe moments are all we get." He turned his gaze toward the ceiling as if he'd just been blessed with divine inspiration. "Moments of knowing."

"Well, I could sure as hell use a moment. Maybe two or three."

"You know what you want." Harvey moved the glasses from wash water to rinse. "Don't give me that bullshit."

"Right now I think I do. But what if I'm wrong? What about the rest of my life? Isn't that what matters?"

"You live to be eighty, maybe it matters." He held up a glass, squinted. "Die tonight, don't mean shit." He gave me as tender a look as he was capable of giving. "I'm just worried for you, kid. Makes me say things I got no business saying. Truth is, you're the only one can know."

"What about Wolfchild?"

"What about him?"

"Can you know that?"

Harvey walked to the end of the bar, wiped each clean ashtray free of moisture before adding it to the stack. "Evidence seems to point in his direction."

"What evidence?"

"Listen," Harvey said. "I'm no judge and I sure as shit ain't going to argue with you about something I got no say in. I didn't tell the sheriff Wolfchild did it. All I said was, Wolfchild showed up here every Friday night and had his eye on Laurette."

"That don't mean he's guilty."

Harvey threw his hands up. "Did I say he was guilty? Did I?" When I shook my head, his hands dropped. "All I know is Laurette's dead. Maybe Wolfchild did it. Maybe he didn't. But somebody's got to pay." He wadded the towel, threw it in the sink. "I'm tired of all this jibber-jabber. Go on back and make sure your brother's still breathing."

Lee was asleep, as I knew he would be. I sat on the edge of my bed and watched him, remembering the nights we'd huddled tight against the Oklahoma winter that froze our sheets to the wall, the stove-heated rock our mother had wrapped in towels and nestled between the covers gone icy with morning cold. I thought of the nightmares he was given to, the way he'd wake wide-eyed with terror, the clutch of sound in his throat. What sure thing had he ever known? Maybe only that he could sing, and nothing else. Maybe singing was all he had to keep the demons at bay.

The cut beneath his chin had welted and dried. We were a sight, my own face patched with rash. Our mother would have shaken her head, said, "Someday you'll learn." And maybe it is true that this was how we learned, one wound at a time, until we bore an armor of scars, tough enough to fend off the world.

I lay on my bed and thought of Irene. How could she expect me not to wonder? How could I defend her to Harvey and Lee without knowing what was true? There were questions to be answered, matters to be settled—she'd said so herself.

There was still more boy in me than man, I thought. I'd let her lead me too long, let myself be coddled and charmed. I'd go to her, demand the truth. No more guessing. I would *know.*

I turned to the wall, felt myself drifting, slipping in and out of dreams, sat up with a start. Five till twelve.

I woke Lee. He took two minutes to wash his face, rinse his mouth with Listerine. We were waiting at the bar when Raimey walked in. Lee's smile must have given Raimey hope.

"See you're in fine spirits," he announced. "Harvey, pour me a martini, if you would."

"Sample the town last night, Raimey?" Lee asked. "It's got some hot spots. Just got to know where to look and what to look out for. Don't want to end up like my brother here."

Raimey took in my face, the backs of my hands. "I hope to hell it's not catching."

I had my explanation down to three words: "Fishing. Poison ivy."

"Looks like jungle rot. Saw some pretty bad cases during the war."

Harvey perked up. "Where were you stationed?"

"Guam. Didn't see action, just a lot of snakes."

Harvey laughed. "Hell, you can get that much action around here."

"So I hear," Raimey said. "What about you boys? Ready for some action?"

I waited for Lee to answer, but he just sat there.

Raimey eyed Lee's chin. "What horse kicked you?"

"Just a little brotherly love going around," Lee said, and gave me a soft jab in the shoulder. "We'll heal up prettier than ever."

"Well, then. Where's the contract?" Raimey directed the question at me. I took off for the back room, came back with the paper rolled like a scroll. It didn't look to me like anybody had said a word in my absence. "Yes or no," Raimey said, "that's all I need, and then I'm ready to get on down the road. Long drive through Nevada."

"Here's the deal," said Lee. "Talked to the band last night, and they're willing to take the chance. Only one who wouldn't say was Floyd, but I think he'll follow along. So"—he clapped me on the back—"I'm leaving the decision up to my brother here."

I hadn't seen it coming, though I should have. Lee hated decisions of any kind, and this was a big one.

"What'll it be, Buddy?" Raimey spied the ring on Harvey's finger.

I looked at Lee, and then at Harvey. I pulled a quarter from my pocket.

"Heads, we're bound for California. Tails, we . . ." I thought for a moment, shrugged, flipped the coin high into the air, stepped back to let it fall.

"Heads!" Raimey pumped Lee's hand, then spread the contract, pulled a pen from his pocket. The expression on Lee's face never changed as he signed. "A round, Harvey," Raimey ordered. "Now we got something to celebrate."

"What's that?" We turned to see Spud standing behind us.

Lee wrapped an arm around Spud's shoulders, guided him to the bar. "Looks like it's the Palomino, Spud. Raimey here drives a hard bargain."

Spud stepped between me and Lee, one hand on the bar, his face slack. "Guess it figures." He fingered the shot of rum Harvey handed him. "Well, we got something else to drink to, then. Me finding a new job." He knocked back the rum, motioned Harvey with his eyes for another.

"Hell, Spud," Lee said. "The Stables was here long before Buddy and I arrived. You'll pick up another band. You just watch. There's young fellas showing up all the time, wanting to play."

Spud let out a breath through his nose. "Don't feel much like celebrating. Guess I'll head on home." He rambled off through the door, hunched with disappointment.

"That makes me feel like shit. Glad you made the decision and not me, Buddy." Lee was only half joking.

"This is business," Raimey said. "Spud's been around the block a few times. He'll survive."

"*He* will. Less sure about The Stables." Harvey leaned against the counter, arms crossed. "Fact is, I think he's about ready to let it go."

"What about you, Harvey?" Raimey asked. "You look like a man who could run a business."

Harvey grunted. "I'm not even sure why I've stayed long as I have. Feel like a vampire sometimes, never seeing the light of day."

"Well, one thing's for sure." Lee stretched his arms above his head. "It won't take us long to pack. When do we report, Raimey?"

"Yesterday," Raimey answered. "Got a call that the Watchers all came down with the dirty-water scours. Told them to stay away from the enchiladas." He stubbed his smoke, tucked the contract inside his jacket, handed Lee a card. "Plan on two weeks. Come down sooner if you want. I'll put you up until you can find a place." He slapped a fifty on the counter, nodded at Harvey. "Keep 'em greased," he said, then pulled out two one-hundred-dollar bills, laid them next to the fifty. More money than I'd seen in my life. "This will get you down there, maybe buy you a new outfit or two." He looked at me. "Buy the boy something snazzy. We might be able to use him at the door." He pointed at the ring on Harvey's finger, held out his hand. Harvey snorted, tossed the ring toward me, and I caught it in my palm. Raimey smiled, nodded.

We waited for the latch to click before settling on the stools.

"It's the right thing," Harvey said. "What do you have to look forward to here? Look at me." He tapped the cash register, slid the fifty beneath the drawer. "Spud would do just what you're doing

183

if he was twenty years younger. He'll mope around here for a while, but he'll pull out of it."

"California," Lee said. "Shit and fall back in it."

I stared into the empty hole of my shot glass. The calamine was powdering off, dusting my clothes.

"What's Irene going to think about this?" Harvey sucked the pimiento from a green olive.

I shrugged, dipped into the garnish tray, loaded a toothpick with maraschino cherries.

Harvey pointed his gutted olive at Lee. "I wouldn't trust your little brother here further than I could spit. She's got him by the balls. He'll turncoat fifty times before day's end."

"Don't matter," Lee said. "Decision's been made."

Harvey popped the olive into his mouth, sucked brine off each finger. "What about it, Lee? Any of this make you happy?"

"I'm always happy, Harv. You know that." Lee held up his empty glass. "Make me happier."

The ring cut through my pocket, pinched my thigh. I remembered Irene's shoulders in the early light, dappled with the faintest of freckles. I remembered the sweet jam she'd spread onto my toast that morning, how she'd licked the spoon, then kissed me, the sweet stickiness of her lips. I closed my eyes, saw Wolf-child, opened them again. Already I was regretting my recklessness, cursing the flip of the coin.

"You girls got some shopping to do," Harvey said, and pushed Raimey's money toward us. "Stores been open for hours."

Lee ignored the money, walked to the stage, came back with his Gibson. "I think it's time that Buddy started singing again, Harv. Ol' Raimey thinks he'd like to see the two of us do a number." He hit a chord. "Well, when I was a young man never been kissed . . . Come on, Buddy." Lee bumped me with his knee, but it was Harvey who opened his mouth and joined in.

They were still singing "Kisses Sweeter Than Wine" when I headed down the hall to our room. I lay on my back for a long time, trying to believe that what I'd done was right for someone. Irene was always so sure about everything, her decisions based on something more than the flip of a coin. I contemplated the lampshade and its cattle brands. Easy enough to slap a mark on an animal and call it your own. How could I claim Irene?

I turned to the wall, closed my eyes. I rubbed my fingers along the crusty skin of my ribs, feeling as I had when sick with chicken pox, my mother saying, "You'll be scarred for life, you keep up that digging." She'd traded the neighbors a jar of milk for a few chunks of stringy beef, made me a pot of stew, ladled it into me for days. She tied red yarn around my fingers to remind me, but late at night, when I knew she couldn't see, I'd untie the bows and lose myself in the absolute pleasure of scratching.

Light shifted along the wall. What if Irene really did love Wolfchild? Or was it the deputy who was wrong? Like so many others, he probably hated the Indian. She'd taken Wolfchild the food, sat and talked in whispers, maybe even held his hand. The rest the deputy had concocted from his own wishful dreams.

I rolled to my other side. They were all jealous. I had to be better than they were. I had to trust her. But why wouldn't she tell me? Why did she have to keep so much secret? I cupped my eyes, squeezed my temples.

And then I thought of Laurette, how pale she'd looked sitting in the car, as though she were already dead. Wolfchild had claimed he loved her. He cried when they showed him her picture.

I sat up, suddenly sure of what I must do.

I rummaged through the papers Lee kept in a shoe box under his bed, found the title to the Chevy, folded it twice, shoved it in my pants pocket, made for the bar.

"I need to borrow the Chevy."

Lee and Harvey considered me for longer than was comfortable. Lee pulled out his keys, tossed them my way. "See how easy it is?"

"Don't forget your money, honey." Harvey rolled the hundred, stuck it in my shirt pocket. "Come back pretty. And pick me up a paper."

The Bel Air glimmered. I patted the dash, said, "Let's go get us an Injun," pulled onto the highway, and headed toward town.

CHAPTER FIFTEEN

A small crowd of clerks joined the deputy to watch as I led Wolfchild down the courthouse hall. Bail had been set low—who would pay it?—posting it easier than I'd imagined. I'd forged the Chevy's title, pawned it and the ring at Kepper's Trading Post. Kepper, a short, black-whiskered man who never removed his hat, figuring it added a good six inches to his height, didn't ask for my identification, just nodded as I signed, said that he trusted me not to leave town, that I could go ahead and drive the car until payment came due. "Money, metal, or skin," he said, winking at his pale wife, who stood near a back door. "I get what I'm owed."

Sheriff Westin was at the Washington border, making his monthly sweep of the county line. The deputy made a half-attempt to protest, but then stuttered silent. No one was more surprised than Wolfchild, who didn't speak a word but did what he was told, nodding to each person in turn as we stepped out the door.

"I'm taking you to Lapwai," I said. I felt as though I were talking to a child or a deaf-mute, so I raised my voice. "Home. For a while, anyway."

Once on the road, he seemed to relax. He rolled down his window and let the wind catch the heavy length of his braids. I considered what would happen when word spread he was out. I took a quick look in the rearview, gave the Chevy more gas. The faster we got out of town and across the reservation line, the better.

"Want one?" I pointed to the pack of Winstons on the dash. He shook his head. He smelled like flour sacks and sorghum, which surprised me. I'd expected him to be sour, still smelling of ancient campfires.

"You'll have to show me where to turn. Either that, or we can just head straight for Irene's." I watched him carefully, but his only response was a nod.

"Which?"

"There's a place by the river. I'll show you."

Just before we reached the bridge at Spalding, he told me to slow down, then pointed to where a faint trail led to the Clearwater.

"There's a house down here?" I let the Chevy idle down the path, cringing each time we scraped bottom.

"It's not a house."

"Tepee?"

For the first time, I saw him smile, some light come into his eyes.

"You ever sleep in a tepee?"

"Can't say as I have."

"Cook on one side, freeze on the other. Here." He pointed to a thick growth of young cottonwoods, and I made out what appeared to be a duck blind set just up the bank. When I stopped, he looked at me directly, seemed to consider and then decide. "Come on," he said.

I'd gotten used to the haze of smoke—the forests burning and no rain in sight—but Wolfchild coughed as we walked.

"Wildfires," I said. "Big lightning storm a while back."

Wolfchild nodded. Had he seen the flashes, heard the thunder? Or was the jail sealed like a bunker?

The hut was little more than a dome of bent poles draped with canvas top and sides, covered with branches and bark. A bum's shack, I thought, and wondered at my decision. I watched Wolfchild walk to the river's edge, undress, fold his shirt, pants, and underwear into neat squares, burrow his socks into each low boot. Broad shoulders and chest, short bowed legs. He pulled the bands from his hair, shook loose the braids. I was suddenly embarrassed to be watching.

I looked toward the highway, heard a splash, saw Wolfchild come back up, grinning.

"God damn *cold!*" he hollered, than started swimming hard for the far bank. I felt a momentary panic, fear that he might be making a break for it, but he let the current carry him only a few yards before working a diagonal back to the narrow rock beach, where he began gathering dry twigs.

As hot as it was, I couldn't believe he'd want a fire, but he was an Indian and might think differently about such things. I pitched in, tried not to watch his nakedness. Never had I seen a man so at home in nothing but his skin.

He piled the sticks, then stood with his hands at his sides. "They took my matches," he said.

I pulled out my lighter. The fire caught easily, eating up through the dry lichen and beaver-stripped branches we'd gathered. He selected a few nearby rocks, nudged them carefully into the flames, laid on more fuel until the heat drove me back and the stones glowed red.

When he moved toward the hut and lifted the canvas flap, I saw a pit lined with flatrock, scattered beds of fir boughs, and a bucket, which he handed me.

"Fill this with water."

I started to protest, but Wolfchild's face had gone serious. I squatted at the river's edge, dipped the bucket full, felt it grow heavy as an anchor at the end of my arm, then returned it to Wolfchild. Using a forked cottonwood stick, he lifted a rock from the fire, dropped it into the pail. He grew steadily more solemn as he performed the tasks.

"Okay," he said, handing me the stick. "You bring me more." He carried the bucket to what I now saw was a sweat house. He turned to face the river, then backed through the entrance.

I poked and cussed until I'd balanced a small rock. When I elbowed open the canvas door, Wolfchild motioned toward the pit. I rolled the rock in.

"Next time, remember to blow off the ashes. And you should always back in." He flicked a few drops of water on the rock. "Washing the Old Man's face," he said. "Please bring us more rocks."

I relayed five or six more stones until Wolfchild nodded that was enough, then indicated for me to sit across from where he knelt on the pallet of boughs. I felt shy in my clothes and wished for a cold beer or a Coke. Steam rose, the metallic smell of river blending with the incense of fir.

Wolfchild's studied quietness made me nervous, and I felt the muscles in my legs starting to jump.

"Ain't it already hot enough for you?" I covered my mouth against the biting air. "How can you breathe in here?"

"Slow," Wolfchild said. "You get used to it."

"Don't see the reason."

"Sweating gets you clean." He closed his eyes for a moment. "It's a place to share stories, what's inside."

"Doesn't sound like fun to me." I scratched at the raw skin of my arms and legs. The scabs had softened, begun to curl at the edges.

"Where'd you get into so much poison ivy?" Wolfchild asked.

"The creek," I said. "Behind Irene's."

"Should have stayed on the path."

"Irene could have told me."

Wolfchild smiled. "She only tells what you need to know." He stood, rolled his shoulders. "Time for a swim."

I followed Wolfchild to the river, watched him slowly submerge himself. I gave myself over, stripped to my skivvies, took a running leap, whooped when the icy water hit my skin.

Wolfchild shook his head.

"What's the matter?"

"You scream like a girl. Do that, and your woman will leave you."

"What are you talking about? *You're* the one who hollered that the water was God damn *cold!*"

"That was before the sweat. Now it is different."

He walked from the river back to the sweat house. I followed, though I wasn't sure why. My mother would have predicted my death from pneumonia. When I told Wolfchild this, he said his own father had sweated every day of the year, summer and winter, and never knew an hour's sickness.

We sweated, then swam, then sweated again. Wolfchild showed me where a small spring came through the rock, and we filled our hands and drank. At some point I stripped off my underwear, more foolish with than without.

"We should tell a story now." Wolfchild reclined, head propped on one hand.

"Well, I ain't going to start."

He rolled to his back, shining in the cream-colored light filtering through canvas.

"I could tell about the ant and the grasshopper, but that's an old one." He considered a fly that had settled on his knee. "Coyote stories are always good, but today doesn't feel like a coyote day."

"Are your stories all about animals and bugs?"

He laughed, sat up, leaned into the heat. "This is a story came to me in jail. It started in my head, but when I opened my eyes, it was there on the wall, and I watched it happen." He tapped the rocks with a stick. "Two *nimíipuu*," he said, and looked up, "people"—I nodded that I understood—"came upon a magpie caught in a trap they had set for grouse. The greedy magpie had wanted the corn, even though he was smart enough to know it was dangerous. One man said to the magpie, 'You have risked your life for three kernels of corn, even though you have wings to fly. Why have you chosen these three kernels over the fields?'" Wolfchild shifted, tapped the stick one last time, then let it drop, lay back on the bench and closed his eyes.

"That's it? That's the story?"

"That's all I've got so far."

"Can't you just make up the rest?" I could feel the air cooling around us, night coming on.

"Got to wait and see."

"I'm so damn sick of waiting, I could puke."

"What are you waiting for?" Wolfchild looked as though he were settling in for a long sleep, head resting against the pillow of his hands.

"Everything. My life. I don't know." I stretched out. Wolfchild was a good six inches shorter than I was, though I thought of him as at least my height. "Just seems like I'm always waiting for somebody else to do something, like the next move is never mine."

He hummed a little under his breath, rocked one foot against the other. "Bailing me out—was that your move?"

"Yeah, I guess it was."

"Why?"

It was the same question I'd been asking myself. "If it was you who killed Laurette, I want to know."

Wolfchild closed his eyes, grew still, gone someplace deep inside himself.

His chest heaved, and I realized he was crying. I kept my eyes focused on the rough weave of the roof. I hadn't expected this.

"Why'd you have to go to White Bird?" His voice cracked. "No one told me you was going to White Bird."

"I'm sorry." I didn't know what else to say.

"I got to The Stables, and she wasn't there. Nobody told me." He moved an arm to cover his face. "I walked home, and it grew in me. Like a dream. I knew I'd never see her again."

"And that's it? You didn't take her from the parking lot? You didn't hurt her?"

Wolfchild didn't bother to wipe his eyes, didn't pretend. He turned his head, looked at me. "I would've been good to her. She would have been happy."

I started to say that his words were no answer, but the answer was there, in the shadows of his face, the empty curl of his hands.

"Irene," I said. "She believes you."

Wolfchild closed his eyes again. "Irene's been gone a long time."

"She's living right here in Lapwai."

"I don't mean where she's living. I mean Irene. Her."

I raised myself. "I don't know what the hell you're talking about. I just saw her a few hours ago." I stood, too fast, and everything went black. I reached out to steady myself, caught air, staggered.

"The Irene that came here first. That girl. She left and never came back."

"I'm sick of this riddle shit." I opened the flap. "It's too damn hot in here to think, anyway. Come on. We got to get going. There's some folks might not be pleased to see you sunbathing." I looked toward the highway, half expecting to see a truckload of vigilantes, but Wolfchild didn't show a whit of concern.

"You haven't told your story."

"I don't have any goddamn story. None of it makes any sense."

"Stories don't always make sense. Not at first, anyway."

"Then to hell with it. Let's go."

"Where?"

"Wherever the hell you're sleeping tonight." I searched the ground for my clothes, saw that the smoke from the big fires had lifted. Wolfchild followed me to the car, just as silent as when we'd left the jail.

I slowed as we neared Lapwai, waiting for directions. "Which way?"

Wolfchild shrugged.

"You don't remember where you live?"

"I remember."

"Ah, for Christ's sake." I pulled to the side. "Get out, then."

"I'm hungry."

"Well, so the hell am I." I eased back onto the road. "I paid your way out of jail. I sure as hell ain't going to buy you a meal. You should pay for my dinner with some of that government money you get."

Wolfchild didn't look at me, but his mouth twisted. "Oh, yeah," he said. "I forgot."

"How much you get, anyway? Wish to hell someone would give me money for nothing. Life would be a whole lot easier."

"I send my army pension to my sister in Yakima. Not much I need anymore." Wolfchild stretched his neck, scratched beneath his chin.

"Pension? What about treaty money? Whatever the government keeps on paying you Indians for." I waved my hand toward the road in front of us, the sage-covered hills and basalt bluffs. "This."

Wolfchild craned his neck to take in the moonlit view. "My mother was born in the Wallowa Valley."

"So?"

"Father, too."

"You getting at something?"

"It's green there." He closed his eyes, rode like that for a while.

"But you get money. Indian money, I mean."

"Buffalo nickels." He kept his eyes closed.

"Maybe I should get benefits," I said. "Had a great-grandmother was a Cherokee. Maybe that makes me enough Indian to get a free ride."

He sat forward, studied my face, squinted. "The nose," he said. "Cherokee got big noses."

I looked in the mirror. Wolfchild laughed. "Let's go to Aunt Esther's." He nodded toward the road. "I'll tell you where to turn."

"I know where to turn," I snapped. Wolfchild made me feel like I was on the outside of something, something I thought I might actually be in control of. He hadn't said a word of thanks.

Irene's car sat in front of Esther's house. I pulled forward, backed until my bumper nudged the Lincoln's.

"Thinking ahead, uh?" Wolfchild grinned, his teeth showing white.

"Just getting off the road."

"Ayee. Got her penned between you and the shed."

"She can get out. Don't worry."

"Not her I'm worried about."

"Don't be wasting your worry on me." I marched to the porch, rapped on the door. "Irene? Someone here wants to see you." I held open the screen, gave a shallow bow, motioned Wolfchild through.

Irene and Esther sat at the table, drinking coffee. The smell of fried meat lingered. Leftover pork chops and fried potatoes cooled on the counter.

"What are you two doing here?" Esther nibbled a cube of sugar. "Dinner's already been eat."

Wolfchild smiled, hitched his pants. "Looks like there might be some bones to chew on."

"Hah." Esther stirred with her finger, licked it clean. "I ain't waiting on you. Serve yourself."

Irene kept her focus on me. "What's going on, Buddy?"

"Jailbreak." I hitched my own britches. I had her guessing.

"Jailbreak, my butt. Get out of the kitchen, all of you." Esther fired the burner beneath the skillet, shooed us into the living room. "Cold meat and hot gravy. That's all you're getting."

Wolfchild sat on the hassock, licked his lips.

Irene settled on the couch. I started to sit next to her but reconsidered, took the other end. I wanted to watch her face, see if she softened toward him.

"All right," she said. "Tell me."

Wolfchild never took his eyes off the kitchen. "Buddy bailed me out."

Irene looked from Wolfchild to me, saw that what Wolfchild said was true. "How?"

"The ring," I said. "That and some cash."

She considered me carefully, wondering, figuring.

"Look, Irene. He's here. You don't have to go visit him at the jail no more. At least for a while." I clasped my fingers behind my head, a little queasy. "You two can just enjoy some time together."

"Some *time* together? Buddy, this isn't about spending time together. This is about a *life*."

Wolfchild followed Esther's movements like a dog waiting for scraps.

"Hell, Irene. I thought you'd be happy. Guess I should have known better." I slapped both knees. "I laid down every dime I had." I stood. "Guess I've done all I can do. You all take it from here."

Irene followed me out into the dusk, the moon just beginning to rise. "This isn't some Saturday matinee, Buddy. This is serious."

"Visiting a man every morning in his jail cell's pretty serious, ain't it? Feeding him muffins." I puckered my lips. *"Oh, he's got a wittle bit of jehwy on his face. Here, let Irene get it."*

The slap came so fast I didn't have time to unpucker. Not a slap but a hit, hard against my cheekbone. I fell backward, landed in a bed of hollyhocks. Irene came after me, sat down on my middle.

"I should knock the holy crap out of you!" Fierce, fist drawn back, aimed for my nose. I bucked her off, rolled with her across the gravel until we'd wedged ourselves tight against the Chevy's front tire, neither of us willing to let go or admit to pain, even as the rock dug into our backs and thistles nettled our necks.

Esther yelled from the door. "I ain't warming this more than once." She peered at us through the dark. "You two lovin' or fightin'?"

Irene stared me down. "We're lovin', Aunt Esther."

"Well, then. That's all right." The screen clapped shut.

I pushed away, brushed my butt and thighs, the backs of my arms. My jaw ached.

Irene paid no attention to her own wounds. "I thought you weren't like that anymore, Buddy. I thought you'd learned to know when people were feeding you lies."

"All I know is that I'm leaving for California. Send me some smoke signals when you get time."

"You're so goddamn ignorant." Something new had come into her voice, anger fading to sadness, a hint of regret that made me hesitate, take a hitch in my own rage. But I couldn't stop this fight now, having never known how before except to walk away.

I stepped toward the Chevy. "I'm not nearly so ignorant as I used to be. You've taught me some things, Irene." I turned. "Like how to make someone believe you love him when you really don't give a rat's ass." I gunned the engine, spraying gravel as I fishtailed onto the street. I took one look in the rearview, but it was too dark to see her, only the lights coming from Aunt Esther's windows, Wolfchild at the table, bent over his food.

My hunger was gone. I hit a steady sixty, rage filling me scalp to toes, a slow pulse of heat. Even with the moonlight, it was too dark to make out anything more than the shoulder of the road, but I found the trail to the river, the sweat house as we had left it, the rocks gone cold. I scuffed a mound of leaves and grass against the canvas, watched the flare of my lighter eat into the cloth, the burn gaping like a mouth. No one would notice the smoke, blending with the acrid wind coming off the mountains. I stepped back, watched the whole of it ignite, the poles collapsing. The flames lasted only a minute, the canvas old and dry as birch bark.

Back at The Stables, the doors were propped open. Word had spread that these were Lee's last nights, and the crowd had pushed into the parking lot. I idled around back, climbed through the window rather than risk being seen, dropped onto Lee's bed. I lay there, listening to the music, the vibration of drums and boots and high heels come up through the floor and into my bones. I closed my eyes, tapped my knuckles against the wall, feeling I had proven something, though I wasn't sure what.

I didn't know I had fallen asleep until the lights flicked on.

"You think just because I let you use my car, you can have my bed, too?"

I grabbed the mattress with both hands as though trying to steady a boat. "Jesus, Lee. Turn off the light."

"No, sir. You got to get up. We got business to attend to."

I squinted from beneath my hand, cast an eye at the clock. Two a.m. "What business?"

"*Girl* business." Lee ducked to see himself in the nail-hung mirror, combed a neat wave off his forehead. "Thought you might like someone more your own age. A little bit fresher." He pocketed his comb. "Let's get going. Don't want these gals cooling off on us."

I watched him smooth both hands across his temples. "I got to use the john first," I said.

"Blow your nose and wipe your ass. Let's go."

Harvey smirked as Lee and I walked past. The girls were waiting just outside the door, two blondes, so alike they could have been twins.

"Where the hell is my car?" Lee held out his hands in a gesture of helpless frustration.

"'Round back. I'll get it." I pulled the keys from my pocket. I felt I'd been asleep for weeks, that I'd awakened into some other part of my life that had been going on without me. Ignorant, Irene had called me, and maybe I was. I looked at the two girls. Maybe *this* was the real world.

"You go ahead and drive, Buddy. Linda here's going to keep me company in the back, ain't you, sugar?"

Linda sidled closer, tucked herself beneath his arm. "Sure." She dipped her head like a turkey drinking water.

"Buddy, this other pretty gal here is Becky. Both from Spokane. Can't find a thing in this town that pleases them. Said we might be able to help." Lee patted Becky's shoulder. "You go on around with him and get the car. We'll wait right here."

I slowed my pace to let Becky catch up, wobbling through the gravel on her heels. "Lee says you guys are brothers."

"Can't deny it." She smelled like lemonade, sweet with an edge of sour. I held open her door, saw a flash of bare thigh. "You go to school in Spokane?"

"Just finished. I'm going to take some more classes, though. I can already type sixty-eight words per minute."

"Really? That's pretty dang good." I drove around, caught Lee and Linda in the headlights. Lee already had his hands under Linda's dress.

"Jeez," Becky said, and covered her eyes.

The car filled with the smoke of four cigarettes. Lee passed around the apricot brandy he'd pulled from the shelf in the bar. Girls, he'd always asserted, heat up on brandy.

I took a drink, tasted the strange mix of fruit and lipstick.

"Hey, we heard some girl got murdered in the parking lot of The Stables," Linda chirped. I heard Lee tip the bottle.

"Where we headed?" My voice was louder than I'd intended. Becky flinched.

"Now, that's a good question, Buddy. Where you girls staying?"

"We're staying with Becky's brother," Linda said. "Jeez, he's fifty years old."

"Russ is only twenty-nine," Becky protested.

"Might as well be fifty. All him and his wife do is sit home and watch their new television. Don't know how to have fun no more."

"That won't be a problem here, I can guarantee." Lee took another swig. "Let's head for that park on the hill, Buddy. We can sit and watch the moonlight. You girls got a curfew?"

"We're eighteen." Linda sucked on her Winston, bounced up and down like a child needing the bathroom. "Besides, what's Russ going to do? Whip us?" She leaned forward, gave a loud laugh. "I'd like to see him try!"

"What about you, Becky? Park okay?" I'd seen the nervous movement of her hands, pleating and smoothing the folds of her skirt.

"It's okay." Her hair flipped up in a starched curl just where it touched her shoulders. She was pretty enough, I told myself. Small nose. Long neck. The large ribbon she'd tied around her head made her look like an oversized doll, her voice a doll's voice, high and nasal.

I led them to the spot in the park where Irene had found me dreaming. The lights of Snake Junction flickered and winked below us. "This *is* a nice park!" Linda swung her white purse like a picnic basket. "Don't you wish we had a blanket?"

Lee flipped away his cigarette. "Got just the thing," he said, pulled off his shirt and shook it out like it might cover a football field.

Becky looked at me. I looked toward the lights. "Let's walk a little," I said.

"Damn, he's smart." Lee bowed to Linda, who curtsied and crumpled onto the shirt. Becky and I hadn't gotten twenty feet away when we heard his voice turn husky, Linda's low murmurs.

The narrow drive Becky and I followed circled the park. If I didn't change direction, we'd find ourselves right back at the place we'd started.

"You from here?" She had taken off her high heels, dangled them by two fingers.

"Oklahoma."

"That's a long ways away." Her words still held a childlike lilt.

"You sure you're eighteen?" I asked.

"Nineteen, actually. You sure you're eighteen?"

"That matter to you?" I kicked a pine cone, heard it knock against the trunk of a tree.

"No, guess it don't. Unless it matters to you."

"Years don't mean a thing to me."

"Me, neither." She giggled. "Well, I guess it might. I mean, I'm glad you're not ten."

I found a place where two sycamores shielded us from the road. We sat with our legs stretched out. I liked it that she didn't seem to care whether her clothes got dirty. Not a word about a blanket or a shirt. She just plopped down, began chewing a blade of grass. "I don't know that I've ever dated a boy younger than I am."

"Now's your chance." Not my words. Lee's. I knew every cue.

"You sure you're interested in an older woman?"

I looked at her quickly. "Always been my dream."

She trailed a finger along my shoulder, then drew back her hand. "What's the matter with your arm?"

"Poison ivy."

"Should I touch it?"

"Only if you want."

She gave a tentative poke. "My daddy always said Listerine was good for poison ivy."

"I've got medicine."

"Poor Buddy." She kissed the tip of one finger, pressed it against my goose-bumped skin. "Are you cold?"

"A little, I guess."

"We don't have to stay. We can keep walking." She retreated an inch.

"Is that what you want to do?" Back to the car, I thought. Lee can find his own way home.

"I want to stay right here with you." She rested her hand on mine. "Lee said you guys are leaving for L.A. real soon."

"Guess so."

"I probably won't ever see you again." She lay back on the grass. "It's kind of like you're going off to war or something." She sat upright. "What's that noise?"

I listened. A scurry in the branches above us.

"Squirrels, maybe. Owl. Bats."

"Oh, God. I hate bats." She pinched my elbow, pulled me back down with her. "I'm scared."

She pressed her thigh against mine, gave a little moan of fear. I worked my arm beneath her shoulders. Her lemony smell blended with the grass, her breath edged with apricots.

"Better," she sighed, and laid her face against my chest. Laughter drifted to us on the light breeze. A train whistled downriver, its thrum barely distinguishable from the constant lull of the mill.

She turned more fully, her hips brushing my groin. I tested a kiss, ran my hand down her throat, worked my fingers between the buttons of her blouse.

"Nobody has to know, do they?"

"Nobody has to know." I ran my palm up the inside of her thigh, touched between her legs.

"Don't," she said. "Don't touch me there."

"Why?"

"It's . . ." She gave a tight shake of her head. "I just don't like it. It doesn't feel good."

I hesitated. It wasn't worth it.

"What's the matter?"

"Nothing. I mean . . . I don't want to get you pregnant or anything."

"Linda gave me this." She held up a Trojan. Bereft of excuses, I unzipped my pants, worked the condom down. She raised her hips to meet my first thrust, then lay still.

I looked down into her face. She was staring into the branches of the tree. She smiled. "All done?" Doll voice.

"No, I haven't . . . I can be." I started to roll away.

"Oh, no! I didn't mean you had to stop. I just thought . . . You can keep going."

I pretended a moan, stiffened. I pulled off the condom, threw it and its wrapper into the tall grass. Becky burrowed beneath my arm.

"I'll always remember you," she said. "Will you always remember me?"

"Sure."

"I could stay like this all night." She sighed. "My brother says Snake Junction ain't the best place for a girl. I think he's crazy."

I shrugged, felt her head rise and fall.

"Is it true about that lady who was murdered? Russ said they found pieces of her in the mill pond." She shivered.

"She wasn't in pieces."

"Well that's what Russ said. Said the Indian cut off her head first, then . . ."

I sat up. "Best we get going. Linda might be wondering."

"Do you want to do it again?"

"No more rubbers," I said, and gave her forehead a little kiss.

We walked back to find them already in the car, Lee behind the wheel, drinking the last of the brandy. When I opened the door to crawl in back, the overhead lit up the interior. Linda's blond hair was tangled, lipstick smeared across her mouth. She looked swollen, blurred around the edges.

"D'you two have a good time?" she slurred.

Becky giggled, rubbed her head against my shoulder.

"Say, Lee, why don't you let me drive?" I tried to sound jolly. "Don't get the chance much."

He held the bottle in one hand, cranked the steering wheel with the other. "I'm driving." He shifted the Chevy into reverse, hit the brakes, gunned it forward. We skidded around the graveled turnout of the park.

"Come on, Lee. Slow down."

"What's the matter, little brother? You scared?" Lee roared through town, ran two red lights, accelerated across the bridge, headed for The Stables.

Becky grabbed the seat. "Tell him to slow down, Linda. Please."

Linda leaned her head all the way back, gave a loopy, upside-down smile. Her body heaved once before she vomited into Becky's lap.

"Jesus H. Christ!" Lee veered onto the right shoulder, then back across both lanes, locked up the brakes. The Chevy bumped hard across a barrow pit, came to rest against a fence studded with barbed wire. A horse and a goat stood frozen in the headlights a split second before bolting for the pasture's far corner.

"Palomino," I said.

"Get her out of here!" Lee pushed Linda out the door,

knuckled open the glove box, dug for rags. Becky gagged twice, then threw up the brandy and at least three maraschino cherries, perfectly whole.

"Aw, Jee-zus!" Lee pulled out his handkerchief, began swabbing the upholstery.

I stepped out of the car, pulled off my soiled shirt. My pants had remained miraculously clean.

"Buddy, where the hell you think you're going?" Lee shouted. "Get back here!"

I bore to the left, away from the road, outside the beam of the Chevy's lights, to the back of the pasture, heard the gelding nicker softly in recognition.

"No apples tonight, boy." I rubbed the velvet of his nose, felt the warm exhalation, the deep animal sigh. Behind me, I could hear Lee's voice rise in anger, the women crying. "Maybe tomorrow."

I looked up and saw an orange-red aura topping the hills to the north. At first I thought it was the moon, but the glow grew brighter as I watched, and then I could see the flames, cresting the ridge, licking into the draws.

"Fire," I whispered to the horse.

I stood with the warm muzzle in my palm, mesmerized by the lava-like flow that followed the ravines—hawthorn, locust, bunchgrass, and thistle sucked dry by a summer's long heat. The hills were invisible against the black sky, the fire sketching downward in meandering lines of brilliant red. When I closed my eyes, I could still see it, branding the dark.

A string of lights moved slowly up the spiraling highway— farmers, ranchers, neighbors working their way toward the flames. The acreage was outside the town limits: any fighting would be done by bucket and spade.

"That's something," I said, and I realized I was talking to Irene. She was the one who would welcome my observation, acknowledge the strange beauty of the world. I wanted her there with me, watching the fires burn. I closed my eyes, breathed in, believed I could smell the spice of her.

I gave the horse a final rub, began walking. By the time I reached Lapwai, the hills would be black, the fire quelled by wet gunnysacks and shovels just shy of the town boundary, where firemen waited with their tankers and hoses.

I stayed low past The Stables, stopped for a moment to gaze down the dark trail leading to the sweat house. "I shouldn't have done that," I said aloud. For a moment, I thought to take to the river, let it cleanse me or drown me, but I needed Irene more than I needed purgation.

What if she'd left with Wolfchild, headed for Canada? The possibility made me walk faster, and then run, gravel chattering beneath my boots. The wind felt good against my bare chest. I spat, ridding my mouth of the taste of apricots. My stomach growled and I thought of Esther's pork chops, Wolfchild smothering his potatoes with gravy.

"I'll eat," I said to the dark. "I'll take whatever you'll give me."

CHAPTER SIXTEEN

Burdock. Beggar-ticks. Cocklebur. Pitch. I'd taken
across the fields to save time, climbed the pine-pole
fences, waded the thick clumps of weeds to the cabin. I sat on
the bed in my underwear while Irene picked the sticktights from
my pants.

"Turpentine's under the sink," she said.

I worked at the pitch smearing my hands. "Smell of turpentine always makes me think of being sick."

"Why's that?" She finished one leg, started on the other.

"Mama used to make us take a swig for cough or sore throat.
Burned like hell going down. Cleared you out, though."

"I don't remember ever being ill when I was young. I remember wishing I could get sick, just so someone would feel

sorry for me. Here." She threw the pants on the bed, shook her head at the pitiful state of my socks.

She hadn't said a word when I showed up on her doorstep, had stood back and let me in, as though she had been expecting me all along. When she told me to take off my pants, I hesitated, fearing she might smell what I'd done in the park, then skinned down to my underwear and pulled a blanket across my lap, took a few quick sniffs of the air wafting up from my crotch. Just because I couldn't smell anything didn't mean she wouldn't. Lee often spoke of a woman's uncanny ability to detect the odor of infidelity. "They'll dig through a week's worth of old laundry to get to dirty underwear," he said. "No shame at all."

I couldn't imagine Irene doing such a thing, but I figured she would come to know about Becky, if she didn't already, in that way animals know that something has happened long before word reaches anybody human. I'd thought to confess, but she might think me only foolish instead of failed.

"Wolfchild's staying with Aunt Esther," she said. "I think that's best, especially when word spreads that he's out on bail."

The hair on my arms had gummed and matted. I rubbed harder, winced. "They related?"

"Aunt Esther and Wolfchild? Probably, somewhere down the line. Same tribe. That's enough." She snapped a sock, turned it inside out. "Some ways, tribe's no different from family."

"You related?"

"To Leopold?" She looked at me over her glasses. I still hadn't gotten used to seeing her wearing them, and I found myself staring.

"Yeah. To Wolfchild."

"No relation."

"He said he's known you for a long time." I rinsed my arms in the sink.

"We played together that summer I was here with my grandmother. Me and him and Danny. We were children. Are you going to put your pants on?"

I considered my options, decided to hold my ground. "Danny was . . . ?"

"A little bit older than me."

"That's not what I mean."

Irene took off her glasses. "What is it you want to know, Buddy?"

I tried to lean on the counter with some nonchalance, realizing too late that I should have taken on the authority of my pants before begging her full attention. "I want to know what the Indian is to you."

She bent her head, sat quietly, her fingers gleaning from ankle to heel to toe. She smoothed the sock along her thigh. "I'm going to tell you the truth."

"I wish you would." My voice was hoarse, my throat so dry I couldn't work up enough spit to swallow.

"Early on, before I was really sure about you . . ."

I coughed, a sound like a dog choking on a chicken bone.

"Are you all right?"

"Fine. Keep going."

"The night Laurette disappeared. I saw him walking, gave him a ride back to Lapwai. Things just kind of happened." She looked at me, a deep sadness in her eyes. "We've been friends a long time."

"You sleep with all your friends?" I hacked, held my throat.

211

"Let me get you some water." She started to stand.

"I don't need no goddamn water, Irene." I gave myself over to a full fit of coughing, stepped to the door and spat. "Smoke, that's all."

"It's been bad."

I wiped my mouth. "Everything's bad." I looked down the narrow road, wondered why I didn't leave right then, never look back. A mess, my mother would have pronounced. You've gotten yourself into a real mire.

When I turned, Irene was sitting with her hands in her lap, her eyes following my face. No shame. What kind of woman would do such a thing?

"I didn't mean for this to hurt you," she said. "It was just that once."

"Figure that you can sleep with every man in the county one time, and somehow that doesn't add up to anything?"

"I haven't—" She stopped, her jaw working. "You wanted the truth, and I'm giving it to you."

What I wanted was to throw a chair, bust a window, tear the legs from the table. I felt the muscles in my arms working, the clench in my fists, and I knew that I wanted to hit her, too, just once, hard enough to knock the calmness from her, rattle her voice of reason.

"I hope they hang him tomorrow."

She rose from her chair. "You can't say that. He's not guilty of anything, no more than I am. You want him to hang, you want the same for me."

My teeth felt soft, as if I could grind them to powder. I could not say I wanted her dead. "If you and him were together, then why ain't he a free man? Huh? Why didn't he tell the sheriff he couldn't have been the one killed Laurette?"

She let out a long breath, eased back down in the chair, picked up the sock, scraped at an arrow of cheatgrass. "He won't tell them. He's trying to protect me."

"From what? What's he protecting you from? Think he's going to *ruin* your *reputation*?" I felt my lip curl. "Seems like I'm the last one to know the truth about you."

Her hands went still. "I've got trouble in my past, Buddy. Bad trouble. If the sheriff finds out . . ." She moved her eyes to the window behind me. "Well, you wouldn't have to worry about any of this anymore. But maybe that's what you want."

My hands unfisted, my shoulders dropped. "No. That's not what I want."

"There's only so much I can tell you." She moved her lips one against the other. "It's about me and my brother Danny."

I let out the breath I didn't know I'd been holding. "Your *brother*?" I gave up my stance, let her see how terrified I was. I wanted to plead that she love only me, that no one—father, brother, lover—had ever meant more. I wanted her to say that she'd found her place of happiness and safety. I wove my fingers through hers, held tight, but she pulled free, moved to the sink, stood looking out the window.

"Danny and me, we'd always sleep together. I wasn't even twelve. After my mother remarried, our stepfather said Danny had to sleep on the couch." She crossed her arms. "On the nights when our stepfather didn't come home or was passed out at the kitchen table. Or after he'd been in on me and left. Danny . . ." She wrapped herself tighter. "He held me, made me feel better."

I thought of the long nights listening to Lee cry, how I tried to comfort him, yet could do nothing, finally, but turn away.

Irene sat on the bed beside me. "It was like he was taking away some of the poison." I felt her starting to crumple, fold in on herself. "One morning, our stepfather found us together, dragged Danny out of the house, kicked him until he spit up blood. Held a gun to his head, told him never to come back or he'd kill us both. I watched him walk down the road, went back in the house, took our daddy's straight razor, cut myself. Didn't go deep enough. That was my mistake."

I let my eyes find the whiteness of her wrists, saw for the first time the twin scars.

"He dragged me into the kitchen, belted me to a chair, stitched me up with Mother's embroidery silk. He wanted me to live more than I wanted to die, I guess."

"You shouldn't guess." I felt myself wanting to hold her, and my desire surprised me. "You should know."

She wiped her eyes, gave me a sideways smile. "You see? Sometimes it's better not knowing."

"No. It's never better. Nothing's changed. I just need time to adjust, that's all."

"You've had to do a lot of adjusting for someone who should be worrying about which girl to ask to the prom. Which reminds me—you don't have to cover up what you do. It's not that I like the idea of you seeing other women, but I can't ask you to be faithful when all I got to offer is a ride in my car or a night in this place." She stood, filled the percolator with water, added coffee.

"I don't want any other girls, Irene. I want you." I walked to where she stood, nestled up behind her, drew her tight against me.

She turned to face me. "You've got to have a life, Buddy. More than I can give."

"You can come with me to California. There's plenty of work I can get down there. I might even sing with Lee, get my own contract."

"That would be wonderful. But I can't go to California. I've got to stay here for a while."

"What's keeping you here, Irene? Danny's dead. Aunt Esther can take care of herself. What's this place got to hold you?"

"I've got to help Wolfchild."

"I thought *he* was the one protecting *you*." I sat down hard on the wooden chair, felt the bite of old paint against my bare legs.

"There's something else. Something I can't say."

Something else. I weighed my need to know against my desire to know no more.

Irene wadded a sheet of newspaper and stuffed it in the stove, added a few pieces of kindling. "Down to our last two matches." She struck one, let it catch the paper. "Coffee will take a while." She scanned the cupboard, pulled out Aunt Esther's biscuits, laid two on a plate and brought it to the table. She brushed the burrs into her palm, fed them to the fire, wiped her hands down her hips. "If you get mixed up in this, you might never get out."

"And what about you? What do you want?"

Irene stared into the fire. "I try not to think about that."

"Think, Irene. A house of your own, a real one. A family. Me."

She closed her eyes. "In my dreams, sometimes. I let myself imagine such things."

"Why not make it real, Irene? Let me make it real."

She opened her eyes, searched my face for some truth she had missed before. She looked down, shook her head.

"What, then? You plan to stay here the rest of your life?"

"I don't plan on anything." She centered the coffeepot, waited for the water to boil.

"Maybe that's the problem. You need a plan. I've got just the one."

"You sound like Lee."

"That can't be all bad."

She laughed. "No. Not all bad."

"Come with me, then. I'll keep you happy. Lee will keep you entertained."

"I don't think Lee would care much for me tagging along."

"He's just mad because you're with me. He'd take my place in a hot minute." I snapped my fingers.

Irene's face softened. "I don't believe that, Buddy. Not all men see me the way you do."

"They all think you're beautiful." I wrapped one arm around her waist, stepped a light waltz.

"That's not all they think. It's what you know that would send them off." She put her hand on my chest. "Yet here you are."

"I won't go to Los Angeles. Not without you." I led her into a two-step, the smell of coffee reminding me that the sun would be up any minute. None of it mattered, I told myself. She was mine now. I'd heal all the hurts, love her the way she needed to be loved. This was why we'd found each other, what had been fated long before she walked into The Stables that first time. I was meant to take care of her, make the old wrongs right.

She rested her head on my shoulder. I kept moving, gently danced us to the door and back, slow circles around the stove where the pot chugged and whistled. Through the window, I could see the sky beginning to pink, a sliver of gold across the top of the near hills, smoke feathering the ravines.

"I need a handkerchief." She turned her head away.

I found my pants, fished the pockets, waited while she wiped her eyes and nose. "Let's have some breakfast," she said.

We sat at the table, me in my underwear, her in her robe. I ate the biscuit, drank the scalding coffee before it cooled. The shock was leaving me, replaced by a pleasurable drowsiness.

Irene traced her cup's handle with one fingertip. "I can't imagine how hopeless he must have felt, lying there in that jail. Like I used to feel, waiting for my stepfather. Only thing coming my way was punishment I didn't deserve."

I relaxed back into my chair. Even with the coffee, my head bobbed, my toes and fingers tingled. I jerked upright, blinked hard. I jiggled my feet, stretched, yawned. But there was no fighting it. It was as if the blood had been drained from my veins. I made my way to the bed. Even as I drifted, I was aware of Irene close by, watching me for a long time, it seemed, smoking, thinking. Then I felt her snug against me, breathed in the sun smell of her skin.

"No matter what happens," she said, so low I almost could not hear, "remember this." She kissed my ear, ran her hands along my chest. "Remember that this moment is true and nothing can ever change that. Sleep now," she said, and I did, and didn't awaken until well past noon to find her already gone, on the table a note scratched with the head of a burnt match. "Come back tonight, 11." The head of the match had broken, but there, etched at the bottom of the paper, I could still read it: "I love you."

"I love you." I said it aloud, then folded the paper, stuck it in my pocket with the handkerchief. I wanted a shave and clean clothes before the night's meeting with Irene. I nabbed the old chamois shirt from its nail, buttoned the last few buttons, left the neck open. I was sure Lee wouldn't let me borrow his Chevy again, sure, too, that it would be sitting in the parking lot, seats scoured, doors opened to dry.

I set off on foot, hitched a ride before I'd gotten a mile down the road. It wasn't until the truck had pulled over that I realized it was the rancher I'd nearly killed a few days before. I ducked my head, said I'd just jump in back.

"Suit yourself," he said. "Where you want dropped?"

"Just past The Stables," I said. "Pasture with the palomino." I didn't want to claim a nightclub as my home.

He nodded. I felt the truck pick up speed as I rearranged the tools and empty feed sacks to make a comfortable space for myself. To the south, a bank of clouds wisped into vapor; the north hills were charred, mottled. I wondered if any of the Nez Perce knew how to dance for rain, remembered that my mother could smell rain coming hours before it hit. There were other things she knew: how to pull the poison from a bee sting with a poultice of baking soda and water; how to blow tobacco smoke into an ear aching with infection. My longing for her at that moment hit me like an elbow in the ribs.

"I sure do wish you was here," I whispered. "Somebody needs to tell me what to do."

I knew what she'd say—that I had already made my bed and now must lie in it. She'd say, too, that the Lord always provided a way to set things right.

"I'd marry her right now," I said as the sacks flagged and snapped. "I'd make it honest." But good intentions were never enough. Best thing, the saving thing, my mother would say, would be to walk away. I leaned my head back against the cab, knuckled my hands together. "I can't. Please."

The blare of the truck's horn jolted me out of prayer as we passed The Stables—Spud in his car, darting in front of us and into the parking lot. I waved as we jalopied by, saw the surprise cross his face. My chest tightened at the thought of leaving Spud and Harvey, the place they had made for me.

I could stay in Snake Junction, find real work, live with Irene if she'd have me, let Lee go on alone. Autumn along the creek would be beautiful, the cottonwood leaves turning over and over, jingling like coins. We'd add extra blankets to the bed, stopper the stove's cracks with tinfoil. Maybe I could plumb in a bathroom, hang another cupboard, talk Irene into an overnight drive to Las Vegas. I'd seen two gold bands at the pawnshop, and I quickly checked my mental list of belongings for something worth trading. My boots might bring two bucks. I wished for Raimey's ring and the hundred dollars back, more than enough to cover a wedding.

And then I remembered the fifty that Harvey had stashed. But even as I began a plan to filch it from the till, I knew I could never do that to Harv. I'd wait, earn some wages. We'd walk down Main Street to Weisfield's Jewelry, find a thin band with a row of diamonds.

When the truck slowed at the pasture, I jumped out, hollered my thanks as the rancher geared up and headed toward town. The gelding raised his head, grass tufting his mouth. I clucked my tongue, scratched behind his ears. "Wish I could ride you right out of here," I said. The goat nosed in, the slit pupils of his eyes widening with interest. The horse laid back his ears, and the goat high-stepped a few feet away.

"Wonder what you'd cost?" I looked west of the pasture,

where a cedar-sided shack sat dark in a grove of black locust. "Wonder."

The gelding followed me along the fence, watched as I took the porch and knocked. From inside came a scurrying like rats running for cover. When the door cracked open, I saw a small white-haired woman peering at me, her eyes clouded with cataracts.

"Whosit?"

"Ma'am, I was wondering if that's your horse. The palomino there." I pointed in the direction of the pasture.

"Ain't but one horse in that pasture. Other's a goat." Her mouth puckered around her toothless gums. I took a step back from the smell of clabbered milk and cat shit.

"It's the horse I'd like to inquire about. If you own him."

"I own this whole damn place and everything on it. Who said I don't?" She leaned further out the door.

"Are you interested in selling? The horse, I mean?"

She swiveled her head, squinted to where the gelding was scratching his rear against a post. The goat had taken his station atop a low-roofed hutch, bleating and pawing for feed now that the woman had appeared.

"That's my husband's horse."

"Is he around to talk to?"

"Dead three years. Won't do no good to talk to him."

"I'm sure sorry." I bowed my head. "Lost both my folks a while back. Me and my brother came to Snake Junction to find work."

"You ain't working standing here. And I ain't getting my dinner et." A tomcat slithered out, balls the size of crab apples. She gave a kick. "Go kill something. Earn your keep."

"I was wondering about the horse. . . ."

"How much?"

"Well, he's a little cow-hocked. Needs to be trimmed and shod."

"That horse is worth more than the farrier you'd take him to. Good lines. Stud until my husband died. Had to have him cut. Always tearing down the fence, trying to mount the goat. Nearly killed the poor thing." The billy bleated, bearing witness to the sad truth of the tale.

"I can pay you twenty dollars a week. One hundred for the horse."

"You're crazy."

I grabbed the door before she could close it. "It's for my girlfriend. I'm going to ask her to marry me."

She rattled the door loose from my grip. "Your plans don't concern me. You want that horse, you pay for it. Two hundred."

"I don't have that kind of money." I remembered Wolfchild's bail, wished I had it to do over again.

"Then you ain't got no horse, either."

"I'd pay you some every week. I could do work around the place. Set fence. Pull weeds. Anything."

She studied me, gauging the strength of my back, the likelihood of my word. "That ringworm you got growing up the side of your neck?"

"Poison ivy. I was fishing. . . ."

"What do you know about working a place?"

"I'm off a farm. Oklahoma. Raised broomcorn and cotton. Had some stock."

"Where you staying?"

I started to say The Stables, then thought better of it, just as I had with the rancher who drove me in. "With relatives. In Lapwai."

"You Indian?"

"No, ma'am. Just that that's where my aunt and uncle have their farm."

"What's their name?"

I quickly ran through the names I had seen on the wooden arrows pointing directions at every back-road intersection. "Hogue," I said. It sounded white enough. "Just up Cottonwood Creek."

She nodded slowly. "Heard of them. Don't know what kind of people they are."

"Good people," I said. "They've been real kind to me."

"Family should be. Ain't no one else you can rely on." She relaxed, let her banty shoulders drop. "Two daughters, grown and gone. Don't know if they're living or dead. Never thought I'd raise such kind." She snorted away her grief. "That horse would fetch more at sale. Got good cow sense. Turn on a dime."

"How old is he?" I asked. "Fifteen? Sixteen?"

"Prime," she huffed. "Young enough to go all day, old enough to know better." She leaned against the door jamb, let her milky eyes wander. "Billy won't like it a bit. Lonely as hell."

"Maybe we can find him a nanny. Something more his size."

The woman's mouth twisted into a smile. "Don't need no herd of goats to feed. You do that?"

"What?"

"Cut him. He stinks. You get Billy done, I'll consider it down payment." She crossed her arms, nodded toward the shed. "Ain't locked. Should be some liniment. Rope. Probably best use your own knife. All mine are dull as dirt." She looked to where the cat stood, backed up to a corner of the house, spraying its urine. "Get hold of them toms, too. Must be ten of them. Nasty things." She stepped into the house, closed the door, leaving me to contemplate my knowledge of castration.

Billy eyed me warily as I made my way to the shed, the gelding at my heels. "Let's move you out of the way first, big fella." The horse lipped the cuffs of my shirt, let me lead him to the hawthorn at the pasture's northwest corner. "I wouldn't watch if I were you." I slid my palm over the dish of his face. "Bad memories."

Rope coiled off several long nails, each loop sacced with spider eggs. Dust smoked up from the floor, feathered off the swaybacked shelves. Axle grease, charcoal, hoof paste. No antiseptic. "Well," I said to the walls, "we'll see which of us survives, and then worry about infection."

Billy had taken up with the gelding, the two of them butt to butt, the goat smart enough to take advantage of the horse's shoofly tail. I wound one length of rope, pinched it beneath my belt, knotted the other into a lasso. How long since I'd worked a lariat, sung it through the air? This one was stiff as old leather. I made a few practice throws, noted the lack of alarm in the goat's snaky eyes.

"Here, goat, goat, goat. Here, Billy." The goat was gone, quick as a deer. He led me around the fence line three times before I lost patience and began running, the rope shedding fiber, prickling my hands. "Come here, you son of a bitch!" I stopped to catch my breath, heard the screen door bang.

"Thought you might have sense enough to use that new horse of yours," the old woman called. "He's got the better head."

I stomped into the shed, dragged out the saddle, bridle, and reins. "This tack's about rotted!" I yelled back, slapping the stirrups over the horn to keep from clapping my shins.

"You work hard enough, I'll throw all that crap in on the deal. Ain't nothing a little oil won't fix." She banged into the house.

I shined the bit the best I could with my shirttail. "I'm sorry about this." I soothed the horse, who took the bridle without hesitation, didn't flinch when I hoisted the filthy pad and saddle onto his back.

I hadn't sat a horse for over a year, and the inches I'd grown made it easier to swing up. I rocked to center, felt the pinch of raw skin on the insides of my thighs, resisted the urge to shove a hand down my pants and scratch. I stood in the stirrups, adjusted myself, wondered if the itching would ever stop.

"Okay," I said. "Let's go rope us a goat." I made a few practice figure eights. "Got any oats you want to sow before we get on with this business?" I gave a light kick and we jumped to a trot. "Faster," I said, leaned forward, giving him rein. The gelding bunched a little but then legged out, and we were loping easy, marking back and forth across the pasture, the goat forgotten.

I drew him to a walk, both of us blowing. "What we going to call you, huh?" I patted his neck, buried my nose in the cream-colored mane. All the names of all the horses I'd ever known came back: Pepper, Brownie, Paint, Star, Silver, Velvet, Moonshine, Jake.

"Color of butter," I whispered against the horse's ear, "but Butter won't do." I caught movement out of the corner of my eye, saw the goat making for the open shed.

The minute Billy saw us coming, he clattered through the door, disappeared inside. I circled the horse around, tapped on the single pane of glass. "Scat!" I said. "Hee-ya!" But the goat held his newly claimed ground. I dismounted, walked warily toward the door. Buckets clattered, then silence. "Come on out, you bastard." More clattering. Remembering the billy's horns, I kept my body clear, hung my head around the jamb. The goat blinked back from his perch atop the workbench. I grabbed a dirt clod, lobbed it in, then went for a sharp rock, hit him square between the eyes. He bolted, hit the rear wall, came at me full tilt. I had left my lasso and could only stand back as he busted by, swung a tight circle and aimed for me again. I jumped into the shed, slammed the door. Nothing. When I dared a peek, there they were, two old friends, sharing a hummock of clover.

"Pat Garrett." The gelding stood accused, indifferent.

I latched the door behind me, walked toward them, and they both tore off, the horse farting, tail high. I saw the screen yaw open, but she didn't even bother to show herself this time.

"Now you got 'em," she announced loudly. "Yes, sir."

I kicked the dirt, wanting to kill all three of them.

"There's carrots in the garden. Looks like you'll have to cheat."

"They're the ones cheating!" But the screen clipped shut.

I filled my pockets, scraped one carrot with the knife, left its greens, chomped loudly. Heads came up. I gazed toward town, letting them believe they no longer warranted my interest, crunched and smacked, enjoying the sweet carrot still tasting of earth.

The horse snorted, cantered forward. I let him mouth a root from my shirt pocket, eased the reins off his neck. He snapped the carrot in half with his sharp front teeth, as if his jaws weren't long enough to accommodate the full length. "Head as big as a suitcase," I said. "Too bad no one bothered to pack it."

Billy hadn't taken the bait. I hoisted myself up, hipped back in the saddle. "You think you can help me out a little here?" The horse swung around, side-eyeing my pockets. "More if you get this job done. Not before."

The minute I hefted a loop of rope, Billy booked for the shed, then pulled up short. I hauled after him, made a limp cast, hit dirt.

"What in the hell are you doing?" Lee rested his arms along the top fence rail, hands dangling.

I tried to hide my surprise at his sudden presence. "I'm roping a goat."

"The hell you are."

I nudged the palomino to the fence. The horse nosed Lee's hand, looking for treats, and I feared that the animal would like him better. Dogs, cats, even the pet raccoon we'd kept close by, feeding it fish heads—all had preferred Lee, ears pricking, tails wagging, the coon upright on its hind feet at the sight and sound of him.

I scratched beneath the gelding's mane for good measure. "Where's the Chevy?"

"Just up the road." Lee pointed west. "Drove past on my way to town. Thought it was you I saw. Pulled over just to make sure my eyes was right. Whose horse?"

"Mine, if I can get that goat tied." Billy had turned his attention to the carrots that littered the ground, marking my erratic chase.

Lee hitched one leg, scratched a thumb across his forehead. "That's a pretty good deal."

"Old woman"—I gave a quick nod toward the house—"she wants him cut. Tomcats, too."

"Ho!" Lee laughed. "You're going to need more than a piece of rope to get *that* job done."

Just then the screen door rattled. "Who's that now?" Her hair reflected the sun like spun glass.

"It's okay, ma'am. Just my brother."

"I'm not offering to pay him nothin'. And you ain't earning a freckle off that horse by sitting there."

"What's the deal?" Lee wore a short-sleeved shirt that showed his scripted biceps, the tattoo a mistake, he said, the name too damned long—"Pattianne"—now with a single bold line inked through.

I told him how I'd wanted the horse, pledged to work off the price. "First job is the goat. Like trying to corner a weasel."

Lee and Billy considered each other across the pasture. "Goats got more sense than most people. Too smart to bait. Might as well keep those carrots for this guy." He stepped back to take measure. "Nice-looking horse. Little cow-hocked."

"I need to get going on this." I didn't want to hear Lee assessing the horse's faults, especially now that those faults were part of what I owned. The rope threw dust as I coiled and gathered.

"Hang on." Lee bit his cigarette between his teeth, unsnapped his shirt, hung it on the nearest post. "Let's see if that old fart can outsmart two of us." He climbed the fence, made a last small leap over the barbed wire. "We got to have a plan," he said, surveying the pasture, the hawthorn grown tight against the fence. "Can't get into that shed, can he?"

"Not anymore."

Lee flipped his smoke to the ground, gave a hard dig with the heel of his boot. "That all the rope?"

"It's rotten." I pulled the second length from my belt, tossed it his way.

He yanked it between his fists. "Here." He motioned me toward the tree. "Let's try something. You and Ol' Yeller stand between me and Billy. Goat's going to want to see what's going on, and we don't want him to."

I watched as Lee fashioned a slipknot, pulled a large circle, placed it on the ground and scuffed it with dirt. "Just hold there a minute." He climbed into the tree, taking the rope's tail with him, his boots skinning bark. "Am I hid?"

I backed the horse ten feet. "You can see the rope coming down."

Lee worked the slack to the back of the tree. "Now?"

"Good."

"Take a few easy turns. Throw him a few carrots, get his mind off where I've disappeared to. He's no fool."

The gelding bucked his head when I tossed the carrots. "There'll be more," I said, guiding him into a lazy inspection of the pasture's four corners. The goat chewed, still wary. After a few minutes, I reined between Billy and the house.

"Go on. Move." I clucked, keeping a little distance. The goat snorted, lowered his head, pawed, then looked toward the tree. "Nothing in there but birds. Hee-ya. Ha!" He spun for the shed, veered off toward the hawthorn. I kept to the rear, directing the goat between me and the fence. "He's coming your way!"

Lee yanked the rope, caught the hind legs. The goat gave a bleat, went down hard, scrabbled back up, but Lee kept the noose tight, the hooves just shy of the ground. "Tie him!"

I jumped down, grabbed the curved horns, threw the billy to his side, tugged enough rope to twine all four hooves into a tight bundle.

Lee dropped from the tree, wiped one arm across his forehead. "Got your knife?"

I pulled out the souvenir of our night in White Bird, and Lee grinned. "That ol' boy had a mean right hook, didn't he?" We laughed together, squatted at the goat's hind end, smelling the piss that matted his belly, the horse shit we'd walked through, our own sweat. I examined the billy's scrotum, unnerved by its familiarity.

"Can't be much different from a bull calf," Lee said. The goat bleated miserably. "Pinch behind one of the balls."

I poked, felt my own gut flip-flop. Billy tried to heave up on his knees. Lee moved to his head, pushed one knee against his neck. "Don't take all day. I might have better things to do."

Prodding with my finger and thumb, I separated one ball from the other. The goat grunted, shat a puddle the length of my arm.

"Animal's going to die before you get done."

I wiped my arm against the butt of my jeans, clamped down with my fingers. The second the blade touched the tight skin, the testicle popped to the surface. I thought I could see it throbbing.

"Now slide it out and cut the cord," Lee said. "Maybe fray it a little. Might bleed otherwise."

I threw the bloody ball over the fence, a treat for the cats, a taste of what was coming. The second one was easier, the nut sac collapsed, the blood not as much as I'd thought. The goat, having exhausted himself, lay walleyed and still. I ran the blade beneath the rope, stepped back, watched him roll to his feet, stumble toward the corner closest to the house.

"By tomorrow, he'll have forgotten all about 'em," Lee said. "Got to wonder what good they do any of us."

"Not the kind of life I want to consider." I walked to the galvanized trough. "I'm getting in. My crotch is on fire." I left my pants and shirt in a pile with my boots.

"Ain't a bad idea." Lee looked toward the house. "Give the old lady something to dream about." He stripped to his skivvies, legged over the rim, settled in to his neck. Together, we faced the highway, the cars headed east and west, the mill just upriver, the smoky blue hills. Lee tipped his head back enough to keep his cigarette dry. "Bet you can't do this in L.A."

"Nope."

"Remember the swimming hole back home?"

I nodded.

Lee's eyes wrinkled with the pleasure of the memory. "Remember them carp we'd catch and sell to that old colored man? Damn, them fish was good barbecued up that way. Carp sandwiches."

"Bones and all." My mouth watered.

"Mama couldn't stand the stink. Made us wash our hands with gasoline. Remember when we got the lice?" Lee began to laugh deep in his chest. "She about killed us with that sheep dip. Shaved us bald, crotch and all, then set us on fire with that stuff. Damn."

"That was right before the hailstorm."

Lee got quiet. "Seen Daddy come runnin' across the field, hollerin', 'Get the boys to the cellar!'"

"He could sure run."

"He was running that day, I'll tell you. And the sound of that hail. Like a train coming."

I closed my eyes. "Sky solid black."

"He threw us down in that cellar. Remember?" Lee chuckled. "Didn't even take time to check for snakes. Just slapped us down there, hauled Mama in, then slammed the door."

"Then it hit," I said. We were telling the story together. I could feel its rhythm, its harmony. "Sounded like a stampede right over the top of us."

"Beat the roof in," Lee said. "Killed every cow we owned. And the hogs. Killed the hogs."

"Chickens lived because they'd gone in to roost. Thought it was night coming."

"Ate every one of them. All we had left." Lee took a deep breath. "We've survived quite a lot, little brother. We've survived quite a lot." He began to hum in the back of his throat, stopped abruptly, pulled himself straight, rubbed the knobs of his knees.

"So. You going or staying?"

"Ain't sure yet." I scrubbed my face with my hands, squibbed a finger in each ear.

"What's Irene going to do?"

"Whatever she wants."

"Never doubted that." Lee smiled, puffed on his cigarette like he'd lit a stogie. "Fact is, I don't think I'd mind having her along."

"I don't want to hear this." I stood, my underwear sagging to mid-thigh.

Lee grabbed my arm. "Sit down, you stupid shit. I don't mean nothing but that she'd make good company and keep you happy."

I let myself be mollified, slid my back down the cool metal, felt the bottom of the trough furred with algae. "I don't think she'd come, anyway."

"Why's that? You two fighting?"

I considered the word "fighting." Sometimes I longed for my time with Irene to be that simple. "We ain't fighting. She's got her own life, that's all."

Lee snorted, stretched his arms along the rim of the trough. "Wouldn't seem quite the same without you. We've been on this trip together for a long time."

I didn't look at Lee, didn't want to risk emotion. "I want to do what's right," I said. "I'm just not sure what that is anymore."

"Wish I could tell you." A logging truck roared past, the scent of fresh-cut cedar in its draft. "What did you do with the ring?"

"Pawned it."

"The hundred?"

"Gone."

Lee squinted at the sun working its way west. "That how you sprung Wolfchild?"

I shrugged.

"I figure you had your reasons."

"I'm not sure the reasons are mine."

"Irene?"

I nodded, scooped a yellowjacket from the water. "Irene says they'll hang him."

Lee leaned his head back until the water lapped at his ears. "Probably will."

"Don't that bother you? If he's innocent, I mean?"

The yellowjacket blundered across Lee's clothes, disappeared into the folds of his Wranglers. "Don't know what anyone can do about it. He's in the law's hands now." He wiped his mouth, blew water from his nose.

I thought of Wolfchild in the sweat house, eyes covered, chest heaving. "But what if no one did it? What if she did it herself?"

"I need another cigarette."

I snagged my shirt, pulled out two, waited as Lee took as much smoke as he could in one draw.

"We're brothers, ain't we?"

I nodded.

"We fight, but we fight like brothers. Don't mean nothing."

"No."

"Listen, then, 'cause I got a truth to tell you. Can't nobody else know."

Behind us, I could hear the goat snuffling for the last bits of carrot, the horse stomping away flies.

"We've made a decision to try for bigger things," Lee went

on, "and I'm ready to do that. Me and Linda, we might have something good going. I like her. I don't want nothing to scotch that. You understand?"

"She puked in your car."

"Don't be a smart-ass. You understand?"

"Yeah, I understand."

"It might not look like much to you, but it's the most I've felt for a gal since Pattianne."

It was the first I'd heard him say her name since leaving Oklahoma. "That's been a long time ago."

"Hurt like that's hard to get over." He splashed his face, rubbed his eyes. "She said some awful things. Always stayed with me."

I remembered the letter, Pattianne's reasons for falling out of love. What she wanted was a man with a steady job, good prospects, who believed her reason enough to come home at night.

"Maybe she wasn't really the one," I said.

"Don't matter now." Lee leaned his head back. "Me and Laurette. We was spending time together. You know"—he waved a slow circle with his cigarette—"we was together."

"I didn't know that."

"I didn't want you to, nor nobody else. Dean might have killed us both. Floyd was the only one had an idea. Never told him outright. Asked him to keep Dean tied up a few hours every now and then. I just wanted to help her. That's all."

"You thought screwing her would help?"

"I wasn't just *screwing* her. Goddammit, Buddy." Lee grunted, lifted himself to a straighter sit. "That's not what I was doing. I held her a lot. She cried all the time. I was just trying to make it better. Thought I was doing the right thing." He flicked the butt of his cigarette, forced out a long breath of smoke. "Here's the truth. And by God, I'll kill you if I find you've so much as thought about tellin' a soul." He glared at me, then softened, pointed his finger at my chest. "No. You swear. Swear on Mama's grave."

"I swear."

He laid his head in his hands, rubbed his brow. "That night before White Bird, she'd told me." He worked his head back and forth, trying to shake memory. "That baby was mine."

The smoke I'd inhaled began to burn. "How'd she know it was yours? Maybe it was Dean's." I remembered the day Laurette and I had skipped rocks across the river, the story she'd told, the baby.

"Dean was shootin' blanks. Been that way since the war."

"Maybe it was someone else's."

Lee looked at me, anger darkening his eyes. "She wasn't a whore."

"I didn't mean that." I swallowed the pain gathering beneath my breastbone. "I know she wasn't a whore."

He let his chin sink to his chest. "I think she did it to herself, Buddy. I think she believed Dean would kill her if he found out."

"But she could have gone somewhere else. You'd have helped her."

"Where, Buddy? Where's a girl like that going to go?" He held up an empty hand. "She'd already been through that once. She didn't want to go through it again."

"She could have . . . You could have taken her somewhere, to a doctor. You could have married her." The thought of Lee and Laurette together made sense—black hair, blue eyes. They would have been good together.

Lee looked toward the highway, jaw set.

"She'd have done that, wouldn't she? You guys go off somewhere Dean couldn't find you. You weren't afraid of him, were you?" There was more hope in my voice than I'd intended.

"Yeah, she'd have done it. That's what she wanted." He blinked hard. "But I couldn't, Buddy. Hell, I wasn't afraid of Dean." He slapped the water. "I just wasn't ready to settle down like that. If I'd wanted to get married, I'd have asked . . ."

"Somebody else?"

"Don't make it sound that way. I feel like shit as it is."

I wanted to say that Laurette wasn't feeling anything anymore, that Wolfchild was going to feel a lot worse before it was over. But I kept my tongue.

"That doesn't mean she killed herself."

He closed his eyes again, slid a little further down in the water. "She told me."

"Told you what?"

"She told me that's what she was going to do." His eyes opened, focused on something in the distance. "I believed I'd talked her out of it."

I remembered Laurette that last night, sitting in the car, making up her mind right then. Lee must have known what she was thinking, yet all he could do was offer her coffee.

"You were wrong." I stood, shedding water as I stepped from the trough, shook the dust from my clothes. Lee sat silent, swaying. I stared at the back of his head. "You got to make this right."

"I can't."

"The hell you can't. You go to the sheriff right now, tell him what you know. There's a man's life resting in your hands. Maybe you couldn't save Laurette, but you owe, Lee. You *owe*." I wanted to spit but tightened my lips. "Right now. I'll go with you."

"I can't," he said again, and I thought he might cry.

I pulled on my pants and boots, bundled the shirt. The palomino held as I fisted the reins. The goat shied into the shadows cast by the shed.

"Don't do it, Buddy. Don't take it away from me. You swore."

"You're a coward, Lee. If anyone killed Laurette, it was *you*."

He looked at me like I'd shot him, then lowered his gaze to the water.

"You go on," he said. "Do what you got to do." He closed his eyes, and for the first time I saw the grief he suffered, not just because of Laurette, but because he knew he'd lost all the people he loved in the world.

The horse sidled against the gate, remembering, and I lifted the latch. The woman was waiting at the door.

"Goat's done, ma'am. I'll work the cats next time. My brother's just cleaning up."

"He's not planning to hang around, is he?" She craned her neck, sounded almost hopeful.

"No," I said. "He's headed back."

"Your aunt and uncle, they need any tomatoes?" She reached into a paper sack, pulled out a tomato the size of a grapefruit.

"They might take a few." I laid them on my shirt, tied it into a bundle.

"That horse." She pointed, her trajectory not quite true. "He carried my husband many a mile. Do right by him." Her chin quivered.

"Yes, ma'am."

The palomino stayed calm as I directed him across the highway to the weedy path above the river. I kept my eyes forward, remembered the yellowjacket, hoped it had nestled snug in the crotch of Lee's jeans. I believed that he deserved that pain at least, unwilling as he was to carry the burden he'd brought on himself.

It would be one of the last times I would see my brother, but I didn't know that then. If I had, I might have offered some word that would have held between us, carried us through the years to come. Instead, I passed on by, intent on what came next, how I might undo some of the wrong that had been done.

I patted the horse's hot neck, finger-combed his mane. "Got to get you some feed," I said, and settled into the saddle, letting the strong hind legs rock me. "Got to find you a name." I glanced only once, saw how small Lee looked, only his head and shoulders above the water. I closed my eyes, thought of all that I had to tell Irene.

CHAPTER SEVENTEEN

"Whole world's falling to shit." Harvey stood just inside the door of my room, stared at the radio, shook his head. All the news seemed bad.

I sat on the edge of my bed, scrubbed and shining, fishing cucumbers and onions from a bowl of vinegar. "Made too much," he had told me. "I'll be shittin' fire for a week if I eat all that." He'd sliced the big tomatoes, set them alongside, sprinkled them with margarita salt.

"It's that goddamn NCAA two-point conversion that started it. Not even the same game anymore." He swung his towel at a fly, missed. "Campanella gets in that car wreck, Celtics lose the NBA. Things like that happen, entire country goes downhill."

"I'm hoping Oklahoma will come back," I offered. The onions didn't even bite, they were so sweet—straight from Walla Walla.

"Can't believe they let Notre Dame beat them. You got to watch them Catholics." Same fly, another miss. "Figure they got God on their side. Almost got to believe it. Okies had won how many games?"

"Forty-seven. Hadn't lost since 'fifty-three."

"Damn. See? This is what I'm telling you. Weird stuff's happening."

I handed him the empty bowl. "I'm headed out. Thanks for supper."

"You best find some gum or something. Your breath's enough to knock the buzzards off a gut wagon."

I blew into my cupped hand, sniffed.

"Take that goddamn horse with you. He's cribbing the door frame." Harvey moved down the hall toward the music, the sound of his name being called.

Out back, the shade between the building and the overhanging limbs of locust had made the heat bearable. When I huffed into the horse's nostrils, he wrinkled his upper lip and blinked. "That good, huh?" The double loop of leather I'd cast over the old pump handle hadn't cinched, meaning he'd kept still. I'd need a good halter and lead, I thought, remembering my father's warnings about tying a horse by its reins. "Dumb as they are big," he'd say. "Don't have better sense than to know that bit will break every tooth in their head if they sit back."

I'd had no choice, and I was relieved to find the gelding's mouth intact. I let him work out the snaffle, slid the bridle down around his neck, led him to a place where the sun hadn't burned the grass to straw. "Eat up," I said. "That's all I got for now."

He snorted away the twigs. "It's a wonder your kind don't all starve to death," I said, "picky as you are."

I leaned my ear against the rumble of his gut, knocked the dust from his shoulder. "You might be a whole other color under all this dirt. Probably bought me an albino."

I went back in the building, found Lee's clothes brush, spent an hour grooming the horse's neck, ribs, and rump. The lights of passing cars had begun to flick on by the time we crossed the highway and started south, but I was in no hurry. Still two hours before eleven.

I ambled the horse along the edge of the asphalt, the clop of hooves keeping time with my whistled rendition of "All I Have to Do Is Dream." My hands were rope-burned, but the rawness felt good, a reminder of my afternoon's labor and the new knowledge I was carrying to Irene. I'd sworn to Lee on the grave of our mother, but I believed she'd know what I was doing was right.

Pressing a knee to the gelding's shoulder, I steered him down the path leading to what was left of the sweat house. "Hope you can see in the dark better than I can," I said, but the horse kept his head down, intent on picking his way through the rocks. "Just a little," I cautioned, pulling him back from the water before he could swill more than was good. He pawed his impatience. "You're still hot, ain't you?" I looked out over the vast black ribbon of the river. Irene would do it, no doubt. "You up for a swim?" I slid down, clenched the reins in my teeth, worked off my clothes, then turned to the saddle and blanket. "You bolt, and we'll both be eating gruel."

The horse's hide against my still-raw crotch felt like the old rope in my hands—coarse and bristled. I flinched, but the scratch was good.

I stretched along the length of the gelding's neck, felt the throb of his heart between my knees. "All horses can swim, can't they?"

He raised his tail, dumped a pile of manure. "Good," I said. "Don't need all that weight taking us down."

I nudged him, kissed and chucked when he hesitated to step in above his knees. I felt the moment his hooves left bottom, that second our anchor gave way and we were moving with the water, his strong legs working their rhythmic march against the current. I let my body float up, my fingers woven with leather and mane.

I heard the horse's hard breathing, my own tight respirations, and the rush of water all around us. I could see nothing but black, the crest of waves rising and falling, the pinpoint flash of car lights in the distance. We were washing downstream, the palomino's tread no match for the river's swiftness. But it was late summer and both banks had shallowed out toward center. "We'll make it," I whispered. "This is the worst of it. Just a few more yards."

But how could I tell? In the dark, I had lost my sense of direction, no longer knew how far we'd swung off course, how wide our crossing. "You can smell it, right? You'll get us there." I bobbed under, came back up, felt my fingers numbing, the cold working up my wrists. I worried that the air, still vaporous with smoke, might foul the horse's senses. Or maybe my own breath, sharp with vinegar. "Keep your head," I said, to the horse and myself. "Steady."

The gelding snorted water, and I could feel his body lose its easy gait and begin to labor. I remembered the story Irene had told me about the Horse Latitudes, how an ancient ship had become caught in the doldrums, its sails useless without wind, how the captain had called for all the portaled horses to be brought forward, roped, and whipped overboard, where their churning legs were caught by the lesser currents and they began to swim, to pull the great ship forward. When the ship's sails filled with a new breeze, the horses were cut loose, still swimming the widening wake, watching, calling as the only world they knew crested and disappeared from the horizon.

"Come on," I said. Then louder, "Come on!" They'd find us, horse and rider, still entwined, floating near the mill pond, just as they had Laurette. And maybe this was how it happened for her, not a decision but a chance, a way to risk something, not knowing the end. I imagined her with her arms raised above her head, hands overlapped, the strong push off rock, the slip into water, a knife through butter.

The horse went under, fought its way back, grunting with the effort. I surfaced, let my body float out like a pennant. My head thrummed. The second time the horse went under, I thought to let go, but my fingers were numb. I flapped my arms to free myself from the knot of hair and reins, my lungs near bursting. But then the horse came up under me, stepped onto shore, stood trembling.

I slid to the ground, stumbled, went down in a heap. The gelding coughed, blew a fine spray of snot across my back. "My fault," I said, catching my breath. "You might want to go ahead and step on me." His nose nudged my arm. "Carrots," I said. "Tomorrow. Lots of carrots."

The sand in the crack of my ass drove me to stand, and it was only then that I realized what I'd done—left my clothes and the saddle on the bank a quarter-mile away. I didn't dare risk the return swim. The bridge upriver floated luminescent, but it would take too long to walk our way over and back.

"Well," I said to the horse. "Guess we took a shortcut."

I was grateful for the late hour, the cover of darkness, the minimal traffic. Each time a car approached, I turned the horse up the bank, into the field, behind a small clump of willow. My bare thighs were chafed, my crotch galled by the time we reached Lapwai.

I considered Irene's reaction should I show up on her doorstep naked. The offering I brought to her was serious, and I wanted nothing to compromise my ability to convince her of the truth. I thought of clothes, and I thought of Aunt Esther.

Esther's house was dark. I circled around back, ground-tied the gelding, figuring he was as loath to move as I was. The door wasn't locked.

"Aunt Esther," I whispered as loudly as I dared. Nothing except a few nervous clucks from the henhouse. I stepped into the kitchen, my way made a little easier by the neighboring yard light. I snatched a tea towel from the sink, held it in front of me like a matador's cape.

"Esther!" Creak of bedsprings. "It's Buddy."

"Buddy?" A light came on down the hall. I positioned myself behind a chair.

"Wait! I need some clothes."

There was a momentary pause. "Again?"

"Lost them at the river."

"Pants? Shirt? What?"

"All. Some shoes, too, if you got them."

I listened to her mutter, open and close drawers. "I ain't got no men's underwear. Threw 'em all away. Some things not worth getting sentimental over."

"That's okay. Pants are enough."

"About all I got. Next time, you'll be leaving out of here in bloomers and a skirt."

She squinted her way toward me, laid the clothes on the

table. In the half-light, she looked younger, almost pretty in her flowered robe and scuffs. The horse whinnied. "What's that?"

"That's my new horse. I'm bringing him to show Irene."

She hit the kitchen light before I could dodge for better cover. "You rode over here naked?"

"Not on purpose." I hunched over the towel, gathered the clothes. "I'll just go on outside. I'll get these back to you."

Her eyes looked past me, and surprise crossed her face. She pointed, held her hand to her mouth. "Oh my gosh!"

I spun around, saw nothing.

"Gotcha!" she said, her guffaw so loud I figured the neighbors would all be knocking in to join the fun.

I clapped a hand across my bottom, then dropped the clothes. "Okay," I said, and raised my hands in the air. "This is it. Everything. Here's Buddy naked." I turned two circles. "Now can I dress in peace?"

"No one's keeping you from it." She folded her arms, worked her tongue around the edges of her teeth. "I'd get some balm on that rash, I was you."

I gathered her husband's old work shirt and pants, smelled the camphoric odor of cedar, wondered if she missed this about him, the sight of his nakedness.

"You want to stay for some hot chocolate?" She swept a finger toward me. "You can get decent first."

"What time is it?"

"Half past ten, I'd guess."

I stepped into the pants, shucked the material away from my balls, buttoned the shirt. "I meant to ask about shoes."

"You asked. Don't got none."

"Can I borrow a comb?"

"Bathroom's down the hall. Use what you find."

Mentholatum and talcum: two smells I recognized. And something else, like cut roses left too long in the vase. There was little space between the toilet, the sink, and the tub. My knees knocked porcelain. I stooped to the mirror, used a blue rattail comb to smooth my damp hair. The shirt was the color of mustard, a miniature black-and-white crest sewn on one pocket. The navy blue pants drooped in the crotch. "Look like I'd sell snake oil," I said to the room. I remembered to put down the seat and flush, wash my hands in case she was listening. Just as I was ready to open the door, I spied the green tin of Bag Balm, dipped two fingers. The ointment caused the pants to stick, but it eased the burn.

When I came back into the kitchen, she was heating milk, a plate of oatmeal cookies on the table. "I tied your horse," she said. "Looks like he could use a good curry."

"Just got him today. There's a lot of things he needs." I sat, helped myself to a cookie, something to quiet the vinegar and onions.

"Don't see many palominos around here."

"Got him from an old woman past The Stables."

"Mrs. Blood. Thought that horse looked familiar. Figured you'd stole him." She set down two steaming mugs, opened the freezer, spooned a dollop of vanilla ice cream into each.

"Made a deal. Her name's Blood?" I bobbed the ice cream with a spoon.

"Mrs. Thad Blood. She tell you how her husband died?"

I shook my head.

"Riding that very horse in the canyon. Trail gave way and the horse went down, landed on top of him. Drove the saddlehorn right in underneath his ribs. Gutted him like a fish."

I slurped a spoonful of vanilla. "Wasn't the horse's fault."

"Didn't say it was. No one shot the horse, else you wouldn't have him right now. Just telling you how it happened, that's all."

"What about the Celery King? How'd he die?"

She blew across the top of her mug, took a hot sip, looked out the dark window as though she meant to see something. "About as hard, I guess. When the farm went down, he had to take a job at the mill." She inhaled deeply, stirred a finger through the cocoa, licked it clean. "Worked pulling green chain, just like all new men. But he was too old for that kind of labor. They should have put him on inspection." Her eyebrows knitted, and I saw an anger rekindle. "He'd come home so tired I'd have to undress him, help him into bed. I think that's the reason . . ." She hesitated. ". . . that's the reason he fell. Got dragged by the conveyor. Wasn't much left to bury. Funeral man said to burn him, and that's what I did." She pointed to a small metal box on top of the refrigerator. "Listens to the news with me every night."

"That's awful." I didn't know if I meant the story or the ashes or both.

"I got a settlement. Enough to pay what we owed the bank. Priest said the Lord would provide, but since Lou hadn't been to confession for years, the church wouldn't guarantee a single blessing." She leaned her elbows on the table, sighed. "Tribal elders came and performed a ceremony over him. That helped. I haven't been to Mass since."

I eyed the metal box, wondered what it weighed. "Irene says everybody should be cremated. Takes up less room."

Esther laughed, then grew serious again. "Danny said the same. Too much prime real estate going to graveyards."

"What was he like?"

"Danny? Well, he was a lot like his sister, I'd say. Real hand-some boy. Smart as a whip. And stubborn as a mule, just like Irene. He'd have done anything for that girl."

She broke a cookie, dipped it in her cocoa.

"He wasn't perfect. Drank too much. Too many women. But he had a good heart. He looked after me as long as he could." She cupped her chin in one hand. "You're just as headstrong as them two. Bent on making your own way." The edges of her eyes soft-ened. "He'd have liked it that you care so much for Irene. He'd have seen right away that it was genuine."

"He'd probably have beat the snot out of me."

Esther nodded, smiling. "He'd have done that first. Then made friends."

"You think I'm too young for Irene?" I heard the gelding cough, the thunk of a hoof hitting dirt.

"Sure I do. You're too young, she's too old. But I learned a long time ago"—she rose, gathered the cups and spoons—"that I don't make the rules. And neither does anyone else. Some people only think they do." She wiped her hands on the towel I'd aban-doned. "There's always consequences, sometimes just for being alive."

"You don't believe you can buy good with good?"

"I think you can be good all your life and reap only sorrow. I think you can be the worst man ever lived and be filthy with money and luck."

"What about heaven?"

"Don't believe in it."

"Hell?"

"That neither."

"What keeps you from doing evil, then?"

Esther set her hands on her hips. "Why is it you think that people are only kept good by the threat of burning in hell? Seems to me, the chances of staying good are just as likely as the chances of going bad. Fifty-fifty, maybe. It all evens out across a billion or so lives." She dropped a cookie in my shirt pocket. "Seems to me, good for the sake of good is a lot more holy than good for the sake of escaping punishment."

"I'm going to ask Irene to marry me."

Esther tipped back her head to see me better. "Marry you."

"You think she will?"

She pressed crumbs from the table, licked her finger. "Why marry? Why not just keep things the way they are?"

"It just doesn't seem like I'm doing right by her. I want to make it honest."

"Got a ring?"

"Got a horse."

She brushed her hands together. "Hang on a minute." She disappeared down the hall, came back carrying a candy box. When she opened the lid, I caught a faint whiff of cherry cordials, saw the glint of glass and gold, and then she was holding up a thin band with three diamonds, the center one the largest, set high. "This was her mother's, given by the man who was their true daddy." She held it out to me. "I wouldn't put it in my pocket if I was you. Can't keep your clothes found long enough."

I tested the ring on my little finger, snugged it over the top to the first knuckle. "I won't lose it," I said. "I promise." I looked at the old woman, her dark eyes both sad and pleased. "I'm not sure how to say thanks."

"You just did. Now get on. You and that horse are going to have the neighborhood woke up." She shooed me out the door.

I led the gelding to the porch.

"You're cheating," she said.

"Getting old, I guess." I stepped up, gave a jump, straddled the broad back. The horse lifted his head to the smell of oatmeal.

"Here." She palmed a cookie beneath his nose.

"Shouldn't let him eat with the bit."

"Tell him that." She smiled, waved me off, closed the door.

I lifted my hand, licked the diamonds, rubbed them against the soft shirt. I couldn't believe that what she'd said about right and wrong was true. I'd made the decision not to steal Harvey's fifty from underneath the till, and now I had a ring and the horse. I adjusted myself, trying to ease the chafe. "If we keep doing good," I said, "my boots and your saddle should still be there to-morrow." The thought brought back the death of Thad Blood, and I wondered if it was the same saddle, the gore washed clean by a kind friend or the widow, or simply saturated with dust, the stain absorbed. I wondered what he had done to deserve such a fate, but then I remembered my mother, good all her life, taking all the bad my father could hand her. "Maybe Aunt Esther's right," I told the horse. "But tonight, I just can't think so." He was tired, ready for a roll and a night's sleep, and I had to keep my heels to him. "Hard day, huh, fella?" His head had dropped, his eyes nearly closed. "I'll make it up to you. Molasses. Sugar cubes." I leaned close to one ear, crooned, "Watermelon."

A half-moon had ascended above the trees as I turned the palomino down the lane to Irene's cabin. Any tiredness I felt had been replaced by a trill of excitement that made me lightheaded. I wanted to whistle, dance. "Better than whiskey," I counseled the sagging head. "But you probably don't remember all you knew about love." Silence. "Out there with all them pretty mares, one for each day of the week." I thought I could feel the shoulders slump further. "But now you've got the life. You'll see. We'll have some good times together. I'll get you another goat, or maybe a steer. You two can commiserate."

No lights from the little house. I led the horse to a cottonwood. "This won't take long," I said. He closed his eyes, grimaced an oat from beneath his tongue.

The ring didn't come off easy. I sucked my finger, tasting metal and the leftover sweetness of chocolate. It would be safe in my pocket for a few minutes, and then it would be on her finger.

"Irene?" I whispered at the door. "It's me."

A small light flickered at a corner of the window. I started to lift the latch, then stopped, caught by the sound of voices. I pressed my ear to the door. A woman's voice, and then a man's. The rhythmic rub of metal, the thump of wood.

I backed up three steps, kicked as hard as I could with my bare heel. The old latch gave without resistance. Candlelight showed me all that I needed to know: Wolfchild holding himself above Irene, his long hair lank with sweat, Irene gripping his shoulders, her eyes on mine full of a fierce wildness—not fear, not even regret, but a terrible intensity that caused me to stop dead, forget my fists.

The candle guttered in the silence. I pulled out the ring, thought to throw it at them as hard as I could, but placed it instead on the table with exaggerated care.

"Your mother's," I said. "She'd have wanted you to have it."

Once I'd taken my eyes off them, I couldn't look again.

Maybe it was the coward in me. Maybe it was some last remnant of modesty. Maybe it was a grief so great I'd never lift my face again.

I raised my arms as though to fly, let them drop, walked out, closed the door behind me.

"Taught me well," I said as I reined the horse around, pointed him toward town. "She taught me well."

CHAPTER EIGHTEEN

That night, the fires that had burned deep in the forests receded, stifled by the cool after sundown and a light morning dew. But by noon, the temperature had risen to one hundred and five, the ground moisture evaporating to a fugitive mist. The smaller fires spread, joined boundaries, converged on the isolated logging towns, sounding an alarm three states wide. The greasy wind carried with it the remnants of giant ponderosa, blackened threads of alfalfa, cinders still sparking that bred new fires miles from the original blaze. Loggers and millworkers were pressed into service to dig lines, cut breaks, set the backfires meant to check the confluence of flames.

"We should all be out there," Spud said. "Every man who can swing an axe."

"Shit. They'd be carrying me and you out on their backs."

Harvey clicked off the radio he'd hauled in from the back room, niched between the vermouth and the Rose's lime.

"It's like a war. Can't believe how many boys we've lost." Spud damped his cigarette. "Got to wonder if it's worth it."

I'd heard the numbers, too: more than a dozen dead, most from a single unit of smokejumpers. But the dead meant little to me. I was deaf to any grief but my own.

"Fire's a hell of an enemy." Harvey poked my arm, motioned toward Lee, who slouched over his red beer, nursing a hangover and favoring the yellowjacket sting to the inside of his thigh. "You two thought about volunteering?" Harvey continued. "Load you down like pack mules, legs you got. Probably earn some good money."

"We're leaving for L.A. in the morning." My statement of the obvious was meant only to take up space, put some distance between me and Harvey. As far as I was concerned, it could all burn.

"That's right, Harvey. We need to think about good things here. Might be the last time we see these boys." Spud raised his rum. "Here's to the Palomino Club—those dirty sons of bitches."

"I'll drink to the boys here, but not to that bastard Raimey." Harvey squinted one eye, pointed a finger at Lee. "You watch him."

Lee raised his chin enough to take a swig. "I ain't drinking to nothing but going back to bed."

"Who'd you top last night, anyway?" Harvey asked.

"Nobody. That's the problem." Lee hazarded another sip, worked himself up to his elbows.

"Shit. You need a steady gal, like Buddy here. Although from the looks of that mug, he might have got denied last night hisself."

Lee's hangover was nothing compared with the anguish that had kept me awake, kept my head and stomach swirling. I'd risen at dawn to take the horse some celery from Harvey's bin, fill a bucket with fresh water. The gelding had nickered when he heard the door open, still remembering my promise of better things. We'd made the trip back to the river, found the saddle and clothes just where we'd left them. But I couldn't see it as luck. Nothing seemed like it could ever be good again.

Spud licked the last of the rum. "We ready for tonight?"

"Got extra everything," Harvey said. "Might use another case of Ten High. You know they'll be drinking their good-byes to this bunch."

"Call Beverly?"

"Yup. She's willing to work till close. That'll give us four. Figure if things get too crazy, you can give me a hand behind the bar." Harvey surveyed the shelves. "Think we'll need extra ginger ale?" He looked my way.

"Don't think I'll be around tonight."

Spud and Harvey exchanged looks. Spud leaned back a little, tapped his glass. "It's your going-away party, Bud. Can't miss your own party."

"I ain't the one they're wanting to see."

The door swung open, a wedge of hot light we shielded our eyes against. Lee groaned.

"It's the law!" Harvey held up his hands. "I give up! Don't shoot!"

Westin peeled off his hat, wiped his forehead. "You boys getting kind of a late start today, ain't you? Half past noon."

"Well now," Harvey protested, "Lee here's just getting primed. And Buddy"—he patted my arm—"you know he's still too tender an age. Spud's holding his own, and I got work to do. And here you are in your civvies. What's the occasion?"

Westin straddled the stool next to mine. "Got two days off. Figure one for pleasure, one for pain."

"What's your pleasure?" Harvey slapped down a napkin.

"Whiskey soda. Lots of ice."

"Anybody else, while I'm pouring? Lee? You ready for something more manly?"

"Another beer first. Lay off the red."

Spud tapped his glass. "One more, then I got to make a money run." He turned to face Westin. "Bankers. Ought to be a law."

"Jail's full as is." The sheriff swirled his ice. "Picked up Gaylord's boy last night for pissing on Mrs. Martin's rosebushes again."

"Boy ain't right, is he?" Spud speared a brace of green olives with a toothpick.

"Nope. Still, can't be wagging his dick around. Damn roses are almost dead."

"At least they're getting some water. Any of your boys on the fires?"

"Not mine. They called up some recruits, I hear. Airport's hopping. Jess Dyer couldn't be happier."

Spud went for a pickled onion. "Jess Dyer thinks the sun rises and sets by how many planes he can flag in. Guess that's why he manages an airport and I'm stuck here with this crew." He followed the onion with two cherries. "Don't take much to make Jess happy. Ever seen his wife? Face like a bulldog. Scare me to go home."

"You going to eat every garnish I got?" Harvey swatted at Spud's hand. "Get out of there. You're worse than Buddy. Bunch of damned rabbits."

"I'm ready, Harv." Lee pushed away his empty beer glass, attempted a stretch. "Remind me to stay away from gin. Stay with the colored stuff." He yawned, winced, opened one eye. "You seen Buddy's new horse, Sheriff? Bought him off the old lady down the road."

Westin tamped a cigarette against the counter. "Horse, huh?"

"Pretty little gelding." Lee contemplated the shot Harvey set before him. "Tell the sheriff here what you had to do to get him, Buddy. Hard work." He managed a wink toward Harvey.

"That right?" Westin turned his head my way. The red indentation left by his hatband circled his scalp, shone through the gloss of thin hair.

I didn't feel like talking, but my sulk would only make things harder for me. I wanted to work my way out of the conversation, make as common an exit as possible. "I'll be taking the horse back this afternoon," I said. "I've decided to go to California with Lee."

Lee belched. "Probably find a way to trailer him down there. Old lady might figure the work you put in on that goat was enough. Might have enough time this afternoon to catch you some cats."

"Cats?" Westin wasn't really interested, only being polite. He kept looking toward the door as though he expected someone.

"This woman had a billy goat. Wanted him cut. That was the deal. That and about a dozen tomcats prowling the place." Lee was warming to the whiskey, making friends again. "I happened by just about the time the goat was getting the better of him." He chuckled. "Hard to say who was roping who."

Harvey fluffed his belly. "Spud here's the one to do the roping. Bet you still can swing a lasso, can't you, Spud?"

"Ain't had a rope in my hands since I was a kid. No desire to, neither." He backed off his stool, straightened his pants. "Hate to say it, but I got to go to work."

"Hold a minute, Spud." Westin hadn't touched the drink to

his mouth. "I've got some talking I need to do. Might be best if you stay."

Spud stood deflated, arms to his sides. "What now?"

"Nothing about you or this place. No trouble."

Spud's shoulders came up a little. He rubbed a hand above his belt buckle, soothing. "Harvey, get me a spoonful of bitters." He hiccuped. "Better back it up with some soda."

"I can tell you I ain't in dutch. Never left this place last night. Come to wish I had." Lee cleared the rasp from his throat.

"I'm not here to get nobody. I just got some information to give. Felt like you people needed to hear before the newspapers start tearing it up." He hiked one elbow on the bar. "About Mrs. Fletcher. About Laurette."

I didn't dare look at Lee.

"Buddy here woke up one morning thinking he was the Good Samaritan," Harvey said. "Having that Indian loose hasn't come to more trouble, has it?" He handed Spud the bitters and soda.

Westin shook his head. "Only trouble's been from a couple of yay-hoos down at the Pair-A-Dice. They got a few others riled up last night, thought they'd go get Wolfchild. Guess someone called their wives. Not much of an uprising. This town's always been more bark than bite." Westin sighed. "One thing to be glad for, I reckon. But Buddy here will be getting some of his money back. I've already seen to it." He shuttered one eye. "We've got reason to believe that Wolfchild is innocent."

"Give me a rum, Harvey. Bitters aren't working." Spud ran a finger across his lips. "Thought he confessed."

"Never confessed to nothing but love." Westin wiped sweat from each eyebrow.

"What's he saying?" asked Harvey.

"Ain't him. It's what somebody else is saying." Westin let his gaze fall on me. "This might be hard for you to hear, son."

I shrugged, blinked slowly.

"It's the redheaded gal. Irene Sullivan."

My head jerked up. It was the first time I'd ever heard her last name, strange, unfamiliar. Suddenly, she was no one I ever knew.

"Says she was with Wolfchild the night of Laurette's disappearance. Came in this morning, filed a statement." Westin reached his freckled hand inside his pocket, pulled out a folded paper, handed it to Lee.

"What's this?" Lee lipped his cigarette, unfolded the document.

"Believe that's the title to your Chevy. Suspect you'll be wanting to use it to get to L.A."

Lee's mouth slacked open. He looked at me. "Why, you little bastard."

Harvey slapped his hands down between us. "There's more important things here. Save it."

"We told him, Harv. We told him. Wouldn't listen." Lee refolded the paper, slipped it in his hip pocket. "Someone should run her right out of here."

Harvey poured, sat the bottle down. "You do your own refilling. Hold your tongue."

I felt the pity falling on my shoulders, the way Spud and Harvey and even Westin wanted to shield me from my own foolishness. I reached too hard, sent the ginger ale across the counter.

"Guess this means you'll be wanting something else." Harvey mopped at the spill. "Maybe a Jack. Maybe a double." The whiskey appeared before me. I drank it in one easy motion.

"He's entitled," Spud told Westin. The sheriff grunted. Spud went on. "What if she's lying?"

"Hell, Spud," Lee said. "We all knew she was just using Buddy. God knows who else she's been messing around with. Woman like that will take any man she can get her hands on, white or not. That's how she gets her kicks. Probably's got a string of suckers from Texas to the Canadian line."

Westin ignored Lee. "Wolfchild won't say one way or the other. Just sits there like he's deaf and dumb. Her aunt came in, gave a statement backing Miss Sullivan. Seems like a pretty trustworthy old gal. Widow of a man used to farm celery above the river." Westin tilted his head toward me. "Miss Sullivan claims you knew about this, Buddy. That true?"

I stared at the round of my empty shotglass.

"Son, I know this ain't easy, but you got a duty here."

I looked at Lee, who met my eyes. Both of us, I thought, cowards and beggars. "She told me."

"Told you what?"

"Told me she'd been with Wolfchild."

"But you never saw them together?"

I shrugged.

"When?"

I closed my eyes, opened them slowly. "Last night."

Lee whistled. Harvey nailed him with a glance.

"You sure it was Wolfchild?" Westin peered at me intently.

"I'm sure." I felt the saliva pool behind my teeth.

"But you didn't see Miss Sullivan the night of the disappearance?"

I shook my head, swallowed. "Said she passed Wolfchild walking home, gave him a ride."

Lee snorted. "Some ride."

"Might want to pour him another," Westin told Harvey.

"There's more." He smoothed his napkin, took a slow first swig of his own drink, waited.

"Jesus God," Lee said. "You can get her right here for contributing to the delinquency of a minor. Buddy's too young to know any better."

I said it to myself three or four times, *I don't care.* I didn't hate Lee for what he was saying. I didn't hate Westin for bringing the news this way. I didn't hate Irene or Wolfchild, any more than I hated my father and the death he had brought on himself and my mother. What good would it do? I'd gotten weak, let Irene open me up, let the feelings come back in. My fault. No one else's.

"What more?" Spud retook his seat.

"I got on the line to Kentucky. Just a hunch." Westin pinched the pleat of his hat.

I kept my eyes on the bottles behind Harvey's head. I'd settled into sipping my whiskey, smoking. One sip, one drag. It kept things even.

"What'd she do?" Lee's voice was as honest as the moon. The four men around me stood frozen in that moment, even as I clicked my glass down, inhaled.

"She and her brother. Weren't more than thirteen, fourteen years old. Killed their old man. Stabbed him to death, then buried the body in the barn. Guess the dogs dug him up a few days later. By then, they'd both disappeared."

There was a mirror behind the bottles, I saw now. It had been there all along, but I'd forgotten to look at myself, those parts of my face framed by Jim Beam and Wild Turkey, or, if I moved just to the right, brandy and Bristol Cream. The Galliano cast a yellow pall, but if I ducked half an inch, the curaçao reflected blue, the sloe gin red.

"Buddy? You okay?" Harvey moved in front of me.

I nodded, canted my head to see around his bulk. Even the labels held a special fascination: eagles and horses, crests and medallions, wax seals.

Spud put one hand on my shoulder but directed his question to Westin. "Where is she?"

"Don't really matter. No charges were ever filed. Both were juveniles. Guess the old man was one mean SOB. Sounds like wasn't nobody sorry to see him gone." The sheriff pulled a handkerchief from his back pocket, wiped his upper lip.

"What about Wolfchild?"

"Be hard to hold him now."

"Got any more you need from Buddy?" Spud's fingers tensed against my collarbone, relaxed.

Westin shook his head. "Just got to let us know anything comes your way." He leaned in over his drink, worked it around in circles. "Still got things to figure. Guess you knew Mrs. Fletcher was expecting."

I let my eyes focus on the calendar tacked just to the right of the mirror: an airbrushed painting of a leggy young woman walking a miscreant poodle, the leash wrapped tightly around her thighs and calves, a look of helplessness on her face as the wind caught the skirt of her dress, exposing her lace panties.

"Dean said right up front it couldn't be his. Poor bastard." Westin sat back, adjusted his belt, one hand, out of habit, reaching to touch the gun that wasn't there. "Gives us reason to wonder. Maybe the man whose child it was didn't want no one knowing."

Harvey stroked the soft folds beneath his chin. "Maybe she went up to Maggie's Bend to have it taken care of. They do that up there."

Westin shrugged. "Can't really say."

"You know they do, Grady. Maybe she went up there and something went wrong. Maybe she died and they tried to dump the body."

"Baby was still in her." Westin scratched at the faint indentation of his hat line. "Something goes wrong, it's usually after."

"Truth is," Spud said, "I can't imagine Laurette doing any of this. Never saw her making eyes or sneaking off after hours. Never saw her even talk to other men."

Lee's head came up. "Maybe we're looking too hard. Answer may be plain as day." He turned to face us, his eyes shining with inspiration. "Now, we all know Dean had been sobered up awhile. And maybe that's what did it. When all the liquor left him, everything started working again. That baby was *his*."

Harvey lifted his shoulders. "You don't think it was Dean killed her, do you?"

"No, no. Now, here's what I think." Lee earnestly gathered himself closer to the counter. "I think that she was afraid Dean wouldn't believe her. Maybe she was so sure he'd kill her, she killed herself."

Spud looked at Westin. "You must have a take on this, Grady. What's your bid?"

Westin hacked into his handkerchief, blew his nose. "Only two things I know for sure: she's dead, and she was going to have some man's child." He folded the square of red cloth. "I was kind of hoping this boy here might know more. Seems he's been on the inside of some things."

I finished my shot, stepped backward off the stool. "I've given all I know."

I was on my way to the door when Floyd walked in. I'd seen little of him since Laurette's death. He came each night at the appointed time, took his seat at the steel, played without inspiration or comment, left the minute the last set was over. He'd never been a talkative man, seldom drew attention to himself, but his silence had become more and more glum, his few words little more than mumbled hellos and good-byes. He stopped when he saw the sheriff, kept his hands in his pockets, even as the ash of his cigarette lengthened and dropped to the floor.

Spud motioned him to an empty stool, pushed an ashtray his way. "Grady's giving us news about Laurette."

Floyd glanced quickly around. He did not want to look me in the eye but kept shifting his gaze, lips clamped tight. There was an anger inside him, I could see now, something like what I was feeling.

"Sheriff's got some questions," Harvey said. "Maybe you can help him out."

Floyd's eyes darted to Westin, then away. He clinched the material of his pants pockets, bunching the legs into wrinkles. "Already told what I know."

"Maybe that's true," I said, then turned and looked at Lee. "Maybe it ain't."

Floyd licked his lips. "I came to get my paycheck."

Spud nodded. "I'm just headed to the bank. Hang around. Won't take me ten minutes." He looked at Westin. "Keep me posted, will you? Like to see some rest come to this." He disappeared down the hall, and we heard the slap of the back door.

"What's in this, Buddy? You think Floyd's got something he needs to tell?"

Before I could answer, Lee slapped the counter. "Christ, Grady. You've wrung every one of us dry. Floyd was with Dean that whole night, remember?" He pushed away from the bar, motioned to Floyd. "Hey, let's practice a little while you're here. Grady can listen for free. Might be one of the last times he sees us this side of L.A."

"You going, then, Floyd?" Westin asked.

Floyd shrugged.

"Hell," Lee said. "Floyd's the best steel player around. He'll show them city slickers how it's done."

Lee was working now, clapping Floyd's shoulder, softening him. "We're going to make us some bucks, ain't we, Floyd? Maybe get famous enough to go to Nashville. Wouldn't that be something? Money, pretty girls, hearing our songs on the radio." He gave Floyd's shoulder a squeeze. "But I can't do it without this guy here. He's the one brings the feeling into the song. Sometimes just listening makes me want to cry."

I watched Floyd follow my brother up the steps to the stage. Without Lee, Floyd would be stuck in Snake Junction, maybe lose his place in the band. He wouldn't last a week on the green chain, pulling lumber. Without the hours to sing away his blues, he'd end up like Dean, drunk, then dead.

I nodded my good-byes, stepped out the back door before they could protest, lidded my eyes against the shatter of sunlight. The horse whinnied from his place beneath the tree, switched his tail.

"Left the bridle and saddle inside," I said, as though he'd asked. "Don't have any desire to go back in, neither."

Earlier that morning, I'd found a length of marine rope in the storeroom, fashioned a crude hackamore. I unknotted the lead, looped it in one hand, grabbed a hank of mane. "Hold, now." I took two quick steps and jumped, throwing one leg up, hooking my heel over his backbone. I gigged, pulled, and grunted, then slid back to the ground. The horse snorted, bent to snatch a last mouthful of grass. I hiked my pant leg higher. "Whoa. Just whoa." The second time, I got my knee over, pulled myself to a sit. I was wet with sweat. "Let's go see your old friend."

A light wind came up the canyon, bringing with it the smoke, the pewter sky. I ducked as we passed beneath the thorny limbs of black locust, and I remembered their springtime smell, sweet as honeysuckle, the white blossoms dark with bees.

Mrs. Blood was out back, hoeing her garden.

"You come to do the cats?" She wore men's boots without laces, tongues panting out, a stained cobbler's apron, a faded sunbonnet.

"I came to see if we can renegotiate." I pulled a cherry tomato from a vine, felt it burst sweet and warm against the roof of my mouth.

"There ain't nothing wrong with that horse." She worked the dirt around the corn, quick cuts with the whetted blade.

"No. I just got to leave town and wondered if I could send you the rest of the money when I get settled."

She straightened, planted the hoe down hard with one hand, rested the other on her hip. "You ain't going to finish your end of the bargain."

"It's either send you the money later, or give you the horse back now. Sure like to keep him, though."

She looked to where the horse stood, his eyes closed, head dropped in a snooze. "You feeding him good?"

"Mostly grass. Few carrots. Plan to get him some grain."

"Where's his tack?" She raised one hand to her forehead, squinted.

"Like to ride bareback sometimes."

"Where you going?"

"Thought I might try and find work in Missoula. Maybe fight some fires."

"Your brother?" Her shaded eyes looked beyond the horse to the horizon.

"He's headed to California. Don't think I'd like it there."

"Ever seen the ocean?" She bent to her hoe, scraped away weeds, mounded catch basins around the base of the pepper plants.

"Never have."

"Don't look much different from the sky." She waved her hand in front of her face. "Hotter than hell out here. You want to come in for some iced tea?"

"Best I take off pretty soon."

"You expecting to ride that horse all the way to Montana?"

"Thought I'd go up on the Musselshell, cut over." Irene had shown me the old Nez Perce trail that followed the Clearwater before ascending to high prairies and mountains. I swallowed hard with the memory, the way she'd led me along the nearly invisible path, touching the trees scarred by starving travelers—peel trees, she'd called them, stripped down to the soft inner skin, the cambium the last stay against hunger.

"You in trouble?"

"No, ma'am." I shook my head. "Just needing new space, that's all."

"You're leaving the only family you got." She moved to the shade of the porch, sat on the step. "Something's caused that."

I looked upriver to The Stables, wondered what they were talking about now. Me, maybe. Irene. Laurette. The Yankees.

"You don't live in Lapwai." She smoothed a wiry fray of hair behind her ear.

"No, I don't. I've been staying at The Stables with my brother."

"You're ashamed of that," she said flatly.

"Guess I am."

Hummingbirds flitted through lilac. A tomcat skulked beneath, biding his time. "When Thad and me was first married," she said, "we lived for a year in the loft of a barn. Woke up every morning smelling like manure." She stroked a finger across her nose. "Thad was just back from the war, working as a hired hand. We didn't have nothin'. Every night, he'd step outside to smoke, then climb the ladder to bed. No matter how careful he was, I had nightmares about fire. Dreamed that the horses were screaming, flames eating up the ladder. Horrible way to die, fire. Think I'd rather drown. You got an extra cigarette?"

I struck my lighter, watched the way she sucked the smoke in, smiled. "Don't have the means to buy my own. Sure miss it."

I laid the pack beside her.

"Figure that'll buy you a horse?" She gave me a girl's grin.

"Maybe buy me some time."

"You got time. What you ain't got is money."

I reached in my pocket, pulled out the pawn ticket. "This is for a diamond ring. Worth twenty times as much as I got for it."

She waved me away, then snatched the stub. "You done a fine job with Billy. You get settled, you send me a hundred." She dusted her hands. "I won't hold my breath. What'd you decide to name him?"

"Haven't. Can't seem to find the right fit." We both considered the horse, so drowsy his nose brushed the ground.

"Might as well go by the name Thad gave him. Caruso."

"Caruso?"

"Yes, sir. Thad was a fool for opera. Sang me an aria every night." She chuckled, coughed, took another drag. "Enrico Caruso's the name of that horse. Called him Henry for short." She picked up the pack of cigarettes, tucked it in her apron. "Thad would have hated to find I'd had him cut. Had no use for geldings. I always figure that when I get to heaven, I'll just have to tell Thad I made Caruso a soprano." She stood, arched her back. "You go on. That horse is yours now. Looks like he knows it, too."

The gelding had raised his head when I'd said his name. He stood watching me, ears tented forward.

"Where'd you get that sorry hackamore?"

"Made it. Works."

"Wait here." She went in the house, came back after several minutes carrying a pair of saddlebags and a fine horsehair mecate. "Thad braided this himself. Not many know how these days." The bridle felt alive in my hands, supple and smooth. She hefted the saddlebags toward me. "Bread's pretty fresh. Can't say the same of the coffee."

"I appreciate it."

"It's hard going it alone." She looked at me out of the corner of her eye. "Guess that gal said no, huh?"

I shrugged, kept my eyes on the ground.

"Well, she missed out on a good thing." She set her hoe. "Better get on if you plan to make Montana anytime this year. Watch them fires. Hear there's some burning right along the state line."

"Yes, ma'am."

"Damned cats have been pissing on my peppers."

The gelding nosed the saddlebags as I removed the rope hackamore and slid the mecate over his ears. "Bet there's something in here for you," I said, hoisting the bags. I waved, but the woman, like the goat, had turned her back.

When I reached The Stables, all the cars were gone except Harvey's beater pickup, its wheel wells eaten with rust. I stole in the back door, gathered a few clothes, the saddle, the leather bridle. Everything else in that room belonged to someone else. Even the bed I called mine was on loan.

I reached beneath my pillow, pulled out the note Irene had left me, its ashy letters smudged and faded, carefully folded it into my pocket, remembering, as I did, the letter my mother had found in Lee's jacket, how tenderly she had put it back, as though she were removing and replacing his heart.

Lee's pants and shirt lay in a pile, shrouding his boots, and I thought to take them, care for them in a way Lee never would. I lifted the clothes, breathed in the faint odor of Old Spice, smoke, whiskey, so different from the child smells we'd shared beneath winter blankets. We'd needed each other differently then. Maybe, I thought, it wasn't comfort that had held him back all those years, but me. I licked my thumb, rubbed the toe of one boot, saw they'd need to be resoled soon, and hoped that Lee would notice, keep them solid on the bottom, supple on top, like a good horse that, tended well, would carry you many a mile.

I left the boots, walked from the room, feeling as I had when leaving the hospital, like someone had died. I missed Lee's hands on my shoulders, the bread he had fed me, the simple song he'd sung. I stopped by the bathroom, splashed my face, peered in the mirror. "Don't look no different," I said, though I wasn't so sure my hair hadn't darkened, my chin taken on a new sharpness. I thought of Wolfchild's braids, wondered what a woman felt with a man whose hair fell around her like a veil.

"Got to quit thinking," I said to the mirror, and then to the ceiling. "Got to get that stuff out of my head." I rolled the two Pendleton blankets—I'd send money to Spud when I got settled—tied them to the back of the saddle, pulled from one saddlebag an apple rubbed to a shine. I took a bite, palmed the fruit for the horse, who flared his nostrils and chewed with such pleasure that I felt my heart lift.

"Wish it was that easy for me," I said. I snugged the girth strap, checked his hooves for rocks, hoped we'd be into the mountains by nightfall. "Horse is better anyway," I said. "Four legs get you places four tires can't." I surveyed the hazy sky, the sun an orange disk I could look at without pain.

Just as I was mounting, Harvey came to the door, towel in hand.

"Figured," he said. "Could almost have told you."

I reined the horse into a circle, brought him around.

"You owe Spud a word of good-bye," he said.

"I'll let him know when I get to where I'm going. Just don't feel like talking to anyone about it right now."

Harvey wrung the rag, watched a few drops of water hit the dust. "Like squeezing a rain cloud around here." He scanned the horizon.

"Couldn't get much drier," I said.

"Could." He set his fists at his hips. "Plan to ride that horse down the road? People will think you're a cowboy or something."

"Maybe I am."

"Cowboy that's lost his herd."

"I'm just riding, that's all." I reached down, held out one hand. "You've been good to me, Harv. Don't think I don't appreciate it."

He gave a tight grip, held on. "You and Lee need to work this out between you. Ain't no sense you coming this far to go your separate ways."

"Lee's way ain't my way." I gave a final shake.

"What if Irene comes in? What do I tell her?"

I smoothed the palomino's mane. "Tell her I hope it all works out the way she wants it."

"Bullshit. You want her and that Indian to rot in hell."

"No. I don't. Like you said all along, I should have known better."

"Kid." Harvey caught the rein. "You're the last one should be leaving this place for what's happened. But maybe it's for the best. There's greener pastures."

"Guess I'll find out."

He stepped back. "Probably won't let on, but Lee's going to be pretty lonely without you."

"Lee's never alone."

"I didn't say alone. I said lonely."

I looked to the east, squinted to see the bridge, gave the horse some slack. "Take care of yourself, Harv."

"Watch those logging trucks. They'll blow you right off the road." Harvey followed me around front, stood on the steps. The last time I looked back, he was still there, arms crossed. I gave one final wave, settled down in the saddle. We were a mile away before I saw the fifty-dollar bill he'd tucked under the cinch. I stood in the stirrups, slipped it deep in my front jeans pocket with Irene's note, gave the horse his head, sure that he knew the way.

CHAPTER NINETEEN

Killdeer keened up around me, feigning injury. I guided the horse along the familiar trail, the asphalt on my left, the Clearwater on my right. I'd cross over the bridge at Spalding, take Highway 12 east, have a choice: fifty miles of narrow road or a fence ride across broken basalt before I could abandon the pavement and diagonal across softer ground.

"I believe we should stay to the highway," I counseled the horse. "Less chance of snakes."

I wished for a hat, pulled out my handkerchief and tied it pirate-like around my head. Already, my nose felt blistered, my lips dry. Although my face and neck were mostly healed of ivy, my crotch remained raw, and I shifted, adjusted. Cicadas whirred, invisible in the mat of bunchgrass and bull thistle. Along with the smoke came an incense of yarrow, dog fennel, mullein. A covey of chukar took up off the rimrock that bordered the highway's far side, set wing and sailed over my head, disappearing into scrub. "Had me a gun," I said, "we'd be eating roast partridge tonight instead of cold sandwiches." The gelding plodded, loaded down with heat, the sun reflecting off his flaxen neck. I had my knife, could set a trap for grouse, just like the hunters in Wolfchild's dream. I had matches, my lighter, and enough sense, I believed, to keep myself dry and fed if the weather held.

Each car and truck that passed stirred a dervish of dust. The gelding lowered his head, snorted. I resisted the urge to rub the grit from my eyes. Just before the bridge, I turned down the path leading to where the sweat house once stood. "You need a drink," I explained to the horse. I dismounted, let him step a few feet into the river. "No shortcut today. Sometimes the long way's better."

"That's a lot of truth." Wolfchild reclined in a basin of rock, naked except for his braids. I might have seen him had I been looking, or if he'd moved, or if I'd taken the time to search the bank as the horse had done before stepping into the open, but I'd thought the palomino's lifted head and widened nostrils meant only that he'd caught the smell of water.

"Hey," Wolfchild said. "I finished my dream."

I ignored his statement, pulled the gelding's head from the water, reached down one hand to splash my face and neck, trying to quiet the flutter in my chest.

"Want to hear it?"

I toed a stirrup, swung up. I hated his nakedness, the hair down his back, his casual slouch against the rock.

"Maybe it's a dream meant for you," he said.

"It's your dream," I said. "Not mine."

"Want to sweat?"

"There's no sweat house."

"Yeah."

I saw the way he looked to the blackened circle, as though he had just noticed. The gelding hoofed a rock, sniffed the wet sand beneath.

Wolfchild wove his fingers behind his head. "So these *nimíipuu* find this magpie . . ."

I reined the horse to face Wolfchild. "What makes you think I give a shit about your stinking dream?" My ears were hot, my scalp tingling. "Tell it to Irene. Maybe she's got reason to listen."

He looked at me with great pleasantness, and I wanted to murder him. The idea struck home, and I hauled off the horse, took one step, stood glaring. How could I fight a man wearing no clothes?

"We can sweat here," he said, patting the stones around him. "Hot enough without the fire. We'll jump in the river, then steam here on the rocks."

"Get your goddamn clothes on."

"It's no good wearing clothes."

I searched the nearby bushes, found his jeans, underwear, shirt, wadded them into a ball, threw as hard as I could. The clothing fell short, landed near his feet instead of hitting him in the face like I'd intended.

"Thanks," he said, and spread the clothes along the boulders.

"If I had a gun, I'd kill you."

He nodded. "Guess you ain't got a gun, then."

"I wish to God I did."

"Well, if these two *nimíipuu* had had a gun, they wouldn't have had to set this trap. Maybe this means something."

"You make me want to puke." I spat. It was true that what I

was feeling was a kind of nausea, a vertigo, his presence before me colliding with all the anger and grief I'd swallowed.

He smiled. "Sweating might help."

I closed the distance between us in a few strides. I fell on him, pounding, bellowing. He caught me by my wrists, rolled us both across the awful rocks and onto the sand. His weight surprised me, the solidness of his arms and legs.

I didn't care what was fair, what rules might be broken. All I wanted was to feel him give way beneath my hands, feel the collapse of bone, the spill of blood. I bit into the round of his shoulder, heard his grunt and held on, even as we wrestled our way to the river's edge and the water flooded my ears.

Wolfchild wedged one arm against my throat, pushed me away. I bounced along the slick rock bottom, caught a fist-sized stone in my right hand, swung it as hard as I could toward his ribs. But the current slowed my arm, the blow little more than a thump. Wolfchild stood, dragged me up by my hair. I boxed him alongside the head with my forearm. He staggered, never giving up his grip, and I heard a pop, felt a hank of hair tear loose.

"Goddamn Indian!" I screamed. "You're *scalping* me!"

We listed back from each other. I reached up, touched a bald knot starting to rise. He opened his fist, let the few strands fall to the water. I charged, grabbed for the black braids hanging across his chest. Again we went down, deeper this time. I held my breath, pulled against his weight, but the current was stronger, pushing us together, forcing us to swim. I came up for air, felt the tug of the undertow. I flailed wildly, windmilling my arms, scissoring my legs, my movements driving me deeper.

The cold blackness brought a moment of shocking clarity,

and I knew what I had to do. I quit fighting, went limp, let my feet play out in front of me, gave myself over to the incessant pull. I concentrated on holding my breath, suppressing the panicked urge to open my mouth, suck in, cry out. I was on my back, hands above my head, like a man already drowned.

Sun flitted for a moment, then turned to midnight. A rock raked my back; I hit another with my feet, pushed off and kept going. I counted like I knew what seconds of air I had left. At five, I felt a sudden heaviness, my feet sinking. I kicked twice, broke through into a shallow eddy.

I lay on the pebbled sand a long time, waiting for my heart to slow, my lungs to quit their frenzied gasping. When I could, I rose to one elbow, searched the bank upstream. I hadn't gone so far that I couldn't see the horse, hock high in the water, drinking his fill. But no sign of Wolfchild. I looked downstream, then to the highway above. I pushed myself upright, grabbed a nearby limb of willow, bent double and retched. When I straightened, I felt the throb along my spine. I reached back to find my shirt torn top to bottom, a raw gouge the length of my back.

"Not too bad," I comforted myself. "Just a scrape." I took a step, realized I'd lost boots and socks. I stared at my bare feet as if they were new to me, then inventoried the rough course ahead.

I stayed to the water's edge, bruising my heels and ankles. By the time I stood across from where the horse placidly grazed, I was wobbling with exhaustion.

"If you was Trigger," I called, "you'd swim over here and res-cue me." The gelding gave me a second's consideration, went back to his business. "Where's Wolfchild?" I hollered. No answer. I looked at my hand, found a single strand of black hair twined around three fingers. I held it up, let the breeze take it. "Wolfchild!" I called, then louder, "Wolfchild!"

I stepped in to my knees, wondering if I'd have the strength to swim back across, or if I'd be better off to walk the mile to the bridge and back up the other side. I stood shivering from something other than cold, knew I'd never make the mountains before dark, knew I couldn't leave without looking for Wolfchild, or at least telling somebody he might be drowned, that they might get out their poles and hooks and start searching the mill pond. I thought of Irene and felt a stab of shame. No one but his own people would care enough to blame me if Wolfchild was dead. No one but Irene.

Lee would help, I thought. If he knew where I was, he'd come, piggyback me across the rocks to his car, bring me around to gather the horse, judge whether or not I was strong enough to ride the palomino, or whether it was time for him to take the reins and give me the keys, send me home for a drink and bed while he whistled his way along the road, waving at passersby like he was Roy Rogers.

Or maybe I was wrong. Maybe too much had passed between us. Maybe the only thing that had held us together all along had been the suffering we shared. This grief was my own, more like sin than misfortune.

Rather than risk the river again, I began to make my slow way through the goatheads and stones, keeping a sharp eye out for poison ivy. The horse nickered, and I looked over to see Wolfchild, one hand on the gelding's shoulder.

"You okay?" he yelled.

"Thought you'd drowned." It took great effort to heave the words across the roar.

"Comin' back across?"

I shook my head. "Think I better walk it."

"I'll come and get you." He waded into the water, bent down, his hair shining black as mink.

"No!" I yelled, this weakness in front of my enemy making me want to cry. But he was already moving my way, his arms sweeping strong across the current. I stood still, too tired to care anymore. He came out only a few yards downstream, walked across the rock toward me without wincing.

"I sure as hell wish you'd put some clothes on."

He smiled. "I'm a man," he said, "like you. What does it matter?"

"It matters." I saw where my teeth had cut a jagged medallion in his shoulder, the blood still trickling. I licked my lips, swollen from being mashed against his skin.

"Come on," he said. "Hold on to my neck. I'll swim you across."

"I can swim, God damn it." I wiped my nose, resisted the overwhelming need I felt to let my legs fold beneath me.

"But I can swim better." He was earnest now, pointing toward the bridge. "I know this river. Used to dive from up there. Got caught in all the suck holes at least once."

The ribs of the bridge arched forty feet above its base. The climb alone would be enough to scare off most men.

"You try it with me sometime."

"Not today," I said.

He chuckled. "Irene"—he motioned with his chin. "She climbed highest of all."

I gazed at the span, imagined her young-girl's legs pushing her to the top.

"Never scared to jump. Made all us boys hate to see her coming. We knew we couldn't let her beat us."

I realized that Wolfchild understood my love for Irene—what we knew together, what we shared, like blood between us. "But she did," I said. "She beat you."

Wolfchild nodded. "We could climb as high, but none of us could fly the way she did." He scuffed a rock with the ball of his foot. "She had something she needed to let go of. Maybe, throwing herself out like that, she felt a little less afraid." He slapped his hands together. "You ready?"

I turned toward the river. "I don't need to hang on. I can make it."

Wolfchild considered. "Let's walk up a little. Less work." He picked our point, motioned me in.

I walked until my body could no longer resist the current's push, ducked my head, began swimming, keeping myself to slow, steady strokes, lifting my face only to breathe, not looking at how close or how far. I knew that Wolfchild had started in behind me, that he was keeping to my left, just a little downriver, that he was strong enough to catch me and pull me along should I fail. And I was grateful for this, the fight having bled something out of me, the river having taken even more.

It wasn't hard, this crossing, and my fingers scrabbled through sand before I knew how close I was. I climbed out, saw that I'd actually come in a few yards above the horse. Wolfchild stepped up beside me.

"Need a fire?"

"Maybe just a good hot rock."

"You'd feel better if you took off your clothes. Let me hang them to dry." He motioned me to sit where I'd first seen him lounging.

I pulled off my torn shirt, my jeans and underwear, handed them to Wolfchild, who wrung and shook them and spread them across the thick branches of a mountain ash. The water-smoothed basalt radiated heat, warming my back and legs, a comfort I could hardly absorb without moaning.

"You need a poultice for that." He pointed at my crotch. stepped to the river, came back working something between his hands. "Here," he said. "Slap it on."

I took the muddy pie he'd fashioned, shivered at its coolness against my genitals. The relief was immediate.

Wolfchild tied the horse to a high limb of cottonwood, rummaged in my saddlebags until he found a pack of cigarettes and matches, brought along the Thermos and a sandwich.

"Picnic," he said. He took half the sandwich, passed me the other. "Haven't had peanut butter and jelly for a long time." We ate, sucking the peanut butter from our teeth, shared a Thermos top of bitter coffee. Wolfchild lit two cigarettes, passed one to me.

"How long?" I asked. "You and Irene?"

"Since we was kids."

"Not how long you've known her. How long?"

He leaned forward, honed the ember of his cigarette against a piece of quartz. "How long's it been since you came in on us?"

"You mean last night?"

He looked surprised. "That all? Jesus, seems like it's been longer."

"What are you saying?" I sat up.

"There was these *nimíipuu* caught a magpie . . ."

"God damn it! Don't do that to me. Just tell me."

"I'm trying, but you won't let me. They caught a magpie, and when they asked the magpie why he couldn't resist the corn, he said because those three kernels were made more desirable by their rarity. You see"—Wolfchild opened his hands on his knees—"the magpie couldn't see the corn in the field. But these three kernels"—he pointed an imaginary triangle—"they shone like gold."

I lay back, draped my eyes with one arm, too tired to argue. "I still don't know what in the hell you're talking about."

"Yeah," Wolfchild said. "But it sounds good, don't it?"

I peeked out. "You mean you don't know what it means, neither?"

He shook his head. "There's something in it, though."

"What'd they do, then? The men, I mean."

"Took him home and ate him."

"Magpie?"

"Sure. You never eat magpie?"

I covered my eyes. "Hope I never have to."

"Crow?"

"Is this a joke?"

"No joke. Muskrat?"

"Squirrel."

"Rattlesnake?"

"Pig's feet."

"Hell, I've eaten pig's feet."

I took a long drag of smoke. *"Penne all'arrabbiata."*

"What?"

I smiled. We were silent for a while. Finally he stretched, began gathering his clothes.

"Might not recognize you with clothes on." Survival had revived my good nature, everything gravy from here on out.

Wolfchild tossed my jeans across my lap. "You still got time."

"For what?"

"To finish your journey."

I looked to the west, wondered how Wolfchild knew my direction. "Too late. Never make the mountains before dark."

He shook his head, pulled on his shirt. "It's not too late. Irene. She's not my woman."

I sat up, spit a flake of tobacco. "What do you mean?"

He stood wholly dressed, one side of his face already beginning to swell. I wondered if my own face was marked from our scuffle. "Last night. We was doing that just for you."

"For me. That's damned considerate."

"She was afraid you wouldn't believe she'd been with me when Laurette disappeared." He halted, swallowed hard on the name he loved. "Afraid you'd figure out it was a lie, go and tell the sheriff." He threw his hands up, slapped them against his legs. "She said all we had to do was just lay there, just be in bed when you came. You'd see us and believe anything. That's all we had to do."

"I still ain't understanding what you're saying. You mean you weren't really"—I searched his face—"making love?"

"We was waiting for you. But being there next to her like that . . ." He bowed his head. "Been a long time since I been with a woman." He held up his palms, confessing, asking forgiveness.

"I don't want to hear any more." I grabbed my jeans, let the dried mud drop to the ground. "Give me your boots."

"I got to walk."

"You think I give a shit? Give 'em."

I left him barefoot in the sand, kicked the horse straight up the embankment, forgoing the trail. The gelding scrabbled for purchase, tearing loose a slide of sand and sage. We clattered across the railroad tracks, turned east on the narrow hump of land bordering the highway.

Heat ribboned up off the asphalt, the air hot enough to dry my lips to leather. I didn't care what lay in our path, what marmot holes might catch a leg, what stones might wedge themselves deep in the hooves' soft centers. I whipped the reins along the gelding's flanks, gritted my teeth, felt the muscles beneath me bunch and release, the shoulders shudder with the impact of each forward stride. I imagined Irene loading the suitcase into the Lincoln's trunk, going back into the house for a final look around. Or maybe she'd be at Esther's, wringing yet another good-bye out of the old woman. I slapped the reins, battered the horse's ribs with my heels. "Hee-ya! Come on, you bastard. Go!"

At the bridge, I gave the gelding no chance to hesitate, belted him hard onto the wood-planked floor, kicked with all my might when he shied at the clatter. He'd filled himself with water, bloated up like a heifer on spring grass, his sides distended, enough to kill him if I kept going, but there was no way I could stop, no way I could give up finding her.

Off the bridge, I kept straight, south on 95, taking little note of how my travel plans had changed. All I had to do was get there, tell her I wasn't mad anymore, that I was wrong all along. I'd tell her about Lee and Laurette. I'd tell her I wasn't going to California, that she and I could go to Missoula together, find a place along the Blackfoot, raise a few head of cattle, find us another horse or two. A long way from anybody who might care who we were, ask about our families, where we'd come in from. We'd feed ourselves, swim naked in the river whenever we pleased. I tried to lick my lips, but the wind had sapped the water from me.

The gelding wanted to slow, fought the bit. Specks of froth flew back, tatted my legs and arms. "A mile," I yelled. "Maybe two. We're going to get there, or both die trying."

A wheat truck roared by, horn blaring, trailing a whirlwind of chaff. I coughed, felt my eyes blur. The horse skidded in the pea gravel, caught himself.

"Up!" I shouted, and reined toward the bordering field. He gave a leap, cleared the ditch, found better footing. We were a few feet above the road now, our path clear through acres of hay stubble. I could almost see the turnoff to the little house, knew that within a few minutes I'd be crossing the creek, busting through her door.

And that's when I saw the Lincoln through the haze of smoke and dust, making a slow right turn onto the highway, headed south.

"No! Wait! Irene!" I pitched my heels against the soft inner flanks, slapped the gelding's rump. We tore through the thicket, across the creek and dirt road, back out onto the field, shedding leaves. The palomino was blowing, a deep rasp echoing up through his long throat. Each stride brought a choked grunt. "Sugar," I said, low in his ear. "I promise."

We were nearly there, the swells of the field taking us high, dropping us down, the single shadow we cast appearing and disappearing along the road, between us a barrow pit, a steep V of gravel. A few more yards and she'd have to see us.

Ahead, I could make out a broken plank fence, low enough for an easy jump, then a gravel road, ditched on either side. "We can do it," I said aloud. I focused on the rear window, the silhouette of her behind the wheel, even as the Lincoln began gathering speed.

A cock pheasant and two hens came up in a thunder of wings, but the horse didn't shy. I knew he was giving me all he had, every muscle straining, every ounce of whatever equine will he possessed pushing him another stride forward. I thought of the horses swimming the ocean, pulling the great ship forward.

"Irene!" I pounded the palomino's neck. He stumbled, caught himself, huffed out a strangled breath. Spatters of bright red blood flecked the spittle. The fence, I could see now, was taller than I'd thought, top rail split and daggered. I imagined us sailing high, clean. I imagined the horse failing, the sharp board goring like the horn of a bull.

We could jump the ditch, have a better chance back on the road.

We could take the fence farther up, where it was unbroken.

But even as I weighed my options, I felt the horse weakening, heard the clutch of each breath, and in that moment I knew that I would kill him if I kept going, that I might already have done so.

I remembered the mare, knees buckling beneath my father's blows. I remembered the last awful screams he beat from her.

I eased back in the saddle, felt the horse slow, reined in hard at the fence to keep him from attempting a feeble leap. He'd have impaled himself, died trying to carry me forward, not because of pain or fear, but because he could feel my need for him to do what I, with my two poor legs, could not.

"It's okay now," I said. "Whoa." The gelding stopped, his only response a labored wheezing. His nose dropped slowly. His eyelids fluttered. I watched the Lincoln pull away, disappear from the horizon.

I gathered the reins, slid down, gave a light tug. "Come on. I'll walk you to the creek." He extended one front leg, stood trembling. I leaned into his neck, closed my eyes, felt a shudder run through us both.

"For your own good. This is what we got to do." I broke off a switch of willow, brought it down hard across his hocks. He flinched, settled back. I hit again, hollering, clucking, keeping steady pressure on the head, bringing him around.

"You got to go! Get!" I gave a high kick, drove the point of my boot into the large muscle of his hip, ran forward and pulled. He stretched his neck, curled his lips. I was glad for the mecate, the absence of the bit. The horse hedged forward, moaned.

"Henry! Fool!" I turned, laid the reins across my shoulder, pulled like I was working a plow. "You! Mule! Move!"

An inch, and then a yard, and then we were walking. "That's it," I encouraged, "keep coming." Wolfchild's boots pinched. I felt the blisters beginning along the knuckles of my toes, the air cooling as the last light left the shallow canyon.

"Just to the house," I said. "Then we can rest."

Sparrows flitted through serviceberry. Red-winged blackbirds clung to the swaying fluff of cattails, their drill a harsh chorus to the horse's wet rasp. We turned down the dirt road, but I knew the palomino wasn't safe yet. He had to be kept walking, circling, cooling down, the great knot of river water working through the maze of his bowels.

We made a slow circumference of the clearing, retraced our steps again and again until I could no longer make out the dusky branches of cottonwood or the path leading down to the creek. I thought of Irene, still driving, passing through the sleeping farm towns, the looping drop down into White Bird, the long stretch of highway that wound through the canyon cut by the Salmon River. She'd be headed toward Boise, maybe Utah, or Kansas. I looked to the south, saw a red-orange rim setting the distant hills, the forests still burning.

"Where will she sleep?" I whispered to the gelding. "Who's going to be there to take care of her?" I smoothed the luminous mane, felt that the heat had left him. I looked toward the dark cabin. "I'm going to get you a little water." I tied him, tested the latch. The door swung open, and I could smell her—not just her, but the coffee and biscuits she had fed me, the calamine, the sharp creosote of past fires.

I lit the lamp, saw that the sink was clean, the bed neatly made. In the cupboard, I found sugar and a sleeve of saltines. I pulled the sodden note from my pocket, slipped it and the fifty into an empty mason jar.

Below the sink, I found a dented bucket. The gelding snorted, took several swallows, then turned away.

"Good boy," I said, patting his neck. "Glad someone learns around here." But I knew that by tomorrow he would have forgotten his aching gut and if allowed would drink himself sick again. I opened my hand, let him lip the three sugar cubes. "See? I keep my promises. Sometimes it just takes a while."

I'd brought along a rag, and I began rubbing him from the poll back, rough across his shoulders, gentle down the spindles of his legs. I rubbed the crystalline sweat from his chest, lifted each hoof and felt for stones, working in the dark. "I think you're going to be okay," I said, and brought him around to a place where I knew he might find grass, staked him there. "Maybe tomorrow," I said, "we'll go to Montana."

I kindled a fire, threw a fistful of coffee in the pot, set it to boil, ate the crackers, thought of Aunt Esther, wondered if Wolfchild would be there later, sopping his bread in gravy, telling the story of his sore feet. The coffee was bitter, and I thought to add sugar but poured it out instead. I snuffed the lantern, gingerly heeled off the boots, felt a little hat of skin come off each toe. I knelt on the floor and checked beneath the bed in the hope she'd forgotten something. Even the smells were disappearing.

I sloughed off my jeans and underwear, too weary to stand. My shirt came off in pieces, split down the back. When I turned my face into the pillow, there was nothing, not her, not Wolfchild, just the cotton that smelled like the air coming in through the open windows. The horse heaved a loud sigh. I pulled the quilt to my shoulders and began to cry, for all I had known and not known, and for tomorrow, whose reason I could not see.

CHAPTER TWENTY

I awakened late the next morning, having slept like a stone. I hitched into town, told the sheriff about Lee and Laurette. Westin wasn't surprised, just a little sad, he said, for Lee to have carried that burden so long. If he held any sorrow for Wolfchild or Irene, he didn't speak it but made his notes and nodded that I'd given him enough, then opened the door for me. "Summer like this might never end," he said, and stepped back into the cool stone building.

I spent the afternoon splitting wood, stacking it against the cabin's south side, moved the horse around what might be a small yard, took him to the creek, where I washed him back to the color of cream. I had the last sandwich for lunch, shaved the apple for dinner and ate it off my knife, sitting on the porch, listening to the night birds pick up their song.

Just near dusk, the ash began to fall—tatters of receipts, newsprint, ledgers. I looked up to see a distant cloud of smoke to the northwest, held out my hand as though catching snow, palmed a furled remnant of gold and black, a label I recognized with such sudden clarity that I startled. I checked the horse's tether, ran down the road to the highway, still limping in Wolfchild's boots, caught a ride with the first car whose lights passed over me—a Fuller Brush salesman, just down from a long day on the prairie.

"Something's burning," I said, peering ahead toward Snake Junction.

"I'll say. Whole place is a ring of fire. Came through a line just past Grangeville. Don't expect anything short of snow will stop it this year." He was small, his vision just clearing the wheel. He smelled like gin, or maybe juniper.

Within a mile, we could see the oily plume, the flames brightening the canyon. The salesman stretched his neck upward. "Is it the mill? Town won't survive, that mill goes down. I'd have to move to Portland." He clicked his teeth like a puppet.

"Not the mill." I kept my eyes fixed on the boiling black cloud. There was nothing else it could be.

By the time the salesman dropped me at The Stables, the roof had already caved, the door busted off one hinge, swinging in the current of heat.

"Where's the fire trucks?" I grabbed the arm of the man standing next to me, who shook his head, shrugged, turned back to watch as the corner of one wall leaned in, separating along its seams.

I searched for someone I knew, the faces wavering yellow. At the edge of the lot, I saw Lee's Chevy, the overhead flick on, then off. I walked toward the car, then ran as the engine started, stumbling forward against the shock of pain, leather drawing blood, toe and heel. I reached the passenger door, slapped it hard.

Lee looked at me, not surprised. He leaned over, rolled down the window an inch. I hooked my fingers, held on. The flames reflected off the glass. I could feel the heat at my back, the cool against my thighs. From inside the car came the smell of him, warm and peaty.

We waited, the two of us held in that moment of fire, held by blood and our shared knowledge that we were both kin and not kin, seeing in each other's eyes our need to hang on, let go, hating and loving each other for all of it.

I could have hurt him then, with my hands, with my words, and I wanted to hurt him—hurt him so bad he might never heal but carry the wound with him like a suckling child to be gauzed and tended. I wanted him to take what hurt in me, take the bitterness and fear and regret, take it away with him. I wanted to say, *You've got to take care of, take care of, take care,* but all I could do, his blue, blue eyes on me empty of any promise, was step away, feel the slide of chrome beneath my fingers, the gentle glide of polished metal.

I watched the headlights sweep through the haze of smoke and dust, waited for the turn west, toward the ocean and L.A., but the Chevy banked east, disappeared down the highway, though I could hear it for a while longer, the strong acceleration of the 283 four-barrel kicking in.

I'm here now, I thought. I whispered, "This is where I am." I tried to hear it the way it sounded, a good thing, lasting.

When I walked back toward the crowd, I saw Harvey kneeling at the edge of the gravel, wondered how long he'd been there, what he'd seen.

"Hey, kid." His voice was heavy and rough. "You about missed it."

I looked around at the men, their empty hands. I had forgotten that it was reservation land, outside the town limits. Even with the river close by, there was nothing to be done. The few buckets of water thrown at the fire evaporated in midair.

"Where's Spud?" I asked.

"Somebody's gone to call." Harvey rubbed his forehead with two fingers. "Should have been here by now."

I peered into the blaze. "But he's out. Everyone's out." A *whump* and a long, high-pitched whistle. Like the Fourth of July.

"If not, they ain't never going to be."

I moved forward, but Harvey caught my arm. "Don't do nothing foolish. It's too late for anything."

I pulled away, walked behind the crescent of men and a few women to the back of the lot. A local farmer was working a plow along the slope, cutting a fire line. I got as close as I could, felt the hair of my brows and lashes singe.

"Too late," I said to myself, then turned to see Mrs. Blood, bundled in a man's cardigan as if she'd just stepped into the cold.

"Grateful for that," she said, motioning to the tractor. "Wouldn't take much for this fire to come my way. Got a cigarette?"

I patted my pocket absently, handed her the pack and lighter.

"You meaning to buy another horse?" She took two cigarettes, tucked one down her blouse. "Where is Henry, anyway?"

"Lapwai."

"Not working him too hard, are you?" Something sizzled and spat, went dead.

"No." I pulled my attention from the fire. "He's been doing nothing but eating."

"Didn't make Montana, I see."

I shook my head, watched in silence as the back wall of my room fell in. There was nothing to save now, not the lampshade with its brands or the bed on which I'd first made love to Irene.

"I got something for you." She searched the sweater's pockets, pulled out several wads of tissue, a stick of Doublemint. "Somewhere here." She patted her bosom, fingered out the cigarette, slipped it back in. "Here it is." She extended her empty palm.

"What's that supposed to be?"

She turned her hand over and the diamonds flickered, a horseshoe of flame.

"Looks good."

"Does." She tilted her head, waved the hand like a wand, then tugged off the ring. "I'm leaving. Got to put some water on my corn. Corn won't make without water."

She held out the ring, but I folded it back into her hand. "I think I might run it out of luck."

She shook her head. "Maybe that gal will change her mind." She opened her palm.

I took the ring, thought to throw it as hard as I could into the fire.

"Heavy, ain't it?" She held the smoke deep in her lungs.

I weighed the ring up and down. "Sometimes a thing like this ain't worth keeping."

"Might be worth something to your kids someday. Maybe if

I'd had more to give, my girls might have stayed a while longer." She coughed, said, "Stop on by, I got tomatoes coming out my ears," then trudged off into the darkness.

I made my way back to Harvey. "What day is it?" I asked.

"Sunday, kid. It's Sunday." He thumped my shoulder. "You missed a helluva party last night."

The crowd was beginning to thin, though some would stay until dawn, a few out of curiosity, others to snuff the rogue sparks with gunnysacks and shovels.

"Don't think that brother of yours ever sang so pretty. Made a lot of folks cry."

"Always did."

"True." Harvey straightened, popped his back. "Got a place to sleep?"

I nodded.

"Irene?"

"She's gone."

"Women like that can tie you in knots for a long time." He studied my face, looked back to the fire. "Sometimes they're worth it, I guess."

We watched the big sign keel off its posts, sink into the blackened ribs of the roof. "No one ever gave her a chance," I said. I wasn't talking to Harvey but to the flames themselves, the raw heat that washed over us. I wanted to say more, tell him how she'd made it all up, how she knew Wolfchild was innocent, how we all did. I lowered my head, closed my eyes against the sting. "I don't understand why she had to leave."

Harvey took in a deep breath, let it out through his nose. "There's just some people," he said. "Like they've been set on some course from the beginning, and no way out. Like they're being chased from behind by their own lives."

"She was better than any of us, yet no good ever came her way."

"You," Harvey patted my shoulder. "*You* came her way. Take what she offered and get on with it." He gave a hard squeeze. "Got my rig parked across the road. Need a lift?"

"Think I'll walk."

"Come by my place sometime. I'll fix you some liver and onions. Bring a bottle. None of us going to be drinking free for a while." He dropped his cigarette, toed it out. "Haven't heard the baseball score, have you?"

I shook my head. I hadn't thought about baseball for a long time.

"Yankees," he said, "all the way." He rolled his arms, imagined the bat, brought it through the strike zone, visored his eyes. "That one's gone!" I could hear him whistling as he crossed the road, then nothing but the fire rumbling, people breaking into smaller groups, the story of that summer already forming: the rodeo queen, the Indian, the red-haired woman who brought the heat and the trouble with her. Someone pulled out a flask, said, "Let's drink to The Stables, biggest dance floor this side of the Mississippi!" Feet shuffled the gravel, someone called out a jig. I thought how much better Lee might have done it, found some way to get himself above the crowd, maybe even stood on the roof of his Bel Air to sing the words out, toe tapping metal as he pointed to the couples: "*You* there! Hold that pretty gal tighter, or I'm cuttin' in! Charlie! You're looking younger every day, son! You sure you're old enough to be here? Harv, better check his ID!"

I stepped away from the bright flames and loud voices, took

my time along the path, turning every now and again to watch the flames recede, the glow off the canyon wall dimming, giving way to stars. The mill droned on. A row of glass-roofed green-houses were lit one at a time from the inside, then went dark, like a string of Christmas lights, and I knew that the nurseryman was making his rounds, the seedlings and saplings tender in his care.

CHAPTER TWENTY·ONE

It took some time for the town's grudge against Wolfchild to settle. When winter came, early and all at once, people turned their attention to the business of frozen pipes and dead batteries, forgot about the woman who floated down to them on a summer current, whose body had caught and swirled in the water that now eddied beneath the feet of their children playing broom hockey, the ice swept clean.

I joined the Air Force that Christmas, put in my four-year hitch. By the time I got back to Snake Junction, Harvey was dead, felled by a heart attack while shoveling a winter's record snow. Spud died of cancer a few months later—the two of them like an old married couple, one unable to live without the other.

When I tried to pay Mrs. Blood for pasturing the palomino, she scoffed, said Billy had been the happiest she'd seen him since losing his manhood. She helped me find work with a rancher who had attended college with her husband in Butte, where both men had studied mining before deciding they preferred the open skies of Idaho.

As we mended fence together, shagged the stray calves home, the rancher told me the story of his life, how he'd been undone by a lovely young teacher he'd thought he might die for, until she took up with a bronc rider, moved to Cheyenne. And so we had this loss in common, though he had left his longing for the teacher when he left Montana, married his high school sweetheart, fathered five children, all girls.

His love of horses was matched only by his lasting love of books. He fed me the volumes one at a time, and I read them by the light of the oil lamp as the days shortened and the cold seeped beneath the door of the cabin. Each morning, as I carried fresh water from the creek so that Henry might drink, I'd look toward the road, expecting the Lincoln at any moment, Irene's voice saying, "Come on. Let's go for a ride."

I wanted to tell her the stories that stayed with me into dream, how she became part of them, how she had ignited a hunger in me to know more than I'd been given. It was Irene I was thinking of when, with my GI Bill, I began taking classes at Lewis–Clark Normal School, and there, in the library, found the recordings of Caruso singing *La Traviata, Il Trovatore, Otello.* Again and again, I was struck by the narrowness of my escape.

If not for Irene, I might never have awakened, left that back room, stepped out into the larger world. I might never have known what grace resides in those moments of decision, when we must embrace the awful freedom granted us, in the face of so much gone wrong, offer the simplest, most complex of answers—*no*. I hear it still. I repeat it each day, each day, as it is, occasion to despair, except for her belief, engendered in me, that with each act of resistance, we redeem ourselves, and each other.

Even now, in bed beside the rancher's youngest daughter, whom I have loved into middle age, I dream of Irene, that she is listening, waiting to hear something true. I want to tell her that I've been to Italy, that I sat in a café and drank a bottle of Barolo while an old woman behind the bar sang "Nessun dorma." I want to tell her of the Englishman I met in a pub in London who'd had both arms shot off in Germany and tipped his glass back with his teeth. Because he was too drunk, he had me walk him to his apartment one night, where we sipped dark beer until the sun lightened the streets, and I told him about Irene and that I would never get over her. "Like my hands," he said, moving his shoulders up, then down. "I wake up at night and think they're still there. I'm not dreaming. I touch my thumb to each finger. I can feel the sharpness of each nail. Every morning, I lose them all over again, and I grieve."

Aunt Esther, Mrs. Blood, gone. Only Wolfchild remains, an old man who rises at dawn to sweat before cleansing himself in the river, even in winter, when he must take his axe and chop through the ice. I've seen him emerge, hair glistered with frost, steam rising from his naked body. Sometimes I join him, though the cold numbs my lungs and limbs, and I stagger to the sweat house, dizzy with premonitions of my own death. Nights, we sit by the fire and listen to the big fish surface and roll. In the deepest holes are sturgeon so old, Wolfchild tells me, that their dens hold the fossils of tigers and mammoths, obsidian arrowheads still lodged in bone. "I know this," I say, and I smile, remembering that day in the park with Irene, when I was too young, too new to this world, to see how the story was just beginning, how I could not will its end.

For a time, Lee sent postcards and photographs—cartoon drawings of sombrero-topped saguaros; the railroad station at Cheyenne; a portrait of him between two pretty girls who wore nothing but boots and bandoliers. On the back of each, he'd scrawl a few words: "Played the Marshall County Fair. Best pecan pie I ever ate"; "Cherokee ain't much of a town, but the girls sure ain't picky." In the last photo, several years old, he is alone on-stage, head thrown back, eyes closed, hair nearly white, even as mine has darkened.

Perhaps he has settled down somewhere, made a family. I wonder if his children's eyes, like the eyes of my own sons and grandchildren, are blue, if he takes his guitar to the porch and sings with them as I do, if he is happy in the land he loves. I think about him when I open the closet and see his boots there—the inlaid wings of red and white—the ones I had coveted so long. I'd found them that night I returned to Irene's from the fire, leaned against the cottage door, as though he had meant a last visit, as though his soul had simply leapt up and away. Each Sunday evening, I take them out, rub them with mink oil, spank them to a shine. They are chamois-soft on top, soles wholly new. Some-day, they will carry me far.

I remember that summer night, The Stables burning, the river so quiet I stopped, held my breath to hear it. It was a part of me now, its surge like the rush of blood. I followed the trail to where the sweat house had stood. An owl called out from the cottonwoods, took flight in a hush of wings. Somewhere, a rabbit held still, believing itself invisible; a rattlesnake furled in a bowl of rock. I reached down, felt with my fingers, closed my eyes, drew back my arm and threw, listened for the plunk into water, heard instead the distant clack of stone against stone. When I opened my eyes, the bridge, silvered with moon, seemed to levitate above the river. In a week, I would be eighteen. I wondered when the Nez Perce boys would jump again, and if I would have the courage to join them.

There was a song coming to me. I felt it building low in my throat, vibrating at the back of my tongue. I slid the ring into my pocket, touched the diamonds as I would the beads of a rosary, each gem a prayer that somewhere, everyone I loved was all right, travelers bound for distant places I could not imagine.